O' Happy Dagger

CJ Love

Mysteries by CJ Love

VERONA'S VINEYARD COZY MYSTERIES SERIES
Juliet & Dead Romeo
O'Happy Dagger
Thus With a Kiss
Stage of Fools

O' Happy Dagger

Verona's Vineyard Cozy Mysteries, Book 2

CJ Love

Secret Staircase Books

O' Happy Dagger
Published by Secret Staircase Books, an imprint of
Columbine Publishing Group, LLC
PO Box 416, Angel Fire, NM 87710

Copyright © 2020 Cynthia Whitten-Love
All rights reserved. No part of this book may be reproduced or transmitted in any form or by any means, electronic or mechanical, including photocopying, recording, or by an information storage and retrieval system without permission in writing from the publisher.

This book is a work of fiction. Names, characters, places and incidents are either the product of the author's imagination or are used fictitiously. Any resemblance to actual events or locales or persons, living or dead, is entirely coincidental. Although the author and publisher have made every effort to ensure the accuracy and completeness of information contained in this book we assume no responsibility for errors, inaccuracies, omissions, or any inconsistency herein. Any slights of people, places or organizations are unintentional.

Book layout and design by Secret Staircase Books
Cover design by Cynthia Whitten-Love

First trade paperback edition: March, 2020
First e-book edition: March, 2020

* * *

Publisher's Cataloging-in-Publication Data

Love, CJ
O' Happy Dagger / by CJ Love.
p. cm.
ISBN 978-1945422850 (paperback)
ISBN 978-1945422867 (e-book)

1. Juliet Da Vinci (Fictitious character)--Fiction. 2. Shakespearean themes—Fiction. 3. Women sleuths—Fiction. I. Title

Verona's Vineyard Cozy Mystery Series : Book 2.
Love, CJ, Verona's Vineyard cozy mysteries.

BISAC : FICTION / Mystery & Detective.

813/.54

To Jax Phillip, the most hilarious boy I know.

"O teach me how I should forget to think."

Chapter 1

"You're still here?"

The shouting came from behind Juliet Da Vinci, and she'd almost dropped the Limoncello bottle in her hand. She twisted around.

"Geez, *Nonna*." Taking a breath to steady her heartbeat, she asked, "Where else would I be?"

"Outside, living your life." The old woman emphasized the word life, pointing out that Juliet didn't have one. Tribly Da Vinci's dyed black hair was still up in curlers even though it was four o'clock in the afternoon. A white cotton dress hung on her narrow shoulders, and she wore a gray sweater overtop. She also wore gray socks up to her knees, because Tribly was all about coordinating her outfits.

"I'm living my life right here," Juliet told her. She tried to keep her voice at a normal tone because sometimes while speaking to her grandmother, she tended to shout too.

They were in the kitchen, near the end of the room, close to the cellar door and wine cooler. However, Tribly was on the move, waving her hand, shouting *Basta, Basta,* and shuffling toward the kitchen island. Copper pots hung over the counter as did dried lavender branchlets and strings of garlic.

Juliet followed her. Setting the liqueur bottle on the island, she rummaged through a drawer for a corkscrew.

Right away, the door to the courtyard opened and a chilly air blasted into the room, making the copper pots bang around like great big windchimes.

Juliet's mother, Italia, stepped into the kitchen with the gust, her wool jacket flapping on either side of her. She was a vision of November in multiple scarves and a folded beret atop her dark hair.

The door slammed shut with the wind, but the copper pots still clanged overhead.

Italia announced, "It's going to snow."

"Like you have the gift," Tribly said. "You know nothing of the gift."

Italia hung her key fob on the hook by the door and then moved farther into the kitchen, her gold lame' ankle boots clunking on the floor. "I don't need *the gift* to know it's going to snow. Dark clouds are building over the lake." She turned her amber eyes on Juliet. "Why aren't you dressed? There's a party tonight."

They were twins, Juliet and Italia, except for their ages and their hair. Juliet had the Da Vinci hair, tight curls as thick as an otter's. "I know there's a party, *Matri*. There's still two hours before it begins." Opening the refrigerator door, she stood staring at the contents. Not much appealed to her at the moment, not the meatballs, the spinach torte, the sausage, or the pasta… eventually, she chose a plate of cheese and shut the door.

Tribly blocked the path to the counter. "You need to get out of this house."

Leaning away, holding up the plate so she didn't hit Tribly with it. "Huh?"

"I have more dates than you do."

Juliet threw a look at her mother. Tribly's love life was a touchy subject in the Da Vinci household.

A slight tremor shook Italia's shoulders.

Stepping around her grandmother, Juliet found a tray beneath the island counter and placed her drink and cheese plate on top of it.

Italia leaned against the opposite side of the counter. "*Nonna's* right. Go out and meet a man. Look how happy your cousin is with her doctor."

"*Per amore della vita!*" Tribly shouted, returning to the counter and pulling a pan from the rack. "The last boy you brought into the house broke her heart."

Juliet made a face and shook her head. "Paris didn't break my heart."

"He's in Boston," Italia told Tribly. "He'll be back, you'll see."

Just thinking about Paris Nobleman made Juliet fidget.

"You're going to spill that," Italia said, eyeing the tray. "You're so restless these days."

Tribly set the pan on the stove and took a wooden spoon from the canister on the counter. "The *diavolo* tried to kill her."

Little wrinkles appeared at the sides of her mother's

eyes. "That devil is dead, and my sweet Ganozza is with God."

Juliet narrowed her eyes on Tribly. Why had she brought up the subject again?

Tribly made the sign of the cross. "*Si, Gesu.*"

Setting the tray on the counter, Juliet crossed herself too.

Italia pressed her elbows into the counter and rubbed her manicured hands together. "You need to dance."

"Ty's not ready."

"Dance with someone else."

"I don't want to dance with someone else."

Her mother stared off for a moment. "You danced beautifully with Paris at the charity ball."

With a sigh, Juliet picked up the tray again.

"You're scared to go out," Tribly voiced. "Larry killed your spirit!"

Oh, great.

"You need to see a doctor about your head."

"There's no shame in it," Italia said, catching Juliet's eye. "Are you scared to leave the house?" She stood straighter. "Oh my God, you're scared to leave the house."

"It's a phobia, it's a phobia."

"I'm not phobic!"

"I'll talk to Dr. Dexter at the party," Italia said in a softer tone. "Maybe all you need is a pill."

Tribly slapped her hip and threw her hand in the air. "Then she will be a drug addict."

"*Dios Mio,* I'm not afraid to go out of the house."

Her mother crossed her arms. "Then why don't you?"

"Because I don't want to go out. All of my friends are shallow twits."

Tribly pointed the spoon at Juliet. "Watch your mouth." To Italia, she said, "She's got a mouth this one."

"Every one of them thought *Papà* killed Romeo, remember? You saw how they turned on us. I don't trust any of them." She moved around the counter and toward the swinging doors.

Italia's eyes followed her, arms still crossed. "You need to be a friend to make friends, Juliet."

"I was a friend, they were my friends, and now they're not." She turned and pushed the doors open with her backside and took her snack to her bedroom.

* * *

Setting the tray of cheese and Limoncello on the balcony table, Juliet fell into a nearby chair. There was still plenty of time before the party began, and she meant to stay in her yoga pants and over-big gray sweater until the last moment.

Matri still has her head in the sand.

It was something Juliet had learned over the summer, how her mother refused to see the reality of a situation until tragedy struck. Even when tragedy struck, Italia didn't join the find-the-murderer movement. No, she went to bed with a glass of wine and hoped justice would win the day, and the police would get their man. Then, when everything blew over, Italia rejoined her gossipy friends as though they hadn't turned their Versace-covered backs on her.

Selecting a cheese slice, Juliet ate it while contemplating the nearby vineyard. The work in the fields had ceased, and the grape-picking machines were parked again in West Portland, at the Renaissance Wine office complex. The cooler weather had turned the vine leaves to burnished gold and brown, and the branches on the trellises showed through.

Have I turned bitter, unforgiving?

Of course not, Juliet told herself. She'd forgiven her friends. Absolutely.

But, I'm not blind either.

They'd all come running back to her side after the news hit that Juliet had discovered who'd killed Mariotto and Ganozza. Or maybe they came back after the *BuzzFeed* article that had gone viral on the Internet. The writer named the piece, *Juliet & Dead Romeo*.

Not wanting to get caught up in those thoughts, Juliet got out of the chair and glanced toward the western side of the house. Her view was blocked by the curvature of the wall, but she heard vehicles arriving in the courtyard. Engines cut off. Metal doors creaked open. "Don't drop that, you idiot. That's the shrimp."

More voices sounded, likely the wait staff had arrived, or the string quartet musicians.

Juliet grabbed one more slice of cheese and her glass of liqueur and stepped through the french doors and into her room again. It was time to shower and dress for the Harvest Ball. She hadn't invited anyone this year. Not even Olive and Emma, her best friends since grade school.

Matri is wrong.

A person didn't need to be a friend to make a friend. No, a person needed friends who shared similar values, such as honesty and loyalty.

Juliet stepped into the adjoining bathroom, gleaming white in the bubble lights above the vanity. Where was she going to find friends who embodied loyalty and honesty?

Juliet supposed she didn't know everyone in Verona's Vineyard. Okay, she knew most of them. Maybe she needed to branch out a little.

She switched on the shower water with a touch of a button.

New friends, that's what I want.

Starting immediately, even at the Harvest Ball, Juliet meant to make new friends. It didn't matter if they were male or female, or whether she'd considered them for a friend previously or not. She'd meet someone and make plans to get together right away.

* * *

Juliet came down the elegant white staircase at ten minutes to six. She'd dressed in a floor-length gown of salmon and coral.

Anthony Yeager stood at the bottom of the steps. As the Da Vinci estate manager, he was in charge of the hired staff for the evening. He spoke to the ten or twelve people gathered around him in the formal living area. His half-balding head glistened in the chandelier light, and his gold wire rim glasses did the same. "I expect you to be observant and attentive, visible and invisible," he told them. "This is not *your* party. You do not mingle, and you won't find your next boyfriend or girlfriend here."

Juliet slipped behind him and went to stand in front of the enormous stone fireplace on the west side of the room. Someone had thrown apple and orange slices into the flames, and a sweet fragrance curled outward like a branch of fruit in the heated air.

Another group of hired help had cleared the

furnishings to make room for the quartet near the two sets of french doors. The instruments squawked and squealed as the foursome adjusted their strings. Then, in unison, they struck up the song, *Song for Sienna*.

Juliet touched her heart. *I love this song.*

The doorbell chimed.

Anthony waved the temporary staff toward the dining area. Then he opened one of the big wooden doors in the grand foyer and stood aside to let the first guest enter.

Paris Nobleman stepped inside wearing a black turtleneck sweater under a charcoal pea coat. His auburn hair was as wild as ever, and scruff covered his jawline. It hid some of his broad and chiseled features. In one hand, he carried a duffle bag, and he leaned toward Anthony and said something.

Juliet's heart pounded. She hadn't seen Paris in six weeks. She'd texted, he return texted, sometimes.

Anthony nodded toward Juliet, giving Paris direction.

He came right at her.

Paris had never been thoughtful about personal space, especially with Juliet.

She didn't mind too much, not usually, but with Paris' sudden appearance and lack of communication, she responded by lengthening her neck and squaring her shoulders.

Paris tilted his head. His green eyes traveled her features. He asked, "Do I still have a room?"

She lifted her shoulder. "You'll need to ask my mother."

He took a breath through gritted white teeth. "What a cold greeting, yeah?" He dropped the duffle bag and leaned toward her. "I'll have none of that. Embrace me."

Juliet leaned away.

He grabbed her around the waist and pulled her to him. After a short moment, he stepped away, his hand still on her waist. "Wasn't that lovely? And, look at you. You're as gorgeous as ever."

Juliet's cheeks heated. "If I'm so gorgeous, why did it take you so long to return my phone calls and answer my texts?"

He smiled, taking in what she'd said. His eyes went from a lighter shade of green to a basil color. "I'm staying for a long time, Juliet. And I promise to return every text and phone call right away."

She let out a long breath, quite willing to forgive him. "Fine."

"Good," he said and gazed about the room. "There's a party I take it?"

"The Harvest Ball." She eyed his coat and sweater. "Did you bring a change of clothes?"

"I know where I am," he told her and lifted the duffle bag. "My same room?"

"Yes, yes, yes," she said, giving in.

Paris turned, crossed the room, and jogged up the staircase.

The doorbell rang again. More guests came through the door. It was a steady stream of men in tuxedos and women in ball gowns.

Geoffrey Leary entered the house, smoking a cigar. Looking at him was like looking at a bulldog. Loose skin draped on either side of his upturned nose. His personality was nothing like a bulldog's, however, because he was the crankiest man Juliet had ever met.

Laughter sounded.

Sebastian D'Angelo stood in the doorway. He shook

Anthony's hand and then took a drink from one of the female servers. "The Da Vinci Sauvignon. Only the best!" He raised his glass, toasting everyone in the room.

Juliet didn't know D'Angelo well. He was a new employee and an important one; Director of Renaissance Wines and second only to her father. D'Angelo reminded her of a pirate, one who'd shaved and showered and dressed well. He had dark eyes and dark hair. Swarthy, that's what he was, and when he smiled, his teeth glittered in the chandelier light.

Someone tapped Juliet on her shoulder and she turned.

The man was the same height as her, only because he wore elevator shoes.

She forced a smile. "Abram."

Abram Fontana had slicked his dark hair off his face with heavy pomade. Who knew he had a widow's peak? Usually, Abram wore a bowl cut that covered his forehead. He smelled quite tangy, as though he'd splashed on *Old Spice* by the bucketful. Abram jerked his chin out, nose up, "Hey."

"What are you doing here?"

"I'm my mother's date for the evening."

"I wouldn't tell anyone else that."

Abram wore a tuxedo shirt without the jacket and a small size vest that was loose on his chest. "I came here to make new friends."

Why yes, Juliet had promised herself to make new friends, but Abram Fontana? Really? She asked, "Ben and Marc Romeo aren't your cups of tea any longer?"

The corners of his thin mouth pointed downward, and he snorted like a horse, a wee little horse. "Ben moved to Buffalo, and all Marc ever does is visit his mother in prison."

"How the mighty have fallen."

"Well, not me," he said with a sharp nod, as though he actually considered himself one of the mighty ones. He pivoted toward Juliet. "Would you like to go bowling next week?"

Juliet winced. "Bowling? Is that your idea of a night out with friends?"

"I can't afford much more than that. Besides, I'm a good bowler."

She smoothed the front of her gown. "Sorry, I don't bowl. Tennis?"

"I don't play fancy boy tennis."

"How about regular tennis?"

"No," he said, thinking. "Oh, I know. They've opened the skating rink. But, we have to go halfsies, Juliet. I'm not a rich man, and we're not dating."

She opened her mouth to reply. Only a squeak came out.

A server passed them, holding a tray full of wine glasses.

"Oh," Abram said and took a flute for each hand. He took a long drink from the first one.

Juliet took a glass too, glancing at the woman.

It was the same server who'd met D'Angelo when he'd first arrived. How she still had her long hair loose and down was anyone's guess. Anthony was strict about such things. There should be no loose hair while serving. None.

Juliet glanced around the room.

The other women and men in server uniforms wore their long hair in ponytails or buns.

But this woman, wow, what a head of hair she had, so thick and black. It was the sort that fell from the neck of a prize-winning horse. Her features weren't beautiful, not really, because her nose took up most of her face, and she had a tiny chin and wide cheekbones. She nodded to Juliet and moved away toward other guests.

"Who was that?" Abram asked, still staring at the woman.

Juliet shook her head. "Temporary staff."

"I want to get lost in that hair like a curling iron."

"We'd have to send in a search party for you."

Taking a long breath through his nose, he lifted his chin again. "Well, I need to mingle and make more friends."

"Right," Juliet said, lifting her glass in farewell.

And she went along too, playing hostess, smiling and nodding as the many guests came through the door. She made small talk and greeted her parents' friends. She met Sebastian D'Angelo and then stood near the hearth and searched the crowd.

A new friend, a new friend…

No, Abram didn't count.

One of the servers offered a tray of *hors d 'oeuvres* to D'Angelo.

It was the same woman, the woman with *the hair*. She certainly was making her rounds.

Juliet was near enough to hear the woman say something to D'Angelo. She spoke in a different language; the intonation and pronunciation sounded like chimes.

D'Angelo leaned back and tucked his chin. He said something in return – in the same chiming vernacular. "I'd rather you speak English," he said, using a clipped tone.

"I ask about son. He is well?"

There was an odd caution in D'Angelo's eyes, as though he were confused or … or scared?

Santos Da Vinci appeared, and he swatted D'Angelo

on the elbow. He didn't seem to notice the server woman. Which was so like her father. The man had no peripheral vision. D'Angelo was the focus, and everything else was background, like splatter art.

"The *Food and Wine* article has upped our sales."

The woman turned away and moved across the room.

D'Angelo kept his eyes on her for another moment and then turned toward Santos. "Yes, yes," he said, his manner absent, as though he still thought about the woman's question.

Juliet wandered away toward the staircase again. Why was it taking Paris so long to change his clothes and come to the party?

Someone in the dining room caught her eye.

Anthony had pulled the female server into the dining area, near a lighted cabinet. "May I remind you, you're not to socialize?" Unlike her father, Anthony noticed every happening in a room. He might be busy in another part of the house, but still somehow knew the woman had spoken to D'Angelo. "And do something with your hair."

The hum of the room grew louder, cutting off whatever else Anthony was saying. He pointed toward the kitchen, perhaps instructing her to grab a food tray.

The woman swung around and pushed open the swinging doors.

Anthony followed her.

Juliet turned toward the party guests again, just as the quartet played *Falling Slowly*.

Someone bumped her shoulder, and she turned.

Paris had shaved and showered and smelled woody and citrusy. "What have I missed?" His black suit coat had been tailored to fit his trim waist and square shoulders.

Juliet inhaled, trying to calm the tingling in her stomach. What was happening to her nervous system? She wasn't in love with Paris Nobleman. The idea was ludicrous. She said, "I'm going bowling with Abram next week. Or is it ice skating?"

His mouth pulled down at the sides. "You're friends with him?"

She bit her bottom lip, not ready to make a full commitment to the idea. "We're giving each other a chance."

Paris took a glass of wine from a passing tray. "I've been gone too long. I've neglected you."

The doorbell rang once more.

Paris took a sip from his glass, his eyes shifting toward the foyer.

Juliet glanced that way as well.

"Is Roseline whom thou didst love so dear?"

Chapter 2

Anthony opened the front door once more, and a cold breeze slipped into the room. It swirled toward the staircase and carried with it the fresh scent of the night, evergreen mixed with subtle and fleeting grape fragrance.

Roseline Gatti, Juliet's first cousin, stepped through the door. Her red hair danced around her gorgeous face like fairy lights on alabaster. She wore a white fur stole across her shoulders and a beige gown that sparkled with sequins. The dress fit her curves like something out of Kim Kardashian's closet.

The roomful of people stopped to stare.

Roseline was used to people ogling her and usually

reveled in it. But, not this night, no, her attention was all on the man stepping through the door behind her.

Dr. David Dexter was fifteen years older than Roseline, and he was tall, six-four, six-five perhaps. He removed his date's stole and handed the furry thing to Anthony. Then his eyes landed on Roseline again. His mouth turned up at the corners, and his eyes softened.

Man, he's got it bad.

Roseline took Dexter's arm tightly, as though she'd never let him out of her sight.

Paris said, "A new man, I see."

Abram was back, standing next to Juliet and gazing at Roseline and the doctor. "How is it that a man as ugly as that can date Roseline Gatti?"

"Don't say that," Juliet told him. "You can't say that."

He held up the palms of his hands. "Sorry, sorry, but what does Roseline see in an old man who looks like Nicholas Cage?"

Paris sipped his drink, nodding at the same time. "It may be that she is unaware that her man is impersonating a celebrity."

Juliet laughed, a horselaugh with a snort at the end.

Perhaps it was the braying laughter that caused Roseline to turn their way. Still clamping Dexter's arm, she dragged him toward the staircase.

And wow, once he was closer, Dexter did look like Nicolas Cage with his long pale face, faint brows, and receding hairline.

"Juliet," Roseline said, breathless from her tugboat routine across the marble. "You haven't met David."

Juliet held out her hand. "Hello, Dr. Dexter."

He said, "Juliet, I've heard a lot about you." He smiled at Roseline.

Juliet motioned to the men on either side of her. "Dr. Dexter, this is Paris Nobleman and Abram Fontana."

He nodded, barely noticing them. "Call me, David, please."

Paris stuck out his hand.

Rosaline's cheeks turned a pretty shade of pink. "David doesn't shake."

Lowering his hand, Paris nodded. "It's nice to meet you."

"Sorry about that," the doctor said. "Professional hazard. I'm careful about germs."

He didn't seem to mind swapping some germs with Roseline, as evidenced by the brush of lipstick on his collar.

Juliet's mother joined their little group. What a vision she was in her gown of deep gold. She'd piled her hair high and let the tendrils fall around her face. She fussed over Roseline's dress and then dragged the couple away to meet other guests.

"I'm surprised my mother didn't gush over you," Juliet told Paris.

"I saw her upstairs. She gushed over me there."

Abram said, "She's never gushed over me."

"For some reason, she thinks you're part Romeo," Juliet told him.

Juliet had turned in Abram's direction, so she had a good view of Geoffrey Leary, the bulldog-faced, cigar-smoking coot, and the same server woman offering him wine. She leaned toward him and said something.

Leary frowned.

And then the woman took a goblet from her tray and threw the contents at him.

But her aim was just a little off, and the wave of red wine splashed the bodice of Roseline's sparkly gown.

There was a heartbeat of silence, except for the violin; it still played *Time to Say Goodbye,* and it was just lovely.

Roseline held out her hands and gaped at her dress. With Roseline, there was always a lead up to the screaming. First, it sounded like *ughhh,* but by the time it exited her mouth, it was at full volume and in the note of high C.

The violin screeched to a stop.

Dr. Dexter dove in between Roseline and the server woman—as though he thought more wine-flinging might be in the offing. He was fearless about it, arms flung out wide, and his white tuxedo shirt exposed to Sauvignon.

Anthony was there in a split second, said something to Juliet's mother, and then pulled the wild-haired server woman toward the dining room.

"Yes, yes," Italia said, draping her arm over Roseline's shoulder. "I'm sure we can find another gown for you to wear."

"It's all right, dear." Dr. Dexter toadied behind, telling Roseline, "You're still beautiful."

Paris leaned toward Juliet. "I've so missed all of the drama in the Da Vinci household."

"I swear that woman threw the wine on purpose."

"Who?"

Juliet nodded toward the dining room. "The server woman. She threw the wine intentionally." She glanced toward the hearth and at Geoffrey Leary.

The old bulldog had gone back to eating his *hors d' oeuvres.*

The quartet started up again, playing Jason Mraz' *I'm Yours.*

Paris pulled Juliet along. "Never mind all that. Let's dance."

"But, the woman …"

"I'm sure she's fired by now." Turning toward her, he held out his arms. "Forget about her and live a little, yeah?"

Every time she danced with Paris, Juliet had fun because he didn't try to hold her tightly or get too close. When he did pull her to him, it was only to swing her around and release her. Juliet felt light as air, which was a first in a long while.

Forty-five minutes later, Roseline came down the stairs dressed in a sheath gown. It was one of Italia's, the blush-colored one, and it fit somewhat loosely around Roseline's tiny waist. But no matter, the girl was glorious as ever, especially with her adoring doctor at her side.

Several people applauded when they saw her, causing others in the room to glance their way.

It must've been the glamour of the descent because Dexter stopped on the bottom step and turned toward his Roseline. He dropped to one knee and held up a jewelry box.

"Oh, what is this?" Paris said, his arm still around Juliet.

"Roseline Adele Gatti," Dr. Dexter said, bolstering his voice so everyone heard him, "Will you marry me?"

Roseline's hands flew to her lips as fat tears formed in her eyes. Actually, she hadn't stopped crying from the wine incident, but these were fresh tears of joy. "Yes, oh yes, David!"

"Oh boy, here we go," Juliet said, meaning the tears might wash them all away.

Paris leaned toward her. "Not in favor of love, Juliet?"

Before Juliet could answer, the guests erupted in applause all around.

Dexter stood, slipped the ring onto Roseline's finger,

and gathered her into his arms.

Juliet's mother congratulated them first and then ushered them into the room again. More waitstaff appeared, this time with champagne on their trays, and the party guests went back to dancing and mingling.

Roseline sought out Juliet. She was still sobbing in happiness, with tears resting on her red cheeks. She was a big apple ready to burst. Taking Juliet's hands, she asked, "Please, will you be my maid of honor, Juliet. Say you will."

Juliet's eyes widened, but she'd half expected the request. Ever since they were children, Roseline planned to marry first with the instruction that Juliet would be her maid of honor. Roseline included the game in all of their playtimes. "Of course," Juliet said, squeezing her cousin's fingers. "I'd be honored."

"Oh, you're such a love!" She threw herself straight at Juliet. "I'm so ridiculously in love," she said in her ear. "I hope you find the same one day." She squeezed hard and then backed away. "David and I need to find Anthony and thank him again for introducing us to each other."

Dexter stood behind his new *fiancée*, grinning like a donkey with a pile of apples.

Paris held up his champagne glass. "Cheers, yeah? Well done, Dexter."

"Thank you," the doctor replied and then pulled Roseline away and toward the french doors at the other end of the room.

Juliet watched them and then turned to Paris. "They've only known each other for two months."

Abram nodded. "Someone pump the brakes."

Paris shook his head. "Some people know right away that they've found the love of their life."

Juliet dropped her gaze to her champagne glass. "I don't believe in love at first sight anymore."

* * *

After the ball, Juliet changed into white pajamas with little navy stars all over them. She pulled on a thick robe and sat on the balcony where a fat yellow moon turned the balustrade gold and the grapevine to burnished bronze. The temperature had dropped into the twenties, but no snow had fallen yet. The dark clouds had remained over Lake Erie.

What Paris had said nagged at Juliet. *Some people know right away that they've found the love of their life.*

She'd never believed Paris when he'd claimed to love her. It was all too fantastic, the part about him falling in love with her photograph. All he meant was that he found her attractive. Being attracted to someone had nothing to do with finding love.

She gazed at the full moon again, so big it seemed to sit right on top of the balcony railing. The Frost Moon, she'd heard it called. She was like that moon, Juliet thought. Frosted over in the emotions department. She'd once been so passionate about love, so sure that she knew what it was all about.

Nicolo …

She and Nicolo had put their relationship on a long pause. It was Juliet's idea. Nicolo had tried to reconcile; he'd texted and asked her out. But she couldn't do it.

I don't trust you anymore.

She shook her head. Where had that thought come from? She hadn't broken off with him because she hadn't trusted him anymore. It was just that Juliet didn't believe in all that gushy love anymore. She didn't love Nicolo, and he didn't love her. It had become painfully evident over the summer. What they'd had was an attraction. But, when all the love sonnets were flat on the floor, Juliet and Nicolo had nothing left to say to each other.

And Paris?

Juliet didn't love him either, although she did care about him a great deal. It was odd how things seemed brighter because he was back in the Da Vinci house.

You were a little too needy, Nicolo.

Juliet would've never admitted such a thing last summer. Her face burned even thinking of describing Nicolo that way. She still had feelings for him. How she'd love to return to the way things were before mid-July.

No, she wouldn't go back, because she would've married Nicolo and would've found out too late that they weren't well suited together after all.

Feeling nervy all of a sudden, she traipsed through the french doors and into her room again. One of the permanent staff had lit a fire in the hearth, and the bedding was turned down.

Juliet wasn't tired, but she was hungry, and her stomach was set on ham and mozzarella fritters down in the refrigerator. She stepped into the dark hallway outside of her bedroom. There was only a tiny light near the stairwell that emanated from the ground floor. Juliet proceeded forward, hurrying a little, until a shadow moved from behind the bend in the wall.

She halted.

Paris didn't. He bumped straight into her.

Taking her by the shoulders, he asked, "Oh my God, are you okay?"

"I will be when you stop manhandling me."

He dropped his hands to his sides. "Sorry, yeah? You surprised me, bounding through the hall like that."

Juliet cringed. "I wasn't bounding…" She touched her nose – the appendage that took the brunt of the run-in with Paris' chest. "Am I bleeding?" She pushed her face toward the little bit of light available in the stairwell.

He bent toward her to get a closer look at her nose. "You'll live." Retaking her arm, he led her to the stairway. "I'm raiding the refrigerator. Join me."

"I was going that way anyway," she told him, her nose still out of joint—literally and metaphorically—because she hadn't *bounded* anywhere. It'd been a majestic frolic.

The up-lighting through the downstairs windows revealed that the furniture had been placed in the living area again. The only evidence that the party had taken place was the serving platters stacked on the dining room table. The remaining parts of the house were completely dark. Everyone was upstairs asleep.

Juliet pushed through the kitchen's swinging doors and flipped on the light switch. The hanging globes over the island counter came on. There was light in the back of the kitchen from the wine cooler.

Paris beat her to the refrigerator. He was in his pajamas too, plaid bottoms and a pale blue t-shirt. He bent forward and studied the contents on the first two shelves. "I don't want any more of those salads on a stick. I want *Italiano*." He said the last word with an accent, which wasn't even close to authentic. Paris was too Bostonian to pull it off.

Juliet reached around him and found the plate of leftover fritters. She pulled it out and set it on the counter.

Paris gazed over her shoulder. "Those look delicious."

"This is for me, get your own."

"Pfft. As if you'd eat all of those by yourself." He didn't bother with a plate or napkin and took two of the fritters in his hand.

Glass shattered on the right side of the room.

Juliet jumped.

Paris nearly dropped his fritters. "What was that?"

She leaned around the wall, thinking the noise had come from the wine cooler. Had one of the bottles exploded?

There was the cooler with its small bit of light. The four bottles inside of it looked intact. The glass front was also in one piece.

She walked toward the corner of the room.

The cellar door was shut.

Where had the noise…?

There was a light on beneath the cellar door.

Her heart gave a small jolt, and Juliet stopped moving. She needed to think through the situation. Tribly's bedroom was down another hallway. The noise hadn't come from that direction. It'd definitely come from the cellar doorway.

So, someone was downstairs, evidenced by the light beneath the door.

"Should we go have a look?" Paris asked, right behind Juliet.

She jumped again. Placing her hand over her heart, she glared at him. "What do you mean?"

"Open the door, yeah?"

Juliet let out a snort. "Yeah right. You first, Plaid Man."

"Plaid Man?"

The light beneath the door went out. Footsteps creaked on the steps. Slowly.

Juliet hadn't lowered her hand from her heart and now tightened her grip on her pajama top.

Paris still had the two fritters in his hand. He lifted both of them as though he meant to toss them if necessary.

The door swung open.

Juliet cringed.

A man stood in the doorframe.

Of course, it's Anthony. Who else would it be?

The estate manager's brows went up; he gazed at Juliet and Paris and at the fritters Paris wielded. "If I want fritters, I'll use a plate and fork, and not have you throw them into my mouth." Stepping farther into the room, he shut the door and locked it.

"We heard glass breaking," Juliet told him, getting out of his way.

He nodded and then bumped his glasses onto his nose again. "So, you came on the attack armed with donuts?"

"Well, what was all the noise about?"

Anthony walked the length of the room, toward the swinging door. "I was putting bottles back on the shelf, and one slipped."

"Oh." That was a little deflating after believing Freddy Krueger was in the basement.

"Sorry to disappoint," he said, stepping through the doors. "Goodnight."

Juliet watched the doors swing shut and then returned to the fritter plate. Selecting one, she placed it on a dish and stuck it in the microwave oven. Thinking while waiting, she said, "How weird that Anthony didn't clean the mess."

Paris finished the food in his mouth. "What mess?"

"The glass from the broken bottle." The microwave dinged, and she removed the plate. With a fork, she cut open the crust. Steam spiraled out of it. "Anthony said he broke a bottle. He didn't have time to clean it up before he came out of the cellar."

Paris shrugged. "Maybe he'll do it in the morning."

"That's not like him." She took a bite of food, breathing in a couple of times to cool the cheese down, and chewed again. She was concentrating on swallowing when she saw the spot on the floor next to her foot. "What is that, blood? Did Anthony cut himself?"

Paris gazed at the spot. "That's wine."

Juliet placed her fork on the counter. "I am a Da Vinci." She pointed to the spot. "That is not wine, *signore*."

Paris' eyes wrinkled at the corners. They were very green in the high kitchen lights. "When did you morph into your father?"

She grinned and took a new paper towel, and wiped the droplet from the floor. She held it out. "Blood."

He shrugged. "There are a lot of knives in here." His gaze went to the knife rack and the several blocks of knives on the counter. "You could film one of those slasher flicks in here."

Juliet saw another drop of blood near the curvature of the wall. She moved toward it and wiped it up too. There, near the cellar door was one more. When she blotted it, a partially dried ring of blood remained on the floor. "These aren't fresh blood marks."

Paris stood behind her. "Might've happened earlier in the evening. Probably one of the staffers cut themselves."

She twisted her mouth back and forth, thinking. "Perhaps there's more blood in the cellar."

"Go have a look, yeah?"

"Come with me?"

"I'm still hungry," he said, pointing toward the other side of the room.

Juliet stepped around him, reached onto the top of the wine cooler, and fingered the cellar's door key. She held it up for him to see. "Come on, Paris. Let's be brave."

He stood aside so that she could get the key into the door. "I'm brave, yeah?"

"Okay."

"And, what's so secretive about the wine cellar? Why is it locked?"

She turned the knob. "There's been a lot going on since our wine was featured in that magazine article."

"Food and Wine. I read the article."

She opened the door. "There's a lot of interest in my father and the company. He has a special fermenting process that people are interested in knowing. He keeps his office locked these days too." Juliet flipped on the light and studied the wooden stairs leading to the underground wine room.

There were no blood spots on the stairs.

Juliet led the way.

The room was finished out in cobblestone walls with wooden racks filled with bottles of every variety of the family wine. High archways separated the chardonnays from the merlots and so forth. The latest addition, the Limoncello was in the farthest little room.

Paris followed her down and then studied the bottles, moving from one section to another. "I heard about the takeover attempt."

Juliet spied the broken glass bottle near the end of the first aisle. "I don't know much about it." She glanced at Paris. "Did you hear that the Romeos lost everything? The same company was successful in taking over Romeo Wines."

"Just imagine, last year at this time, the Romeos would've never dreamed their entire life would get turned upside down."

Juliet nodded, thinking of Nicolo again. Last year things had been very different in her life too. Nicolo had snuck into the Harvest Ball and kissed her in this same cellar.

Stop it. All of that is over now.

She changed the subject. "I don't see any more blood."

Paris moved into the next area, the Riesling section, and he studied the floor. "None here, either… Wait."

Juliet turned around.

Paris had frozen in his spot, staring into a corner. He whispered, "Oh, damn."

A nagging little nerve stabbed Juliet between the shoulders. "More blood?" She came away from the chardonnay and stood beside him.

He nodded toward the wall. "Quite a bit, yeah?"

Her eyes followed his gaze, and then she saw her.

"O happy dagger, this is thy sheath: there rust and let me die."

Chapter 3

The server woman who'd spoken to D'Angelo and tried to splash wine on Mr. Leary lay on her side with her arm thrown over her head. Blood pooled on the floor around her. Her eyes were still open, but she was very, very dead.

Stomach in her throat, Juliet swallowed hard a couple of times, trying to keep the mozzarella fritter down. "That's—oh my God—that's the woman who handed out drinks."

Blood pooled beneath the woman's torso. A lot of it.

Juliet took a deep breath and moved toward the dead woman, looking for a wound. There was a black stain on her blouse, right above the left breast. There, on her hand, the one she'd thrown over her head, was another wound.

"She was stabbed," Paris said. "Look, above the staining on her shirt. Her blouse has been sliced open."

Juliet inched closer and then stepped around the woman's head. More blood stained the back of her blouse, and there was another slice in the fabric too.

Thoughts clicked fast in Juliet's mind. "She threw her drink at Mr. Leary. She spoke to D'Angelo. One of them killed her."

"We don't know that." Paris made a scoffing sound. "There were a lot of people at the party, Juliet."

"But she wasn't throwing liquor at the rest of them."

He shook his head, studying the woman from the front side. "It could've been one of her co-workers, her boss, anyone." He pulled a cell phone out of the pocket of his pajama bottoms. "I'm calling the police." He held up his free hand. "And don't try to talk me into calling your father down here. Remember what happened last time?"

The booming voice came from the staircase across the room, a voice that was rich and accented. "What do you think you're doing down here?"

The question had been directed at Paris.

Juliet leaned forward and stuck her head out from behind the stone archway. "He's with me, *Papà*."

Still dressed in his black slacks and button-down dinner shirt, Santos came off the stairs. "This is not a meeting spot, Juliet." He stepped closer, rounded the corner. His dark eyes went from his daughter's face to the body on the floor. "*Dios mio!*" He glared at Paris—and then smacked him on the back of the head.

"Hey," Paris said, arching away from the older man and

combing his hair down with one hand.

"Every time you show up, someone dies, eh?"

"It's not my fault that your family attracts dead bodies."

"That's not the hot issue here," Juliet reminded them both. "Paris, call the police."

"Hot issue, hot issue?" Santos asked, shaking his gray head. "I want to know how she got *dead* down here." His black eyes found Juliet again as if she knew all about it.

She threw out her arms and put a little Italian in her answer. "Someone *killed* her down here, that's how."

"It's supposed to be locked," he reminded her, throwing an arm out and pointing to the cellar stairs. "Only Anthony has the key to the cellar. Only me, eh? I didn't kill her." He gazed around the room and into the next. "Where is Anthony? He did this."

Paris held his finger in his ear while he listened to the phone. He walked away from them.

Juliet put her hand on her waist. "I'm sure he left the cellar unlocked this evening during the party. He was running in and out and getting supplies."

Santos gazed at the dead woman again. "Who is she?"

"One of the servers."

"Good, *si*. One of them killed her." He nodded. "Case closed. Bury her."

"*Papà!*"

He narrowed his eyes. "*Basta,* Juliet. I don't need this. The police will be back, snooping around our house again, accusing someone in our family of killing her."

"They are on their way." Paris slipped his phone back into his pajama pocket. "The dispatch woman said not to touch anything."

Footsteps on the stairway caused all three of them to turn.

It was Anthony. Once again, he knew there was a disturbance in the family and arrived in the nick of time. He'd changed his clothing and now wore a blue slicker and boots, as though he was on his way to bury a body…

Wait.

Anthony's words came out slowly, with a hint of suspicion in his tone, "What is going on down…?" His eyes went to the woman on the floor. "Oh."

Santos took a step toward him. "What is she doing here?"

Anthony shook his head. The orange lights of the cellar caused his angular face to take on a gaunt look. "I fired her."

"You fired her or you whacked her, which is it?" Santos asked, stepping closer and eyeing him.

Anthony bumped his glasses upward. "I told her to get off the property. Obviously, she didn't listen."

Paris made a strangled sort of noise. "How rude of her."

Juliet made a throat-cutting gesture, and then asked Anthony, "Was the cellar door locked during the party?"

His brows came together, and he shook his head. It was the first he'd ever looked confused about anything. "Not during the party, no."

"Did you let anyone else come down here to retrieve the wine?"

"Of course not," he snapped.

He needed to tone it down a little. Juliet wasn't the one standing there in outdoor gear looking for a shovel to bury a body.

But, she couldn't quite bring herself to believe Anthony killed the woman either. She said, "I'm going to go change my clothes. The police will want statements."

"You want to talk to the police, no problem," her father said. "But we all gotta say the same thing." He held up his fingers, counting, "You don't know nothing, you didn't see nothing, and you don't say nothing."

* * *

The lights from five police cruisers and a forensics van filled the driveway, lighting the six-car garage and some of the grape fields beyond them.

Nicolo Montague stepped through the back door of the house first. Eight more officers crowded into the kitchen behind him. All of them wore khaki pants and black bomber jackets with the words Mayville Police Department embroidered across their chests.

As they all piled into the room, a gust of cold air caused the swinging doors to bump together. Nicolo glanced into the kitchen area.

Juliet sat on one of the counter stools, dressed in loose-fitting gray sweatpants and hoodie sweater. At the sight of her former love, her heart began to boomerang around in her chest.

Sky blue eyes met her. He blinked a couple of times, as though trying to control his expression.

Juliet wanted to control her expression, too, and her emotions and her heart. She dropped her gaze to her fingers in her lap. Why did she still feel such an attraction to him?

"Where's the body?" Nicolo asked.

"This way," Anthony told them. He'd remained dressed in his slicker and boots, which, Juliet felt sure, meant he hadn't killed the woman in the basement. If he were guilty, he would've changed out of the gravedigger outfit and into innocuous clothing.

Juliet got off the stool and followed the officers.

Santos wiggled one hand. "Where are you going, eh?" her father wanted to know. He stood on the other side of the counter with a snifter of brandy in his other hand. "The more you don't know, the better."

"Someone needs to represent the family," she told him. "This is our house, and I'm sure they'll have questions."

"Anthony can answer their questions," he said, bringing the glass to his mouth.

"But this is our house, *Papà*. Do you want to go and represent us?"

He snorted like a bull and then knocked back a mouthful of brandy.

"We need to stay on top of this. We don't need another murder investigation leveled against us."

He waved her away, "*Si, si,* go, go."

Juliet hurried toward the cellar, not wanting to miss anything.

Paris followed her. "You made a good argument, but you're only nosy, yeah?"

"Shh."

The officers had already crowded around the woman on the floor. Most of them stood against the wine racks in the back of the small area.

Juliet leaned against the archway.

Nicolo kneeled and examined the woman. He'd left his officer's cap with fur earmuffs on, his blond hair showing at the edges. "Anybody know who she is?"

"She was a server at tonight's party, the Harvest Ball,"

Anthony explained, eyes on the body. "I fired her for spilling drinks on people and for making a nuisance of herself."

Nicolo stood and pulled off his leather gloves. From his back pocket, he took a pair of latex ones and pulled them on his hands. "What sort of nuisance?"

"Talking to people, interrupting their conversations."

Nicolo nodded and then turned his attention to the men and women near him. "Rope off this entire area and the doorway." He pointed toward the walls and stairway. "Forensics will want to examine the first floor, too. Who saw her last?"

"I guess that was me," Anthony said, stepping forward. "As I said, I fired her."

Nicolo's eyes went from Anthony to Juliet to Paris. "Anyone know her name?"

One of the officers pulled the tape through the shelves and headed toward the stairs.

Juliet moved out of the way. "I don't think she wore a name badge."

Paris lifted a shoulder. "I didn't see her when I first came into the house. And, she wasn't dressed like the other servers."

"She joined the group afterward," Anthony told them.

Nicolo's eyes followed the conversation. "We'll want to take all of your statements. You can go back upstairs." His gaze landed on Anthony. "I'll need a guest list and any surveillance video you have in the house."

Anthony nodded and stuck his hand in his pocket as if to pull out a pencil and paper.

Instead, he pulled out a boning knife.

Eight officers unsnapped the weapons on their hips.

Blinking hard, Anthony raised his hand. "Kitchen knife," he explained. He held it gingerly between his forefinger and thumb. "I forgot I put it there."

Nicolo stepped forward with his gloved hand out. "May I?"

"Of course," Anthony said, dropping it into his hand.

"Why was it in your pocket?"

Anthony dropped his hands to his sides. "Weird story that."

Juliet asked first, "How weird?"

Behind his glasses, Anthony's blue eyes pinched at the edges. "It was behind the curtain in the dining room."

No one said anything, just waited for him to carry on.

His eyes widened as he took in all the men and women surrounding him. "I changed my clothing and came back downstairs to clean up a bottle I'd dropped. When I stepped into the dining room, I saw something shining on the floor. The outside lighting had hit it just right. I bent to see what it was, and it was that knife." He pointed to Nicolo's hand.

One of the female officers held out an evidence bag, and Nicolo dropped the knife into it.

"As I said, I forgot it was in my pocket."

There was a lengthy silence.

Juliet shook her head. "Oh my goodness, Anthony didn't kill her. If he did, you'd never find the body or the weapon." She'd meant that in the best possible way.

More silence and all the pairs of eyes landed on her.

Nicolo tilted his head forward. "So what you're saying is, is that Anthony *could* kill someone?"

Isn't it obvious?

"He's an ex-army ranger, remember?"

Nicolo raised one brow. "No, I'd forgotten that."

Paris whispered over her shoulder. "You're not helping."

She glanced toward Anthony, her cheeks warming. "You know what I mean." She waved her hand. "If he'd killed the woman, he wouldn't just stand there."

Which made perfect sense.

Santos' voice drifted from behind her. He leaned on the cellar stair railing and ducked his gray head to see them. "*Sì*, the girl would be buried by now in the vineyard. Nobody would've called the police."

It dawned on Juliet that she might be on the wrong side of this conversation if she and her father said the same thing.

Nicolo shook his head. "Please wait upstairs, all of you." Then he turned his attention to the woman on the ground again.

In the kitchen, Santos turned on Anthony. "Did you kill her? Tell me now."

Anthony sidestepped him and took a seat at the dinette table.

Juliet sat beside him. "Don't even joke like that, *Papà*."

Santos poured another glass of whiskey and then leaned his back against the island counter. "Joke? I'm not a funny man. I'm not a comedian." He glared at Anthony with his gray bushy brows gathered together like a furry worm. "Did you do it? Say so, we call someone. Nobody knows what happened."

Anthony leaned back in the chair. "I didn't know the woman well enough to want to kill her."

"Of course you didn't," Juliet told him. "It was somebody at the party."

Santos shook his finger at Anthony. "Be careful, my

friend. These officers will arrest you whether you killed the woman or not."

"He didn't," Juliet reiterated.

Santos ignored her. "Perhaps you should visit your family for a while. My helicopter is outside in the fields. Do you have family in Mexico?"

"Oh, for goodness sake," Juliet said, getting out of her chair. "I'll figure out who killed her."

Three pairs of male eyes stared at her.

Her father got his words out first. "You will not chase a killer again, *capiche*? I forbid it."

* * *

Nicolo didn't interview Juliet.

One of the policewomen took her statement, of how she'd seen the blood marks on the floor and followed them into the basement. Juliet hadn't realized she'd disturbed evidence. The policewoman wasn't too happy about it and made Juliet find the napkin in the trashcan.

Juliet didn't get to sleep until four o'clock in the morning. She woke at nine, showered, and changed into a long skirt, ginger spice sweater, and leather boots.

It seemed to hit her more, after waking, that a woman had died during the party. How could that have happened? To see the woman alive and breathing one minute, and then …

She wandered downstairs into the kitchen, forgetting the forensic people who swarmed the bottom floor of the house. She couldn't get to the espresso machine.

Paris stood near the swinging doors, watching the officers dust for prints. His expression matched Juliet's.

She suggested, "How about the Wake-Up Cafe?"

"I'll drive," he told her, pulling keys from his pocket.

Paris' Jaguar was still parked in the driveway in front of the house. He backed onto the main entrance and then put the car into Drive. They were on the road and moving toward *Via Cavour* when he glanced toward her. "How are you and Nicolo doing?"

Her stomach muscles tightened. "We're not *doing*," she said, leaning back in the seat and tightening her seatbelt. "You know I called it quits."

"I do know that," he said, nodding his dark head. He steered the car with one hand, his other wrist resting on top of the wheel. "But I also saw the way you two looked at each other last night when he came into the room." His green eyes stared straight ahead.

"You don't want Nicolo and me back together, do you? Since you're so in love with me." She threw him a quick grin.

He didn't return her smile. "I'm not going to love a woman who loves someone else." He gave her a quick glance and then watched the road again. "And I wonder if you should cut people a break. They were lousy friends, yeah, but you can't stay mad forever."

"You've been talking to my mother." Juliet's top teeth worked her bottom lip.

He nodded. "I have. She said you stay in the house all the time."

"That's not true."

He drove fast toward Verona's Vineyard. "The one thing that I came to appreciate about you over the summer was your faith in your friends and your love for your home town. You were such a free spirit and passionate all at the same time. I'd hate to see you lose that."

"Oh, for goodness sake," she told him, "I'm just a little distrustful of people at the moment. Once I find some new friends, all of that will change."

"New friends, is that the strategy?"

"Yes. That is the strategy."

During the autumn and winter months, the town of Verona's Vineyard wasn't much of a tourist draw. There were no ski slopes in the area to pull in families and athletes. It was the spring and summer times when the swell of visitors converged on the little town, since the temperatures didn't rise above the low eighties and there was always a breeze off Lake Erie.

One of the biggest reasons people visited Verona's Vineyard was because it was built to resemble the Sicilian town of Taormina. There was no Greek theater, but there was the Catholic Church with a courtyard made up of harlequin tiling. The dizzying brick streets wound through medieval architecture filled with shops, bars, and restaurants. Out of the center of the town rose the colossal bell tower of St. Mary's.

Once they neared town, Paris slowed the Jaguar to the city speed limit and then found a parking spot right outside the little cafe.

Juliet said, "I remember you had trouble before you came to visit here for the first time. And now you're back again. Don't you like your friends at home anymore?"

He switched off the engine and turned in his seat to gaze at her. "I did a little reconciling while I was there. I came back because I'm going to move here." Without giving her a chance to reply, he pulled on the door handle and opened his door.

"Holy Saint Francis, what change is here?"

Chapter 4

Juliet practically jumped out of the car. "You're moving here?"

He grinned, waiting on the sidewalk with his hands in his pants pockets. He wore jeans this morning and a long-sleeved t-shirt and jacket. "You're happy about it?"

Her heart was a butterfly flitting in her chest. "Yes."

They stepped through the door of the Wake-Up Cafe. Tables for two were the only seating except for a long leather bench against the plate glass window. The warm air smelled of coffee beans with a hint of butter and sugar and vanilla. Paris' news and the smell of coffee did wonders for Juliet's mood.

Two baristas stood behind the counter; both seemed eager to take their orders. The woman with the pink hair asked, "*Affogato,* Juliet?"

"Yes, please," she answered and moved aside for Paris to order.

Once they had their coffees, they made their way to one of the little tables. Paris asked, "Everyone back to loving Juliet?"

"Doesn't matter. I know their hearts." She took her seat and changed her tone to a happy note. "So, you're here for good?"

He sat too, taking up much of the view with his broad shoulders. "I am. I've got my eye on a few houses."

"A house?" The heart-butterfly missed a beat. "How far away are you moving from us?"

He put his coffee cup on the table. "I'm looking for a place somewhere between Verona's Vineyard and Buffalo."

"You might as well stay in Martha's Vineyard as to move to Buffalo. That's too far away."

"Well, I'm not going to live in your house, Juliet. You didn't really think I would?"

She lifted a shoulder. "But, Buffalo?"

He shook his head, leaning forward. He'd washed his dark wavy hair, and it was thick enough to still be damp. "I didn't say Buffalo. I said between here and Buffalo."

"That's fine," she told him, making a face, indicating it didn't matter to her where he set up house. Paris was like everyone else, wasn't he? "Whatever you want."

He drew his faint brows together. "What I want is for you to help me look for a place."

The butterfly flapped in rhythm again. "You do?"

"I do. I trust your opinion. Will you help me?"

"I suppose I can carve out some time for you."

Paris leaned back in his seat again and gazed around the room. "What happened to Ganozza's bakery? When I left, your father wanted to sell it."

She nodded, holding her coffee cup with two hands, willing the warmth of it to thaw her fingers. "He still does, but *Matri* and I don't want him to sell. It's a little piece of Ganozza that we can't seem to let go."

"I thought it would go to Ty. How is he, by the way?"

"He actually still lives with us."

Paris frowned. "Where was he last night?"

"Up in his room with his cats."

"That sounds healthy," he said, taking a sip of coffee.

"Right? He's better than he was, I suppose. The monkshood damaged his lungs, and he can't get his breath enough to dance just yet, so he mopes around."

The bell over the door rang, and Juliet glanced in that direction.

It was Anthony. He strolled through the door, wearing a long jacket over his crisply creased pants and white shirt. He joined them at the small table. "Can't get a decent cup of coffee with those forensic people dusting everything." He wore real gold cufflinks and a *Movado* watch. Juliet suspected the gold that trimmed his eyewear was eighteen carat. Anthony was attractive because he knew how to spend his money to look good. If he were a poor man, he'd be a bald forty-something of average height.

He leaned forward, gazing to the left and right. "I found out that the woman who died last night didn't work for Abate Staffing."

Juliet leaned back in her chair. "What? You mean she just showed up and handed out drinks on her own?"

"I contacted the owner this morning, and he said all of their staff left in the vans last night. Every one of them are accounted for."

"That explains her ineptitude," Paris added. "So, what was she doing at the Harvest Ball?"

"I have my ideas," Anthony told him. "Let me get my coffee ordered, and I'll fill you in." He came back to the table in less than a minute but didn't sit. "The police said the woman had no ID on her, no credit cards. And, she'd been dead at least four hours when you found her." He nodded at Juliet.

"Four hours?" she asked, her mind ticking the details. "So, she died around eight o'clock." She gazed at Paris. "What time did she throw the wine at Leary?"

Paris shrugged. "I didn't see her throw wine."

"You got to the party at six," she reminded Paris. "Roseline and Dexter didn't get there until after seven. It was after that … It had to be Leary who killed her."

"That's remarkable," Anthony said with a straight face. "You figured out the murder by one clue."

Paris asked, "How did you arrive at Mr. Leary?" He sounded less impressed than Anthony, which was a feat.

Juliet waved them both off. "She spoke to D'Angelo too. He didn't like her. He was suspicious of her. He spoke her language."

"What language?"

She nodded at Paris because that was a good question. "Sing-songy stuff with chirping sounds."

"Bird language?" Paris asked.

Anthony shook his head. "Middle Eastern."

Juliet pointed at him. "You know what I'm saying…"

"I have no idea what you're saying. I assumed it was a

Middle Eastern language because the woman was Middle Eastern."

She shook her head. "Or we can just go with *you* killing her, Anthony."

"Okay, so Leary made her angry, you say?"

Paris sat forward. "Or one of the other hundred people who were there. What about the other servers?"

Juliet shook her head. "I think I'm on to something."

Anthony stuck his hands in his coat pocket. "I had to walk her outside because she wouldn't leave on her own. Twice. I threatened to call the police."

Juliet gazed out the café window. "So she came to the party for a specific reason. To see someone."

"Or some*thing*," Anthony added.

Paris added, "And she wasn't going to leave until she saw that someone or something."

"Right," Juliet said.

The barista called out Anthony's drink order and set it on the glass case.

He raised his finger in acknowledgment but remained with them at the table. "I locked the kitchen and front doors the second time I tossed her out."

Juliet continued to nod, thinking through all the clues. "If she died in the second hour of the party, then she got back inside the house pretty quickly."

Paris said, "Somebody killed her outside and then dragged her in and threw her in the basement."

"There'd be more blood in the kitchen if that were the case. And the security cameras would've picked it up. I wonder if they've looked at those yet?" Juliet gazed at the foam in the coffee cup in front of her. "I say she died in the cellar."

"That means she came back inside again."

"The french doors were open," Anthony reminded them. "She could've gone around the side of the house and strolled right back in."

Juliet nodded. "To throw more wine at Leary."

Anthony took three steps and grabbed his coffee. "I've got to drive to West Portland this morning. I'll ask Geoff Leary if he killed her. Will that help, Juliet?"

She gave him a flat look. "How were you ever a spy?"

He raised his cup in farewell and then headed outside.

Paris leaned in. "Your father *forbade* you from investigating the case."

She laughed. "Forbade."

Paris' mouth turned downward. "So, you are going to snoop around again?"

"Actually, I'm a little hesitant about chasing after a killer." And she really was hesitant, not because her father had forbidden it, but because she'd been so horribly wrong before. She'd been lucky last summer. And by lucky, she meant really badly surprised, because she'd nearly died for her mistake.

No, this time, Juliet meant to let Nicolo and the police handle the dead woman in the cellar.

* * *

Dressed the next morning in a creamy cozy sweater, skinny jeans, and with a wide clip holding up her curls, Juliet poured the espresso into a small cup at the kitchen counter. A pair of Bichon pups sat at her feet. Her mother had named them Dolce and Gabbana, which sounded expensive and well-bred, but they were nothing but a couple of moochers. "You're not getting coffee," she told them. "It'll make you nervous. Nervouser."

Nervouser?

She had the cup halfway to her lips when the first bong of the doorbell sounded.

The dogs took off, zero-to-greyhound, in two seconds flat. Theirs was a continuous bark in the tone of laryngitis. One of them had scratched Juliet's boots on its flyby, causing her to jiggle her cup and spill some of it.

She studied her boot for damage.

The doorbell went off again.

Juliet wasn't going to answer anything until she took a sip.

Bong, bong, bong.

Plodding to the swinging door, she pushed open the left one and waited while Anthony came off the staircase and checked the entryway monitor.

The dogs jumped at the door until Anthony shooed them away and pulled one side open. Then he stepped aside to allow their guests to enter.

Nicolo came through the door first, dressed in his police uniform. Two more officers followed him inside.

Ah, news!

Juliet set her cup on the dining room table and listened from the arched doorway of the room.

Nicolo hadn't noticed her. His attention rested on Anthony. "We've discovered the dead woman's name. Mr. Yeager, do you know Gemma Hakim?"

"So she was a spy," Anthony said, as if he'd suspected it all along.

Nicolo shifted his posture. His chin-length hair was in a knot at the base of his neck. "What do you mean, spy?"

"It has to do with the takeover attempt."

Juliet couldn't see Anthony's face. It seemed he didn't look at Nicolo, but on the floor as if putting clues together.

"Right," Nicolo said, glancing at the officers with him.

Juliet recognized Gary Blanchard. He was as tall as Nicolo and had the belly of a Sumo wrestler. One of the dogs sniffed his shoe and then his pant leg, but Gary kept his attention on the matter at hand and with his right hand resting on his gun belt.

Nicolo said, "We have witnesses who've seen you with a woman who fits Hakim's description."

"Seen *me*?"

"In town, in restaurants." He leveled his gaze. "Dating."

Juliet's mouth fell open. *Anthony dates?*

"I've never met a Gemma Hakim. The first time I saw her was at the party."

Nicolo nodded. "Forensics came back on the knife you pulled from your pocket. It is the murder weapon. Yours are the only prints on the knife, Mr. Yeager."

Juliet's fingers tingled and she rubbed them together, chest level. It was happening again, wasn't it? Someone she loved was being questioned for murder.

Nicolo waved his hand at the door. "We'd like you to come down to the station and answer a few more questions." Without glancing her way, he nodded toward the dining room. "Juliet can tell everyone where you are."

How had he known she was there?

Perhaps he remembered how nosy Juliet was and assumed she was lurking nearby.

After the men moved outside, she slipped toward the dining room windows and watched the officers lead Anthony to one of the cruisers.

Should I go along?

No, she'd never be allowed into the interrogation room.

Ruffling the curtain fabric between her fingers, Juliet thought through what Nicolo had said: Anthony's fingerprints were the only ones on the knife?

He'd claimed he saw the knife in the small light from the window when he came down the stairs the other night. Was he lying?

No, Juliet didn't believe that.

Anthony saw the knife when he came down the stairs, and he picked it up and put it in his slicker pocket. Why had he put on a slicker and boots? And why did he come back downstairs?

Maybe he meant to take out the broken glass to the garbage bins. He put on the slicker to stay warm in the night air, and then came downstairs to complete the chore only to find everyone standing over a dead woman.

Right.

And in the meantime, he found the knife behind a curtain.

If he weren't her friend, Juliet would think Anthony murdered Gemma Hakim.

But he was her friend, and he didn't murder anyone, so …

His were the only prints on the murder weapon, which meant that the killer wiped the knife before hiding it behind the curtain. Whoever murdered Gemma Hakim killed her in the cellar and then came back to the party.

Which was quite nervy.

Who do I know that nervy?

Anthony.

Focus!

What about those drops of blood on the kitchen floor?

The killer cleaned off the knife at the sink, not realizing he'd dripped blood on the floor.

Juliet let the curtain fall back into place.

I'm not a detective. The police will solve this.

Still, she needed to tell her father what had happened to Anthony. She crossed the room, pushed open the swinging doors, and exited the house by the back door.

Juliet hadn't bothered with a jacket, hadn't thought about the still twenty-something degree weather.

"Ohh, it's a little nippy," she said out loud, spying an employee golf cart parked next to the garage. She found the key in the ignition and then blasted toward the gardener's cottage.

It was an uphill journey. The colorful mountains in the east were splattered white with snow. There was a smell of evergreens on the breeze and woodsmoke from one of the chimneys.

The wind chill in the open-air cart was in the teens. Juliet's ears burned.

Can't feel fingers. Can't blink eyes ...

Santos stood outside the cottage in his long wool coat. He spoke to one of the workers and pointed to the espalier pergolas. It was one of his newer ventures, growing lemons for the Limoncello liqueur he'd added to his stock. The fruit trees did really well in the New York climate. Her father babied the trees by lighting smudge pots to keep them warm.

Juliet parked the cart near the cottage.

Her father must've heard the cart engine because he turned, and then threw out his hand. "*Mia figlia.*"

Juliet nodded to the workman. Between the chattering

of her teeth, she told her father, "I need to speak to you right away."

Santos draped his arm around her shoulders. "Sit with me in the office."

Years ago, workers gutted the gardener's cottage and turned it into an office. The kitchen was on one side of the old living room, and there was an office area on the other side. Black paint trimmed the gray walls. A sleek desk sat in the middle of the dark wood flooring.

Juliet didn't sit. She paced the length of one wall and rubbed her arms to slow the frostbite.

"Stop with the back and forth. You're making me dizzy."

She stood still and placed her hands on her waist. "Nicolo just took Anthony in for questioning about the murder in our basement."

Santos slammed his fist on the desk. "I never liked your boyfriend. You're never allowed to date again. Not until you're thirty and married."

"Nicolo is not …"

"Good!" Rounding the desk, he paced the other side of the room. His direction was the opposite of Juliet's. "What am I going to do now? I need Anthony here."

They both stopped mid-pace and faced each other.

Juliet said, "They'll let him go." Her confident tone did nothing to ease her worry. Her father hadn't been guilty of murder either, but he'd wound up in jail.

"*Si*, and in the meantime, my grapes get sour at the warehouse."

"You have other men to see to the grapes."

He paced again.

Juliet marched in the opposite direction. "You should

go to the station and find out what's going on. Talk to the police. Tell them Anthony didn't do it."

Santos stopped again. Now they were on opposite sides of the office. "Me? You think your boyfriend cares what I say? I show up, and he'll throw me in jail, too."

"He will not."

Santos pointed a finger. "Maybe you should make the googly eyes at the policeman, eh? It might keep me out of jail." He paced again. "Anthony is a smart man. If he killed the woman, no one would catch him."

"That's what I said, and everyone got mad." Juliet stayed where she was and leaned against one of the wingback chairs. "We both know that isn't the case, though. I do wonder about a couple of men at the party."

Santos jerked to a stop. "Who?"

"D'Angelo spoke to Hakim."

He narrowed his dark eyes. "Hakim? What do you know about Hakim?"

"Nothing. That's her name, though, Gemma Hakim. The police just said so."

With his hands on his hips, he stared out the many-paned windows. "Here's what we're going to do—we're going to find a new manager."

"Blistered be thou tongue for such a wish."

Chapter 5

Stop acting as though Anthony had something to do with it."

He whipped his gray head around. "The Hakims were the ones trying to steal our information, trying to take over our company. Anthony stopped it once. Now he stopped it for good."

"He wouldn't need to kill the woman. All he needed to do was call the police." She tapped one boot heel on the toe of the other, thinking. "Does Anthony have a girlfriend?"

"What do I know about his love life?"

"I can't imagine him having one," she admitted. "I always think of Anthony here around the house and in the vineyard."

Her father went back around his desk and pulled his phone from his pocket.

Juliet placed her stomach against the back of the chair and watched him. "Who are you calling?"

"I'm texting Anthony."

"He's being interrogated, *Papà*."

"He has a job, Juliet. He doesn't have time for that."

"What about Mr. D'Angelo, did you know that he spoke to the Hakim woman?"

He shrugged. "So?"

"They spoke to each other in a foreign language." She ran her fingernail along the seam on the top of the chair. "Where's he from?"

"Smucker's."

"What?"

He threw out his hands. "He worked for Smucker's Company when we hired him."

"I meant what country."

He dropped the phone on the desk and sat in the chair. "How should I know? Maybe Italy. D'Angelo is a fine Italian name."

"They didn't speak Italian to each other." Leaving the chair seam alone, she placed her hands on top. "Why did he want to leave Smucker's?"

Santos shrugged and then ran a hand through his thick gray hair. "He said something about wanting to be near his son. Anthony is the one who knows these things. That's what I pay him to do, know things."

"Then I'll talk to Anthony when he gets home," she said, leaving her father.

* * *

It wasn't unusual for Juliet and her mother to have lunch together since last June's events. It healed them both a little.

They ate at *Al Saraceno,* on the terrace. They were in the shade, but large outdoor heaters warmed the space. Wrought iron fencing separated the tables from the sidewalk where gas lamps glowed even at midday.

Italia was in a cheerful mood, despite Anthony being questioned at the police department.

Head still firmly in the sand.

Fifteen minutes into the Prosecco and cheese course, Olive and Emma Moretti stepped onto the terrace. Juliet and the Moretti twins had gone to school together and had been fast friends most of their lives. Until last summer. Juliet had put the distance between herself and the twins.

Now it seemed Italia was trying to close the gap for them.

The young women weren't identical twins. Olive was the taller of the two, and she wore her auburn hair straight to her shoulders.

Emma had her brunette hair cut in a pixie style. She was the more stylish of the girls. Today she'd dressed in a long sleeve sweater, baggy jeans, and mustard-colored boots.

Olive was the sporty type. Judging by her outfit, she'd hit the golf course that morning as she'd dressed in a black sports top, black skirt, pink leggings, and *Nike* tennis shoes. Olive was the first to greet Juliet, hugging her, and saying, "I've missed you!"

Juliet nodded and moved her chair over so that Emma could sit next to her.

Olive sat opposite. "We don't see you enough."

"Everyone's busy," Juliet said, sitting back so that the waitress could remove the plate from in front of her.

Italia shook her head. She wore a scarf and large sunglasses, like a movie star. "Stop it, Juliet. You're not that busy. As a matter of fact…"

"Paris is back," Juliet told the girls, faking a smile. Her hands rolled the napkin in her lap, and then she snapped it like a rope, imagining it would look fantastic around her mother's neck right then.

"Paris Nobleman?" Olive asked.

Juliet nodded, her hands on the arms of the chair. "Yes, and he's moving to Verona's Vineyard. I'm helping him hunt for a house." She hadn't done that yet, but Juliet imagined it was going to consume large chunks of her time.

Olive leaned back a little, eyeing Juliet. "I suppose he needs to move somewhere now that his family disowned him."

Juliet blinked a couple of times. "What?"

"Portia told me," Olive explained.

Portia?

That's right, Olive spoke of Portia once in a while. She knew the young woman from … Juliet couldn't remember right then. "Who's Portia again?"

"Paris' sister, of course. I met her in college." Olive bent forward. "I don't know all the details. Portia mentioned it as an aside, but she said Paris had a row with his parents over a woman. He got his affairs in order and moved out of the house."

Juliet gazed at her mother. "Did you know about this?"

Italia hadn't been listening. The waitress returned with their salads, and she'd moved back to allow the woman to put the plate on the table. "What's that, dear? You're going skiing?"

"Skiing?"

Emma nodded. "We've come to ask you to go skiing with us the day after Thanksgiving. We've already rented a chalet. Say you'll come."

"I don't know," Juliet said. Her mother had cooked this up, that was for sure. "Let me check my datebook."

Her mother lifted her sunglasses. "I've already checked your datebook. You're free. And a ticket to the lodge is cheaper than a psychologist. You're going."

* * *

Juliet arrived home after four o'clock.

Tribly was in the kitchen preparing dinner, which was still four hours away, chicken and pancetta by the smell of it. She took the pan off the stove. It still sizzled. "This garlic, don't throw it out." Putting it back on the stove, she told them, "This is Da Vinci gold."

Her father sat at the dinette table with papers in front of him. "Stop yelling."

"I'm not yelling," Tribly hollered.

"Is Anthony home?" Juliet asked, setting her purse on the island.

"No," her father said. "No phone calls, he doesn't answer my texts."

Juliet picked up her purse again. "I'm going to the police station. Come with me, *Papà*."

"Leave it alone," he told her, going around the counter and watching Tribly stir the meat in the pan. "They will inform us, eh?"

"But he's been there for at least eight hours," she said, tapping her inner-Tribly and throwing out her free hand. "They should've released him by now." She turned toward the door. "He'll need a ride home."

"I told you not to get involved in this, Juliet," Santos called after her.

She held the door open. "How am I involved? I just want to know what's happening with Anthony. He's more than a manager, *Papà*. He's our friend."

"Don't make this a big ta-do." Tribly's black hair curled tightly on top of her head, and she wore baggy leopard skin pants and a white blouse. "We know some people. We'll get him out."

"Who do you know?" Santos said, holding out the palm of his hand and shaking his head. "You don't know anybody, *Matri*." He looked at Juliet. "She thinks she's *Mafioso* now."

Juliet walked out and climbed into the Fiat.

The police station was on *Via Cavour*, and if she drove across the vineyard, she'd make it in five minutes. By the highway, it took twenty minutes.

Nicolo's jeep was still in the parking lot. Had he questioned Anthony all day long?

She stepped inside the small outer office. The walls had been painted a dingy green shade, as though whoever had chosen the color decided a criminal's visitor deserved no beauty whatsoever. To the left was a waiting area. Apparently, visitors deserved *Sanka* coffee and uncomfortable seating too.

In front of Juliet was a reception desk with a glass window only a quarter of the way open. Leaning her palms against the ledge, she asked, "Can you tell me if Anthony Yeager is still here?"

Desk Sergeant Donata Zizzo spun her chair around and stood.

Juliet's mood dropped two notches with one look at those maroon-dyed spikes on the sergeant's head.

They resembled knives.

Approaching the window, Donata asked, "You want me to tell you? I'll tell you." She hailed from New Jersey and had never lost the accent. Laying her hands on the desk, she leaned toward the window.

Juliet waited.

The woman's eyes squinted tighter.

Oh, was that supposed to be a question? "Yes. I want you to tell me," Juliet answered.

Up this close, Donata's smoker's lips were much more pronounced. People could sail boats in them. "Mr. Yeager is being held in jail until further notice."

"What?" She pushed off the counter. "He's under arrest?"

Donata sighed as though Juliet exhausted her. "Yes, that's what it means to be held in jail, Miss Da Vinci."

"Is he allowed visitors?"

"Until eight o'clock. But you already know the rules of the jailhouse, don't you?"

That was rich coming from Zizzo when her own cousin, Este Romeo, sat in the state penitentiary for murder one.

But, Juliet was not going to get dragged into the old family feud. She asked, "May I see him?"

Old Zizzo's face fell, presumably disappointed that Juliet hadn't taken the bait. She hit a button on the desk.

The double doors to the right buzzed.

Juliet took off, her shoulder bag beating her across the back. She had only one chance to get through the doors. Zizzo wouldn't open them twice.

There were three cells in the room. Anthony was in the

middle one, leaning against the pale blue cinderblock wall. The place smelled like a cross between bleach and a fun night in Amsterdam.

"Did you bring a nectarine grenade?"

She frowned. "What?"

"Never mind. I do need my cellphone charger next time you come."

"They're allowing you a cellphone?" She moved her purse strap and held onto the bars.

"For the time being and only here. If they move me to another facility, they will take my phone and I'm sure they'll look at the text and call messages." He got off the cot. "I'm here until the arraignment, whenever that is. What are you doing here?"

"I got worried." She waved a hand toward the three jail cells. "This was what I was worried about. It's all happening again. Someone was murdered, a Da Vinci is accused."

"I'm not a Da Vinci."

"Yes, you are," she told him, cross about it. Her brows hurt from gathering them constantly. "And I must say, you do look guilty."

His hands landed on his hips. "Is this you being on my side?"

She glanced toward the door, and then she dropped her voice. "This is me being angry at you for acting so stupidly dumb. You broke the wine bottle in the basement when you saw a dead body, didn't you?"

Hands still on his hips, he leaned away from the bars. "You don't know…"

"You were going to move the body, that's why you changed your clothes."

Anthony glanced toward the door, too, and then at the

bars near the ceiling. Did he think the room was bugged? Moving closer to the bars, he dropped his voice. "Your family does not need another scandal."

"So you were going to get rid of her? For *Papà's* sake? And what about the knife?"

His eyes widened. "I didn't kill her, Juliet."

"Where was the knife, originally?"

"Just as I said, behind the curtain, but I didn't find it when I came downstairs the last time. I found it earlier. I didn't overthink it until I saw a woman dead on the floor."

"You were going to get rid of them both?"

"It would've been easy. But then you and Paris went downstairs and had to call the police."

"Of course we called the police, especially after last summer."

His blue eyes grew hard behind those fancy glasses. "You should've let me handle it."

She took a tiny gasp. "Then you should've told me there was a dead body downstairs."

"Keep your voice down."

"You keep your voice down," she said, even louder.

He closed his eyes for a moment, as though collecting himself.

Juliet lowered her voice. "What do we do now?"

Opening his eyes, he shrugged. "Hope the police find the real killer."

She dropped her hands from the bars and walked toward the end of the cell and back. "You said Gemma Hakim was a spy. When Nicolo came to the house, that was your first response." She stopped in front of him. "At the café the other morning, you said something about having ideas about who she was."

He nodded. "Hakim."

"Right, right. It's the wine company's name, the one that tried to take over our company. But why would Hakim Wine send a spy to our house?"

He placed both his hands on the horizontal bar, where he leaned his weight on his palms. "There are a couple of reasons I can think of. Number one, she wanted to go through your father's paperwork and learn about our fermenting process. That's the prize, that's the information they want."

"It's that special?"

He shrugged. "It seems to make tasty wine."

She paced again. "What other reason? You said you could think of a couple."

"It's the more likely reason. Ms. Hakim was going to meet someone who would give her the information. I told you that she kept coming back to the party, even after I threatened to call the police. I think she had a contact, and there was going to be a hand-off. They met in the basement, and things turned ugly."

Juliet stood in front of him again. "Someone hands her the information, she gives them the money … Why kill her?"

"Tijuana Refund."

"What's that?"

Anthony straightened and then leaned on the bars. "Whoever was offering the information took the money and then changed their mind. They killed her and took the information back, along with the money."

"That's a lousy way to do business."

He shrugged.

"It narrows the field a little, though. The killer is

someone who works for Renaissance Wine and has access to the fermenting process."

"Or stole it when someone wasn't looking."

"Don't the employees working with the wine know the process?" Juliet asked. "It could be anyone, and surely it's not that much of a secret."

"You're wrong about that. It's a very secretive process, one which the employees only know parts of, not the whole. Three people have access to the complete information."

"And they are?"

"Your father, me, and Sebastian D'Angelo. Like I said, someone could've stolen it, most likely from D'Angelo's office."

Juliet raised her finger and shook it. "D'Angelo. He's right in the middle of this."

Anthony shook his head. "He took a loyalty oath, signed a contract."

"If the price was right."

"It'd have to be millions. Your father pays him well."

She paced to the door and back. "What about Mr. Leary? Gemma threw wine at him. That means something."

"Maybe he said something crude."

"I can believe that. He's often crude."

"But why would she throw wine at someone whom she was buying information from?"

Juliet bit her thumbnail before answering, "Maybe she needed a reason to get him alone. He'd have to go clean his shirt."

"If that were the case, she would've made sure to hit him with the wine." He shook his head. "No, Geoff Leary is the one who stopped the takeover attempt in the first place."

"I thought you stopped the takeover bid."

"Geoff was the one who tipped me off to what was happening. He's loyal. He's not a spy."

Juliet wasn't so sure about that. Leary might be loyal, but he had the potential to murder someone. She could tell just by looking into his bulldog face. "Now what?"

Anthony placed his hands on his hips again. He didn't look at Juliet, but stared somewhere behind her. "I will hire a corporate spy. Someone who'll fit in and figure out who stole our information."

Juliet wrinkled her nose, thinking about that. Wouldn't it take a long time for Anthony to hire someone and then put that person into place? "What if I do it?"

His eyes focused on her again. "You?"

Her stomach knotted. "*Papà* has always wanted me to get more involved in the business."

"You're certainly nosy enough," he told her, coming back to the bars. "And, you're reckless."

"I'll just make some friends, listen to gossip, and keep my eyes open. It'll be faster this way, and I already know what to look for."

He nodded. "And, if you see something, you tell me, or you tell the police. No going it alone this time."

"Absolutely. I learned my lesson last time."

* * *

It was dark when Juliet drove home—with the knot in her stomach still tight. She turned on the seat warmers and bent the heat vent toward her feet. In blew the scent of warm honey locust.

There, that was a little better. Tree smells always relaxed her.

Besides, I'm not hunting for a killer. I'm only gathering information.

Her sleuthing had to be done in a low-key manner because, absolutely, she wasn't a detective and wasn't striving to be one. Her going to work for Renaissance Wines would just be her small contribution to the family business. And if the spy turned out to be the murderer too…

The knot tightened.

It would be a good thing, a great idea, because Anthony's name would be cleared, and everything would be as it should.

Pulling the Fiat into the driveway, she hit a button and one of the garage doors opened. She parked and got out of the car.

Now to ask *Papà* for a job. That was the easy part.

She'd just made it in time for dinner. The rest of the family was at the table when she stepped into the dining room. A small fireplace was lit behind her father at the head of the table.

Juliet removed her jacket and hung it on the rack before backtracking to the table. "Where's Ty?" She glanced left and right. "Where's Paris?"

Italia waved Juliet to her side. "Kiss me."

Juliet kissed her on the cheek.

Her mother said, "They went to see a house."

Juliet took a seat and placed a napkin in her lap. "Paris asked me to look at houses with him."

Tribly said, "You weren't here."

"Where've you been?" Italia asked. She still wore her black knit dress and silk scarf.

"In jail," Juliet told her. Her mother deserved no more answer than that, after what she'd pulled at lunchtime.

Italia leaned back and eyed her thoughtfully. "Well, at least you were out of the house."

Juliet ignored the dig and turned toward her father. "Are you even aware that Anthony has been arrested?"

He finished the pasta in his mouth and then wiped his lips with a napkin. "*Sì*, he texted me. That is a fine way for me to learn this fact."

Juliet pulled the pasta bowl to her plate. Taking the tongs, she served herself. "You could've come with me. You knew where I was going."

He shrugged. "He texted me."

Juliet squinted her eyes at him and shook her head. "You just said…" She put the tongs back into the bowl. "Never mind. *Papà*, can I have a job at the West Portland office?" She waited with her hands pressed in front of her as if she was in prayer.

His dark eyes lifted. "What do you mean?"

"Isn't it what you've always wanted? I thought you'd be happy that I want to get involved in the family business." She glanced at her mother.

A huge smile formed on Italia's face. "What a wonderful idea."

Juliet turned to Tribly.

The old woman concentrated on her pasta.

Santos swallowed his food, eyeing Juliet at the same time. Finally, "Has this got something to do with you sniffing around D'Angelo?"

"Sniffing? I never…"

He leaned toward her, fork pointing. "You know what I mean. You asked about him this morning. What are you doing, eh?"

Oh, that's right, he'd forbidden her to get involved.

"It's, well, I'm bored," she admitted, leaning back in her chair. "I want something to do."

He waved the fork in the air, making circles. "Then go to Italy and visit the family." He bowed his head and ate more pasta.

Italia said, "Stop it, Santos. I want her to have a job."

Juliet grinned.

Her mother smiled, too. It was a gentle thing, full of kindness and concern. "I spoke to Dr. Dexter, and he knows a psychologist for you to see."

Juliet stopped grinning.

"Give him a call," her mother said, reaching across the table. "Take this opportunity to work through your homophobia."

"Homo … you mean agoraphobia … *Matri*!"

Italia shrugged and told her husband. "She's scared to leave the house. She will die if she doesn't get out of the house."

"This never happens in Italy." He wiped his mouth with a napkin and threw it on the table. "Why is this happening here? What is wrong with you?"

Tribly jumped in, sonic voiced, "She's scared to die, this one." She pointed a crooked finger at Juliet. "Her head is shrinking on her body. She doesn't leave the house."

Her father's eyes were narrow slits. He jabbed his bread chunk at her. "You will work, *sì*? I will make a phone call. You will work."

*"Unseemly woman in a seeming man.
Thou hast amazed me."*

Chapter 6

On Sunday morning, Juliet sat in the front pew of St. Mary's Catholic Church. Paris was on one side of her and Roseline on the other. Next to Roseline was her fiancé, Dr. Dexter.

Dexter seemed keen on church. He'd lit a candle when he'd first arrived and then sat very still during the call to worship music. Perhaps he prayed, prayed hard for Roseline to stop crying over her engagement ring.

Every time.

Every time she glanced at the two-carat rock, she'd well up, and the waterworks flooded the immediate area.

Juliet's prayer was that Roseline didn't work up to a crying fit in church. The building was too old to withstand rising water. Hanging on the walls, between the stained glass windows, were fading tapestries. Many had come from crumbled churches in Italy.

On the other side of Dexter were Juliet's parents. They'd all leaned in at one point and planned to have dinner together.

Really, Italia should be Roseline's maid of honor. She'd be much better at it than Juliet. Already, her cousin wanted three showers—one each for family, friends, and *close* friends.

For Juliet, it was too much of the old crowd.

She glanced around the sanctuary. The fan-shape of the pews allowed excellent views of the congregation.

Abram gave Juliet an upward nod.

In her head, she heard him say *hey* in his ultra-smooth, *I'm wearing my elevator shoes* voice.

Was this really who her friends were now, Abram and Roseline?

No, she told herself. No, no, there was still Paris. Dear Paris on her left side. She glanced in his direction.

He ignored her and spoke to her cousin, Ty Gatti, on his other side. It seemed they were in deep conversation about one of Ty's cats, William Shakespaw.

Okay, I'm down to Abram and Roseline.

The bride-to-be angled toward Juliet. "Let's go shopping after church."

Thinking she meant wedding dress shopping, Juliet asked, "You're buying your dress in Verona's Vineyard?"

Roseline laughed, causing her red curls to dance on her shoulders. "No, I was thinking of my honeymoon trousseau."

Scads of clothes, just like her scads of showers. Scads of tears...

"Keep the weekend after Thanksgiving open and we'll go wedding dress shopping at Kleinfeld's."

"New York City?"

"Of course. But today, let's go to that darling little shop, Eleanora's."

Juliet nodded, smoothing out the skirt of her gold church dress. She wore camel-colored boots and crossed them at the ankles. "I do need to buy work clothes."

Her cousin leaned away and narrowed her blue eyes. There was a dusting of freckles on her nose, lending to the strawberry and cream complexion. "Work—what are you talking about? You can't work now."

Juliet pursed her mouth. "Why not?"

"Because you're in my wedding. You're my maid of honor." She'd said it loud enough that people in the next row glanced at them.

Juliet focused on Roseline again, noting the welling up of tears in the girl's eyes.

Someone save the tapestries!

"I don't need to be available all day every day to be your maid of honor."

Roseline's lips parted for a long moment. Then, "But, all the decision-making. We need to find vendors, and then there's the showers and bachelorette party, and all the pre-wedding events."

There'll be a bachelorette party too?

Juliet said, "I'm sure I'll have plenty of time to do it. I'll make it my top priority."

And ask Matri to help me.

Roseline seemed to force a smile. "Promise?"

"Of course, but *Papà* needs me to learn the wine

business. It's my duty."

The altar boys moved toward the dais and climbed the red-carpeted steps.

Roseline wrinkled her perfectly tweezed brows. "You've never been involved before."

Shifting in the pew, Juliet stuck her feet beneath the seat. "It's time to find out what happens at the winery." And, that's all she meant to say about it.

"But, it's in West Portland. There's nothing out there but the plant. What will you do for lunch? You'll need your strength with all the wedding responsibilities."

"I'm sure Tribly will pack a lunch for me."

"Well, don't tear up your nails." Roseline adjusted her posture in the seat. "I want you to look great on my wedding day and not have wine stains all over you."

"Wine stains?"

"That's right, don't show up smelling like Zinfandel."

"I'm not packing trucks, Roseline. I'll work in the office. I think."

Roseline leaned back again and eyed her with suspicion. "You don't know?"

"*Papà* hasn't told me what I'll be doing yet."

"You'll come home smelling of cardboard and tape. Don't do it, Juliet. Save yourself."

"Stop being so hysterical. It's only for a little while, and I'll be long gone before your wedding date."

Father John, dressed in a black robe and cinch belt, climbed the steps to the dais, his hands in a prayer position. What a splendid old man he was with his white hair and cherub cheeks. His temperament was as sweet and thoughtful as his features. He was just the sort of priest the Vineyard's congregation needed now.

Roseline's eyes were on the priest too, but she leaned in her seat to say, "Uncle Santos is making you do this, isn't he?"

"No, it was my idea."

Roseline twisted around, ignoring the holy procession.

Juliet felt the weight of her heated stare. She shook her head. "Okay, okay. I'm going undercover, but keep it to yourself. Questionable activities are going on at Renaissance Wines, and I'm going to set things straight."

Roseline's shoulders dropped. "You're not a corporate spy, Juliet. You're not a detective." She lowered her voice. "And it sounds dangerous."

"Believe me, I'm keeping my safety a top priority."

"You just promised to keep my wedding top priority." She glanced at the dais again. "Maybe I need to select a new maid of honor."

"Whatever makes you feel comfortable."

Roseline shook her head. "I want you."

"Then trust me to figure things out and not put myself in danger."

* * *

After the service, Juliet walked toward the car in the late morning sunshine. Birds sang in the nearby garden, now dormant until springtime.

Father John had promised to plant a new garden, with flowers and vegetables.

Her father's voice interrupted Juliet's thoughts. "You start working tomorrow at eight o'clock." His long gray hair looked more silver in the late morning sunshine.

"Wonderful," Juliet said. "What will I do, work in the

office or the warehouse?"

Please say office, please say office.

He'd started to turn away already, but paused mid-step. "One of my directors needs a secretary."

"D'Angelo?"

Please say yes, please say…

"Geoffrey Leary." Her father must've seen the lemon-puckering expression on Juliet's face. "You will behave honorably, *capiche*? No showing up late or leaving early. You will be passionate."

"Can't I work in the warehouse?" she asked, hand on the car door.

"No," he said, finger raised and walking away from her. "Leary needs you."

Juliet doubted that.

She was just about to climb in the car, when…

"Come see a house with me," Paris said, catching up with her. He was dressed in a black wool jacket and slacks. His curling hair picked up sunbeams as he moved toward her.

"If you suffer through dress shopping with me, I'll suffer through house shopping with you."

"You don't want me to find a house, do you?" He got close to her, on the other side of the car door. "You want to keep me all to yourself in that mansion of yours."

She hadn't thought of it as such, precisely. It was true that she wasn't happy Paris was moving away from her. But, she didn't want to admit it. "Fine, take Ty with you to find your own place."

His eyes held hers for a long moment. "What a funny girl you are, Juliet. Are you pushing me away as you've pushed your other friends away?"

"What? No."

He leaned toward her. "I hope you'll remember that I stuck by your side last summer."

She held his gaze. "I know that."

"It's important to me that you like my new house." He didn't move away.

She suddenly had a hard time swallowing. "Okay."

"Stop calling it *suffering* when you help me."

Juliet nodded. "Okay."

"I'll see you later." And then he was gone, strolling across the parking lot toward his own car.

I'm still not going to like any of your houses.

* * *

Juliet bought two dresses from Eleanora's. She chose the mid-length style for her first day at work and wore long leather boots with spiked heels. As soon as she got out of the Fiat, she realized she'd overdressed.

Every employee walking toward the office building, and especially those trudging toward the warehouse, wore jeans and sweatshirts.

No matter. Head high and shoulders squared, she made for the one-story office building with her heels clicking and her Gucci bag over her arm.

The air that morning was chilly and full of gas fumes. Someone needed to get their car fixed … perhaps several people needed to get their cars repaired as evidenced by the amount of carbon monoxide burning Juliet's throat.

Behind the office building was a two-story bottling plant and warehouse. A narrow sidewalk cut through the field where there were no trees, only patches of weeds. A chain-link fence bordered the road.

Juliet pushed on the double glass doors and stepped into the foyer. There was no reception area, just a pot of coffee and a small refrigerator down at the end of the hall. The floor was covered in big blocks of dark blue carpeting, and all the walls were a dull blue.

A head appeared around the bend in the wall … a woman's head. She seemed to be sitting in a chair. Either that or she was three feet tall. "Who are you?"

"Oh, I'm Juliet," she said. She hadn't expected a welcoming committee, but she hoped her father had told someone she was working there. "I'm going to work with Mr. Leary."

The head nodded. She had lovely eyes, big and brown and thickly lashed. But, were there no stylists in West Portland? The young woman's hair was in desperate need of a shampoo and perm. The thin locks lay limp on her head like an overused mop. "Turn left at the fridge. You're two doors down."

The head disappeared.

Juliet made a left at the coffee pot. It had been ten years since she'd visited the office, and she hadn't paid much attention to the layout. The place smelled the same, though, like grilled cheese and baby diapers.

The office door was open, and Juliet paused at the entry. Here was where she'd stage her spying operation. This was another dull area with a desk, chair, and some boxes along the wall. No windows let any sunlight into the office cave. Another door stood on the right. The placard read *Geo. Leary*.

Juliet knocked on the door.

No one was home. Leary probably started later, or

perhaps he visited the bottling plant before coming into the office.

Juliet tried the knob.

Locked.

See there, she told herself. Leary was a suspicious sort, shady, fishy … *leery*! She set her purse on the metal desk and tried out the chair behind it.

She nearly fell out of it because it wobbled so badly.

What dismal surroundings. She'd ask Father John to bless her office and say a prayer over the carpet too, maybe sprinkle some holy water.

No matter. For Juliet, it was only one bit of business to attend to, and that was to catch a spy who might be a murderer.

Where to start?

Placing her purse into one of the drawers, Juliet walked into the hall again and then continued. Around the bend was a double door entry into a much more appealing office.

Sure, D'Angelo was the director, but why did he get the fancy glass doors, Godfrey Hirst carpet, and the smell of Moroccan amber in his space?

Then Juliet remembered that this was her father's office, too, which reminded her of how obtuse he could be at times, and which was something she meant to talk to him about very soon. She'd form a picket line, if necessary, to renovate the office complex. No wonder people came to work in sweatshirts and limp hair. There was no spark of inspiration here.

Beauty beget beauty and all that.

No one sat at the secretary's desk. It was the only spot in the room that was stodgy. Paperclips lay about when there was a perfectly good holder next to the phone. Coffee stains marred the desk calendar. And the calendar? It was covered with scratchy notes and was still set to September.

The placard on the door nearest read S. D'Angelo, Director.

It was a shut door, too, and Juliet twisted the knob ever so gently. If D'Angelo was in, she'd say she'd popped in to say hello.

The door opened without Juliet pushing on it.

And a woman stood there, looking nothing like Sebastian D'Angelo.

First, she was taller than Juliet and filled out the long red sweater and black tights she wore. She had golden hair and her head was down when the door first opened. Then she glanced up–and dropped what she had in her hand.

"Sorry," Juliet said, fast. "So, so sorry." She bent and picked up a picture frame the woman had been holding.

The woman let out an embarrassed laugh. Or, at least, Juliet hoped it was embarrassed and not her usual laugh because it was very high pitched and loud. "I didn't expect anyone to be here."

"Sorry," Juliet repeated, giving back the frame. "I was just going to knock and see if Mr. D'Angelo was in this morning."

"Mr. D'Angelo comes in at nine." She let out a long breath, and her brown eyes focused on Juliet. "You're Mr. Da Vinci's daughter."

Juliet raised her brows. "Yes, I am."

"I'm Beth. I took your dad's phone call regarding your employment. It's nice to meet you." She held out the hand with the picture frame in it.

Juliet gazed at the frame.

"Oh, sorry," she said, laughing again, in the same high pitch.

Oh, no. No, no. Beth needed laugh classes, *velocemente!*

Beth laughed again, her octave going ever higher. She held out the frame. "D'Angelo's son. It needs dusting." She moved toward her desk, and out of a bottom drawer, she pulled a cloth and wiped the frame.

It was a funny thing. This was what Juliet would've looked for in D'Angelo's office if she'd been able to pry. She'd have been interested in the photo of his family, or anything that might give clues about the director's life and espionage or murder habits.

But here was Beth acting giddy over the fact that she held the picture frame, as though she'd been doing something dodgy herself.

Juliet leaned on Beth's desk and said, "I don't think I've ever seen Mr. D'Angelo's son. How old is he?"

Beth held out the frame. "He's in college now."

There was Sebastian D'Angelo standing next to a boy of about eighteen who was dressed in a graduation gown. They were outside, and it looked as though the wind blew hard that day because the boy's robes sailed out behind him like Superman's cape. "What is his name?"

"Amir," Beth said, still holding the frame out for Juliet to see.

Juliet studied Amir. He didn't look much like his father. No, he was of Middle Eastern descent with his black eyes and dusky skin. And, his hair, it was so thick and black and reminded Juliet of someone else: Gemma Hakim. She said, "I've never met Mr. D'Angelo's wife."

"I haven't either." She pulled the frame away and set it on her desk. "They're divorced."

"Oh, that's too bad."

"Right." She gazed at Juliet, smile still in place and nodding. Beth didn't seem to know what else to say. Should she stay standing, sit down? It was a quandary. Perhaps she was awkward because Juliet was a Da Vinci.

Ahh.

Juliet turned to leave. "Well, I'd better go see if Mr. Leary is in yet."

"Stop by anytime," Beth told her, with a note of relief in her voice.

Back in the hallway, Juliet made her way to the dinky office. Laughter sounded from one of the rooms farther down the corridor. She might meander that way later and try to make friends with the office workers, but right then, she had work to do.

Juliet sat behind the metal desk again and flipped on the computer monitor. At least her father had kept the computer system current, and *voila*, internet.

Now, to find Amir D'Angelo.

Flexing her fingers, she set to work with a fire inside her. She'd known all along that D'Angelo had something to do with Gemma Hakim's death. Gemma had asked D'Angelo about "son." At the time, Juliet thought Gemma meant *his* son, not *their* son.

It was so obvious now, now that she'd seen the boy. Gemma Hakim was D'Angelo's ex-wife …

Juliet looked up from the computer screen for a moment. Did that mean D'Angelo was handing over company secrets?

She shook her head and thought back to the party. D'Angelo had been surprised to see Gemma. Juliet had thought he'd been surprised that she spoke a different language, but maybe he was simply shocked to see her there. He hadn't seemed happy to talk to her, and he'd watched her with suspicion when she walked away.

Maybe he'd thought she was up to something. He surely knew her connection to Hakim Wine. Had he thought she was there to get information about Renaissance Wine? More importantly, would he kill her for being a spy, or for being an ex-wife?

"Miss Da Vinci," a male voice said at the doorway.

Juliet's heart rocketed. Anyone would think she'd been caught breaking into a high-security space of Facebook. "Hello, Mr. Leary."

He held a coffee cup in one hand and a briefcase in the other. His overcoat was saggy and beige, and he wore a brown derby on his head. "I told your father that I don't want to work with you."

"O, break, my heart, poor bankrupt, break at once!"

Chapter 7

"I told my father that I'd rather work in the warehouse," she admitted, keeping her hands in her lap.

His large lips made a puffing motion. "So would I, but they stuck me in here against my wishes." He grumbled, something about it being more useful than he imagined. His eyes locked on hers again. "How is Mr. Yeager? I heard the police threw away the key."

Leary gave Juliet a slow burn in her belly. "They didn't throw away the key." She stood and leaned the front of her legs against the desk. "Did you know the dead woman?"

He shrugged and turned toward his office. "How would I know her?"

Juliet came around the desk. Keeping her voice light and inquisitive, she said, "I saw her throw wine at you and I thought there must be some connection between the two of you."

"Oh, she was the wine tosser?" He pulled a set of keys from his coat jacket and stuck one of them in the knob of the door. "Bad luck and bad aim then." He grumbled something else and threw his briefcase and derby onto a chair in the corner.

His room wasn't any bigger than Juliet's office with just a desk, chair, and a bookcase with a few operating procedure manuals on it. He did have a window, though. Outside, the sky was full of low clouds.

Juliet remained at the door. "Her name was Hakim."

He'd gone around to the other side of his desk. "Yes, I've heard."

"Did you recognize her?"

He raised his thorny brows. "Why should I?"

She leaned against the doorframe. "Well, because you turned in the last spy … I thought maybe they were related, since they were both named Hakim."

He shook his head, making his long jaw jiggle. "It was a boy last time. The little twit was so stupid and obvious." He lifted one finger off his Styrofoam coffee cup and pointed it at her. "You're rather obvious yourself. You're fishing for something. Why all the questions?"

Juliet shrugged. "Just trying to help Anthony."

He gave her a bored look. "To business, Miss Da Vinci. Those boxes behind your desk need to be arranged and filed in the cabinets in the hallway."

She pushed off the frame and glanced at the boxes behind her desk. "I think I can manage." She turned back toward him. "What do you do, Mr. Leary?"

He went through one of the drawers of the desk. "I supervise the bottling plant, which keeps me very busy, so I'm in and out of here a lot. You'll have to manage yourself and figure out what to do. I told your father the same thing." He slammed the drawer shut. "Stay out of my office, Miss Da Vinci. I don't want to come back to find you in here."

"All right."

"And shut the door," he barked.

"All right," she repeated and shut his door.

Wow.

Juliet tracked back to her desk and sat in the wobbly chair. If Oldie Locks in there thought he'd hurt her feelings or distressed her in any way because he didn't want to work with her, then bully for him. He'd given her a gift. Juliet would take time sorting through the boxes and have plenty of time to snoop around the office and warehouse.

She sat behind her desk again and wiggled the mouse, bringing up Facebook.

She'd never liked Geoff Leary. Who could?

Juliet met him when she was eight years old. Her father had introduced them to each other and Mr. Leary had said, "What happened, did you stick your finger in a light socket?"

At eight years old, having an adult make fun of your curly-curly hair was hurtful.

Another time when she'd visited, Juliet witnessed Leary eating mashed potatoes out of a pickle jar that he'd brought from home. Sure, she understood that not everyone was Italian and therefore underfed and had to make do, but mashed potatoes from a pickle jar? That meant Leary was gross.

Plus, the hair joke was just hurtful.

Now, why didn't Leary want her in his office? It wasn't as though there was anything in there to see, unless he was hiding something in the desk drawer … maybe he was and maybe he wasn't, but Leary was someone to watch.

Out of the corner of her eyes, Juliet saw someone walk by the office doorway.

That someone backed up and stared at her.

"Juliet?" Nicolo asked, his dark brows raising on his forehead.

She caught her breath. "Nicolo."

He stepped into the office. He'd left his hair long to his jawline, it was gold and white and brown all throughout, and his sky-blue eyes took in the tiny office. He was within smelling-distance, and the scent of sandalwood drifted in the air.

Juliet got to her feet and came around the desk to meet him, almost taking his hands into hers. She stopped herself. "How are you?"

He gave a small nod. "Good." It was as though there was a thin bit of glass between them and any movement might shatter it, but neither one of them wanted to do the breaking.

"What are you doing here?" She sounded a little breathless.

"I was about to ask you the same thing."

"Just learning the business."

His tone was slow, somewhat suspicious. "Really?"

She lifted her shoulders. "Oh, it's super interesting." She pointed to the boxes. "I'm filing."

He nodded, but his eyes were still narrowed. "Does anyone else know you're here to spy?"

She took a sharp breath. "Spy?"

"Well, there's been a death, and all clues point to someone in the wine business because the dead woman's name is Hakim. You won't believe Anthony had anything to do with it."

She'd started to shake her head when he began talking. "No. Just here to file and learn about …" Suddenly she couldn't remember what they sold here.

"Wine?" he suggested.

"Yes."

His mouth broke into a smile. "Uh-huh. Well, keep me informed of things. We don't want a repeat of last summer when you almost *died.*"

"I didn't almost die."

"Because you got lucky." He shifted his stance and tilted his head. "I'm going to go on record here and say I don't approve."

Juliet moved back around the desk. "There's nothing to approve or disapprove of, Nicolo. Now, if you'll excuse me, I need to order a silk plant." She sat in her wobbly chair and wiggled the mouse again.

Just as quickly, she closed out of the Facebook page, in case Nicolo tried to see what she was up to now.

He stepped closer. He didn't look at the screen. "Dinner Saturday night?"

Her heart nearly exploded. "Umm." She stared at the screen. Juliet wasn't sure she was ready to date him again.

"Or Thursday next week." He tried to catch her eyes.

She licked her dry lips. "There's that church thing."

"Then, Saturday?" His voice was quieter than usual.

"I can't Saturday." She gazed at the computer screen, though it was timed out and black.

"Okay," he said, taking a deep breath and standing

straighter. "I'm here to speak to Geoff Leary and a…" he took a notepad from his jacket pocket. "Sebastian D'Angelo."

Juliet took a deep breath too. "This is Leary's office." She moved again toward the door and knocked. "Mr. Leary?"

Leary didn't answer.

Juliet tried the knob. He'd locked the door. "Mr. Leary, a police officer wants to speak to you."

Nothing.

Juliet turned to Nicolo. "That's strange. I didn't see him leave."

Nicolo lifted a shoulder. "I'll come back this way. Which way to D'Angelo's office?"

Juliet nodded at the door. "Turn right. It's the next office down through the glass doors."

Juliet sat again, wobbling with the chair and with a weight in her chest. Maybe she should date Nicolo.

Obviously, I still care about him.

She pulled the chair closer to the desk.

Was she being too hard on him?

I'm so confused.

She reached for her espresso to drown her sorrows in caffeine, but when the liquid touched her mouth, she had to stop herself from spitting it out on the keyboard.

Was there a microwave by the coffee pot?

Getting out of the chair, she stepped out of the office.

Leary rounded the corner at the same time.

She halted fast in her high-heel boots. "Where'd you come from?"

"You may be my assistant, Miss Da Vinci." His long cheeks jiggled with his answer. "But I don't think I need to inform you when I take a bathroom break."

The word bathroom out of the lips of Mr. Leary caused Juliet's shoulder blades to bow inward. She pointed the espresso cup behind her. "But you didn't come out the door."

"Of course I did," he said, stepping around her. He pulled out his keys to unlock the knob again.

She watched him a moment longer. If he'd come out of the office and locked the door behind him, then she would've seen him. But Juliet was going to leave that alone for a moment. Caffeine called her name. It was obvious she wasn't thinking straight.

Glancing left, she looked for Nicolo.

No one was at the end of the hallway, but a high-pitched laugh came from around the corner. It was Beth, no doubt, all nervous and excited to talk to a handsome detective.

"What are the police doing here?" a woman's voice asked from the other end of the hallway.

Juliet twisted around.

Two women walked toward the coffee area. They were both the same height, but one of them was average in size. The other one, well, she was much larger and had the shape of an apple. She'd dressed in baggy jeans and a lavender blouse. Atop the apple was the round face that Juliet had spoken to that morning.

The other woman was a bit more chic in a cropped jacket and ankle boots. A massive pair of round framed glasses sat on the bridge of her nose. Auburn hair as curly as Juliet's bounced on top of her head.

Juliet said, "They're interviewing people who were at a party last week. A woman died." She stepped toward the refreshment area too. Here was her chance to make friends. Smiling, she opened the microwave.

The ladies glanced at one another and then back at Juliet. The apple asked, "Did they interview you too, Miss Da Vinci?"

Juliet blinked. "You know me?"

"Of course."

She gave them her warmest expression. "Please call me Juliet."

Neither woman smiled in return. If anything, the curly-haired young woman grew more distant. "Yes, we know your name, but I'm not comfortable calling you Juliet, Miss Da Vinci, considering you're the owner of the company."

She held up her hand. "Oh no, I don't own it. It's my father's …"

"Same thing," the bigger girl said.

The bowing in her shoulder blades was back. She hadn't thought it would be difficult to make friends. Friend-making had always come easily to Juliet. She asked, "What are your names?"

"I'm Tricia," the woman with the cute boots said. She pointed her thumb toward her companion. "She's Patsy Michelson."

Patsy turned toward Tricia and asked in a clipped tone, "Why did you tell her my last name? Now she'll complain about me, that I didn't call her Juliet. I could lose my job."

Wow.

"You'd better call me Juliet then," she suggested. "Besides, how many people named Patsy work here?"

"Plenty," Patsy said, pulling open the refrigerator. "Now, if you'll excuse me, I'm on my lunch break."

"It's ten o'clock," Juliet said, wrinkling her nose. But,

not everyone in the world was Italian and ate a five-course meal at two.

Patsy nodded. "It's my first lunch. Second lunch is at one o'clock."

"Oh," she said, her voice hitting a high note at the end. She tried to think of something else to say, to keep the friend thing going. "Is there a lunchroom here somewhere?"

Tricia leaned her hip against the counter. Behind her over-big glasses were dark blue eyes that scanned Juliet head-to-toe. "There's a lunchroom in the warehouse with vending machines. Or you can eat at your desk."

"Or your car," Patsy said, closing the refrigerator door.

Juliet blinked a couple of times. "You eat in your car?"

"If I don't want to be disturbed." She'd pulled out a deli wrapped sandwich. The paper hadn't been taped down and a piece of lettuce stuck out at one end. "I may want to yell at my sister, for example."

Juliet winced, and then covered her reaction by pressing her lips together hard.

What else was there to say…? "We need better working conditions."

Tricia glanced at Patsy and shrugged. "Maybe we should make friends with her."

"No. And you know why, too. Think of Delia."

"Who's Delia?" Juliet asked.

"It's too late for you to worry about it," Patsy scolded. She turned toward Tricia. "Let's go eat at our desks."

They were halfway down the hall. Tricia asked, "Did you buy that lottery ticket? It's up to one hundred forty-nine million."

"I'll stop at *Big Bashas* on the way home. Don't forget to give me your half. I want my dollar."

With her spirits bruised, Juliet pulled her cup from the microwave and returned to her desk. Working at Renaissance Wines was going to be a challenge.

She took a sip of espresso.

Ugh, she'd forgotten to heat it.

* * *

The next morning, Juliet arrived at the office wearing blue jeans and a two-toned top. She did, however, wear her cute little blue jean boots because no matter what the office atmosphere, she would not be bullied into wearing ugly shoes.

Pulling her hair back into a fat ponytail, she set to work clearing files and kneeling on the floor while piling paper into an ABC format. The mindless task gave her a chance to think things through. There was a spy in the company, and a killer too. Most likely, they were the same person.

She supposed the killer-spy might work in the bottling plant. How many of them had been at the Harvest Ball—ten? Only the executives and the supervisor had been invited to the party. Juliet thought back. Gemma Hakim only spoke to Leary and to D'Angelo – who Juliet knew of anyway.

I should've paid more attention.

But why would she pay attention? She hadn't known someone was going to grab a knife and go dagger happy on a woman in the cellar.

Sitting back on her heels, Juliet stretched her back. She'd eat her lunch in the cafeteria in the bottling plant and try to make friends. Hopefully, no Patsy's or Tricia's worked over there.

Juliet picked up another pile of papers and began to sort them.

D'Angelo.

She had a strong sense that the man was involved in all of this. After what had happened at the Ball, and then seeing a photo of his son ... well, there was something there. But how to figure it out?

The door flew opened behind her.

Juliet twisted around on her knees.

There was old Woolyburger himself in his yak jacket and matching derby. He didn't glance at Juliet, stormed into his office, and slammed the door.

Yet whatever fragrance he wore caused Juliet's stomach to growl. What was that ... cinnamon streusel?

"Sorry about him," someone said behind her.

Juliet dropped the papers in her hand. She turned.

A young woman stood there. She was a little older than Juliet, but not thirty yet, and she had the sweetest expression on her face, as sweet as the smell coming from the baking tin she carried. "He's not a morning person."

Juliet pushed to her feet and faced the young woman. "Hi, I'm Juliet."

"I'm Delia," the woman said. Her reddish-blonde hair spilled over her shoulders in waves. She wore a long beige sweater, tight jeans on her full-size frame, and leather boots that matched the leather bands on both of her wrists. She held out a cupcake. "My father is abrupt sometimes. Will this help?"

"Thank you," Juliet said, accepting the cupcake. It was warm in its little liner and had streaks of cinnamon on top of the icing. "It looks delicious. Did you make it?"

"Just this morning."

"You're Mr. Leary's daughter?"

"One of the three. I have two older sisters."

Setting the cupcake next to her espresso cup, Juliet turned around again. "No brothers or sisters for me. Just two Bichons and a cousin who needs grooming."

The young woman grinned. She was charming in a confident sort of way. Not necessarily beautiful, but she knew how to apply makeup and dress for her body type. "Your last name is Da Vinci, isn't it? Your father owns the company."

Juliet suddenly felt the need to apologize. "I'm sorry, yes."

Delia laughed, "Well, Juliet Da Vinci, I'm glad you're watching over my grumpy father."

"I don't know about watching over him. He hasn't come out of his office too often."

All of a sudden, Patsy's round face appeared in the doorway. "Hey, what are you doing here?" Her question had been directed at Delia. "You're supposed to bring us cupcakes."

Delia rolled her eyes at Juliet and then said, "Hi, Patsy. I haven't forgotten you."

"Well, get over here quick," Patsy said with a teasing tone. "Tricia is starving." She left the doorway and headed in the direction of the coffee pot.

"It was nice to meet you, Juliet."

She didn't want the girl to go. She was the first potential friend she'd met recently. "Do you bring them treats often?"

"Oh, sure." Perhaps she caught an unguarded expression on Juliet's face. "You just need time to get to know them."

Juliet nodded. "They seem lovely." The words came

out like rocks, but she kept a smile on her face.

Delia grinned and held up her hand in farewell. "See you later."

Juliet returned to her desk and gazed at the cupcake. She hadn't eaten breakfast.

Something caught her attention.

Someone moved toward her.

Patsy pulled the cupcake from Juliet's hand. "You don't deserve this." Turning, she left as fast as she'd come.

"Hey!" Juliet said, jumping to her feet.

Patsy's voice floated in the hallway. "I said you don't deserve this."

Juliet got to the hallway but wasn't sure what to do. Should she steal her cupcake back? Was she back in grade school?

If she were in grade school, she'd run down the hall, grab the fire extinguisher off the wall, and threaten Patsy until she handed over the little streusel cake.

Why does that sound so appealing?

Not into sorting paper any longer, Juliet glanced toward D'Angelo's office. Maybe she should get to know Beth a little better. It was true that she didn't seem any more likable than the other ladies in the office, the streusel stealers.

"Women may fall when there's no strength in men."

Chapter 8

Beth wasn't in her chair or anywhere else in the room. Her desk was just as cluttered as it had been the previous day.

D'Angelo's door stood open.

Juliet moved toward it and then paused at the doorway. A nervous tingle started in her belly. Did she dare?

She put one foot inside the office and then paused to glance left and right.

All clear.

She stepped farther into the room and stood a moment. If D'Angelo or Beth came back, she'd say that she'd just arrived and wanted to say hello.

Sure, that sounded reasonable.

D'Angelo's office was neat. No, it wasn't just neat, it was sparse, as though nobody worked there.

Juliet stepped out of the room again, read S. D'Angelo, Director, and then stepped back inside again. No papers lay about, no jacket on a hook near the door. There was a computer monitor on the desk and a picture frame. Behind the desk was a picture window that overlooked the empty field and the road leading to the office complex.

It was as if the office belonged to someone who wanted to be ready to leave at a moment's notice.

She moved around the desk and put out her hand to open the top drawer…

"Can I help you?" a man's voice said at the doorway.

Juliet nearly jumped out of her cute little boots.

Sebastian D'Angelo stood there, coffee cup in hand. He cut quite the figure, broad shoulders, and slender hips. He was in his forties. Some men age great.

D'Angelo aged great.

"Hi, Mr. D'Angelo," Juliet said, attempting to shovel a load of friendliness into her tone. "I just stopped by to say hello."

"Hello." His tone was welcoming, but his eyes glittered, and he'd narrowed them with a considerable amount of suspicion.

Desperate for a diversion, she picked up the frame on the desk. "Is this your son?"

"Yes, that's Amir." He stepped forward, his free hand fisted and flexed, fisted and flexed. "How are you, Juliet?"

"I'm very well," she told him, replacing the frame and coming out from behind his desk. "I - I also wanted to say thank you for allowing me to work here. I thought it was about time to learn the family business."

He stepped around her, never losing eye contact like a tiger stalking its prey. "Well, it is your family's company, isn't it? You're welcome here anytime." His eyes went to the picture frame, gazed all around it as though thinking she'd done something to it. "Amir is in college. It's his first year. He's studying at the University of Florida."

"Florida? That's a ways away." She reached the chair and stood behind it. It put a barrier between her and him. "Will he be home for Thanksgiving?"

"No, Amir will stay at school. That is what he has chosen to do."

"Oh. You and your wife must be disappointed."

"She's dead."

Juliet said, blinking a couple times, "I hadn't heard. I'm sorry."

He nodded and placed his cup on the desk. "Is there anything else I can do for you?"

She backed toward the door. "Oh no, not at all. It was nice seeing you again."

"Please don't come into my office again without Beth, Miss Da Vinci."

"Of course," she said, her cheeks warm. "I'm sorry I didn't wait."

Juliet walked fast to her office with her heart boomeranging on her ribcage. She sat in her wobbly chair and waited for her breathing to slow down.

D'Angelo had been a little scary, hadn't he? Sure, he had reason to be put out, what with her snooping in his office, but hadn't he been a little over the top?

Did I imagine it?

Putting herself in his shoes, she'd be angry if someone was snooping around her desk and about to open a drawer.

Maybe he thought she was acting on her father's wishes and was snooping for a reason.

Sitting forward, Juliet did a *wikiHow* search on how to get information on someone.

Simple and easy instructions popped up.

She clicked on *Instasearch* and did a public record search on Sebastian D'Angelo. He'd said his wife died.

Juliet paused. That's what had been creepy about D'Angelo, the way he'd said *she's dead*.

But Beth had said that D'Angelo and his wife were divorced. So, when did Mrs. D'Angelo die?

At the Harvest Ball?

Juliet followed the next instructions on wikiHow and pulled up 411.com and did a reverse search. It didn't list D'Angelo's phone number, but it did list an address.

She wrote it down.

Following more directions, she went to the property appraiser's website and searched the address. There was Sebastian's name, but no wife's name.

She typed his name again, into Google, searching obituaries.

Nothing.

Juliet sat back in her chair, staring at the paper all over the floor.

Amir D'Angelo was an uncommon name. Juliet had started to check Facebook yesterday but kept getting distracted.

She tried again, pulled up the social media site, and entered Amir's name.

Amir's photo popped up along with his page.

Hello!

He only had ninety-five friends. Was he a college kid

or not? Didn't a freshman have a five-hundred-friend minimum?

The information popup said he was born in … Iraq. So, his mother is Iraqi.

When was D'Angelo in Iraq?

Must be a veteran.

Juliet studied Amir's information again. "Born in 2003," she read aloud. Scrolling down the page, she looked for photos, hoping to see his mother's face.

No family photos, actually no photos at all, just Star Wars posts, every ten days or so.

"Come on, kid, help me out a little here."

Clicking off Facebook, she put in Amir's name, to see if any other photos or news articles popped up. Then she tried Instagram, SnapChat on her phone, and then LinkedIn.

Nothing.

Okay, so which military operations were happening in 2003?

She typed the question into Google.

Google came back with *the Iraqi Freedom Campaign.*

Juliet bit her lip, her nerves singing. She knew what had happened. She just knew it.

D'Angelo had been in the Iraqi Freedom campaign, met his wife there, they married, Amir came along, and they moved to the US. And if that woman is Gemma Hakim …

Juliet needed to see a birth certificate or a marriage certificate. But, how?

* * *

Juliet ate in the lunchroom of the bottling plant. There

wasn't much to the place, just rows of metal tables and aluminum chairs surrounded by vending machines. There were no windows, only terrazzo flooring to gaze at and more green walls.

She'd arrived just as most of the employees were heading back to work. Everyone ignored her, except for one skinny man who said, "Hello, Miss Da Vinci."

I just can't cut a break.

And she was sure Patsy was the one telling everyone about her. How was Juliet supposed to fit in with the crowd and gossip and find out information if everyone kept her at arm's length because of her family connections?

She ate ravioli and antipasto by herself. Tribly had added *Ciabatta* bread and a cinnamon roll too. All Juliet needed was a delicious Rosé to wash it down. Alas, it was all bottled up around her.

After washing up and returning to the office, Juliet headed to Beth's office in an attempt to make friends again.

She pulled open the double glass doors and slunk inside, hoping to avoid D'Angelo.

Rapid clicking noises came from Beth's desk.

There she was, at her desk, and wearing another red sweater. This sweater had pearls around the collar and sleeves. She'd gelled her hair into a sleek bun, and her lips were as red as strawberry Jell-O. Ramrod straight, she pounded the keyboard with her long fingernails, creating the loud clicking sounds. She didn't notice Juliet. Whatever she was typing had her complete attention.

Not wanting to startle her, Juliet kept her voice down. "Hey, Beth."

Beth about came out of that sweater. A teacup went over the edge, and a penholder spilled.

This reminded Juliet of something. Oh yes, the other time she met Beth.

May need to take away Miss Jellybone's stimulants.

Juliet rushed around the side of the desk to help the girl dab tea off the chair mat.

"I've got it, I've got it," Beth said, with a hint of irritation in her tone.

Juliet straightened and watched as Beth dabbed away.

"Now, it's sticky."

"I'll get a wet towel," Juliet told her, taking a step backward.

"Never mind. I've got wet wipes." She opened a drawer.

Juliet glanced down.

It was Genovese's Drug Store in a drawer. Not only that, Beth had plastered her name all over every box and wrapper with a label maker.

And Matri wants me to see a shrink…

Beth said, "Mr. D'Angelo said you were in his office today." She finished swabbing the floor, stood, and tossed the wipe into the overflowing trashcan.

She jammed her hands on her waist. "Why were you in Mr. D'Angelo's office?"

There were a lot of clipped tones coming at Juliet. She leaned away. "I went in to say hi. He wasn't there at first, and I looked at his son's photo."

Beth retook her seat and rearranged the papers on her desk, as though she didn't want Juliet to see what she worked on.

It seemed silly to Juliet. She could ask her father anything about the company and find out about it. What was the big secret?

No matter. There were other things to talk about, like, "Amir looks like someone I've met. Do you know his mother's name?"

"No," she snipped. "Now, if you'll excuse me."

"You're angry."

"Yes, I am," she said, finally focusing on Juliet. "Are you spying on him for your father?"

That was just what Juliet thought D'Angelo was thinking. How very fishy. What's everyone worried about? D'Angelo seemed more and more guilty every day. She said, "My father wouldn't ask me to do such a thing. If he had questions, he'd come here himself."

Wasn't that the truth? Santos Da Vinci was one hundred percent *gesto*, eh? He'd confront one of his directors all by himself.

Beth got to her feet and planted the palms of her hands on her desk. Eye level with Juliet, she said, "Mr. D'Angelo is very upset. Which makes my job harder. You need to stay in your office."

Things had turned topsy-turvy, hadn't they? She'd come to make friends with the woman, and now Beth wanted to throw Juliet out.

"I'm sorry, Beth. I really am. I didn't mean to get you into trouble."

Her glare faltered, and she glanced down at her desk. "I'm supposed to make sure the door is locked before I leave."

"But – but, you weren't here to make sure, were you? He should've locked his own door."

Beth's dark eyes glared daggers. "Don't you say anything bad about him."

"I wasn't," Juliet said, holding up her hands. "It just seemed a little unfair to expect you to do something when you weren't here."

Beth sat again and reached into the drawer for a Bethlabeled tissue box. "I love my job. I don't want to lose it just because you're nosy."

Juliet ignored the nosiness bit. "Did D'Angelo threaten to fire you?"

"No, well …" She shook her head. "No! I should've been here to make sure no one goes in there."

She relaxed her shoulders. "What's Mr. D'Angelo got in there that's so secretive?"

"Wouldn't you like to know?"

"Beth," she reasoned, pointing her thumb at her chest. "Boss' daughter, remember? I'm not here to steal company secrets."

"Just stop acting so snoopy. It doesn't matter who you are. I will protect Mr. D'Angelo and do my job."

"Okay," she said. "I'm sorry you got into trouble."

* * *

On a One-to-Ten Scale of Unpleasantness, hashing things over with Beth had come in a solid Four.

Back at the jail that evening and asking police sergeant Donata Zizzo to hit the buzzer twice—because Juliet missed the door the first go around—rocketed that scale beyond the number ten and straight to hellacious.

Anthony wasn't in a cell when she finally got to see him. He was in a separate room down the hall, reading a pamphlet of some sort. A police officer sat on an aluminum chair outside the windowless room. The paint was the same green color as the rest of the building, but this space smelled like brown bananas and armpits.

"What's going on here?" Juliet asked, setting her Boho bag on the table.

Anthony gazed up from behind his eyewear. The smell and color of the room caused him to look a bit less elegant—though his pants were just as creased as any other day. His muted striped shirt, impeccable.

"They gave me a choice of recreation this evening." He set the pamphlet on the table in front of his knees. "A class in anger management or a 'Quest for Authentic Manhood' lesson."

Juliet's mouth parted. "How'd you get in here?"

He tapped the paper on the table. "This is a GED Preparatory booklet."

"You graduated from West Point."

He raised a brow. "What have you learned?"

"D'Angelo did it."

"Did what exactly?"

"He murdered Gemma Hakim."

He tilted his head, causing his wire glasses to catch and twinkle in the overhead lighting. "You're looking for a spy."

"Same thing."

"D'Angelo can't be the spy."

"Why not?"

He shook his head, brows together. "Because he already has access to the processes locked in his office. If he wanted to sell them, he'd open up the safe and sell them without any of us ever knowing about it."

Oh yeah.

"There'd be no cloak and dagger, placing the Hakim woman at the party to break into your father's office and then killing her in the cellar."

"All right, all right," she told him, holding up one hand to stop his flow of logic. "But he might've killed her anyway."

He tucked his chin and deepened his frown. "Why?"

"Well, let me explain," she said, trying desperately to remember because Anthony's speech took away some of her reasoning powers. "His son is Amir D'Angelo, who was born in Iraq during the *Iraqi Freedom* campaign. The boy's photo is on D'Angelo's desk, and he looks very much like his mother, Gemma Hakim."

Anthony eyes flickered, just a tiny bit, as if impressed.

That was precisely the reaction Juliet wanted. It spurred her on. "Remember the conversation I overheard between the pair of them? Gemma asked about a son. *Her* son, *their* son."

"Gemma Hakim is his wife, you know this?"

"Nnnnno. I haven't got the proof yet, but Amir's hair looks exactly the same as Gemma's."

"And the conversation you overheard," he asked with an intense gleam in his eyes, "she said *our* son."

"Well, no. Gemma just said *son*, but work with me on this. It's the only lead I have right now."

He pursed his lips now, his eyes upward and to the left. "War brides."

"What?"

"I was there, stationed in Dubai, and flew missions into Iraq. A few of the guys had war brides and brought them home. Well, some of them did. Some had children, never married the woman, and then left them there."

"What if D'Angelo brought Amir home and left Gemma in Iraq? She finally makes her way over here and confronts him about their son, and he kills her."

"I doubt that very much. What man do you know who would take a child on by himself?"

Juliet had to give him that one. "Okay, so D'Angelo

brought his wife and child home, which means I'm right."

"You have no proof." His cellphone pinged on the seat beside him and Anthony picked it up. After reading the message, he said, "All you've got is the idea that the boy's mother was Gemma. The rest is potluck and guesswork."

She nodded and shrugged simultaneously. "That's why I need to see a marriage certificate or a birth certificate. Was D'Angelo married when he came to work for us?"

"Yes."

"And that was what, six months ago?"

"It was in June."

Juliet leaned back in her seat. "Surely you would've known, we all would've known if his wife died. He would've taken bereavement time, right? "Maybe he didn't like her and went on with life as usual." He studied his phone again.

"Another reason to kill her," Juliet said, nodding. "Did you ever meet her?"

"No, I never met his wife. I did know Sebastian, however, when we were young. We were based at the same station during the war. I didn't know him well enough to meet his wife. But your father did. I did all the reference and background checking. Your father wined and dined him."

She sat forward again, at the end of the chair. "Right, I'll ask *Papà* then."

Anthony put his phone in his shirt pocket and paid attention to Juliet again. "Why do you think Mrs. D'Angelo is dead?"

"Because I found her in the basement."

He raised a brow.

"D'Angelo told me she died. No, let me rephrase. He

said, *she's dead*, using a Jack the Ripper voice."

"No one's ever heard Jack the Ripper's voice," Anthony said in a flat tone. "And maybe D'Angelo's been married a couple of times, did you consider that? Maybe one of his wives did die."

"Oh, right." She stuck her feet out in front of her and crossed them at the ankles, thinking. "Tell me about Beth, D'Angelo's secretary."

"He brought her along with him from Smucker's."

Juliet raised her brows. "Did he? Where is Smucker's anyway?"

"In Florida." The pocket of his shirt buzzed and he reached for his cell phone.

"That's a long way to follow a boss."

"He said she was the best assistant he'd ever had. They both passed background checks."

"Then Beth knows his wife's name. She claimed that she didn't."

"She's being a good secretary and keeping his information private."

Juliet rolled her eyes, and then narrowed them. "Who are you texting? Do you have a girlfriend on the side?"

He stuffed the phone in his pocket. "What?" His tone had changed, a little higher than usual.

"The police say you've been seen around town with a woman. Where'd you meet this woman, Tinder?"

His face moved as if she'd slapped him. "I am not on Tinder. No wonder Beth is protective over her boss. What a question."

She gave him a brilliant grin. "I suppose you could've used Ugly Schmucks or Meet an Inmate." She heehawed a laugh at her own joke.

"You certainly know a lot of dating websites, Miss Da Vinci."

Now she knew she'd hit a nerve. She'd provoked the *Miss Da Vinci*.

Reclaiming her purse, she asked, "When is the arraignment?"

"Thursday or Friday. I expect a ride home from you."

* * *

Taking a deep breath for courage, Juliet pushed open the door to the police station's foyer to face Sergeant Zizzo again.

Donata sat in her usual spot, but someone leaned on the counter.

Detective Nicolo Montague.

*"Being purged, a fire sparkling in lovers' eyes;
Being vex'd a sea nourish'd with lovers' tears."*

Chapter 9

Butterflies flew up from Juliet's stomach and filled her chest. They batted each other around and banged against her heart.

Nicolo's pale eyes narrowed. "Visiting Anthony?" Pushing off the counter, he faced her.

Donata's quilled hair turned toward her too. Her lip curled.

Juliet continued toward the exit. "Yes." She turned before opening the door. "He told me that his arraignment is Thursday or Friday. It seems like a long time to wait."

"It's the holidays, and people are on vacation. Will you be there?"

She pushed the bar on the door, letting in a swell of cold air. "I told him that I'd give him a lift home. I have to work that day too."

The news nearly knocked Zizzo out of her chair. "Work?"

Nicolo took his cousin's defense. "It does sound funny coming from you."

Juliet pushed the door all the way open and stepped outside.

Nicolo followed her. "What have you found out?"

She faced him on the sidewalk. "About…?"

"I know you're spying. Admit it." Nicolo was a man who didn't move a lot, physically. His eyes did most of the communicating. Right now, they memorized her face.

Juliet let out a breath and watched the vapor float in the air between them. "I don't have anything I can prove at the moment. What about you?"

"Nothing I can share."

Her mouth had gone watery, and she swallowed. Was she over Nicolo, really? She might be if he weren't so very devastatingly handsome.

They stared at each other for a long time.

Juliet came to her senses first. "So, was Gemma Hakim a US citizen? Or can you tell me?"

He shook his head. "Her passport said she was born in Iraq. She must've been here visiting someone, but we don't have any names. It takes time to get information out of a foreign government."

Her nervousness turned into excitement. "But she is Iraqi. That's fantastic."

"Is it?" He asked. "We don't know if she was part of Hakim Wine or not."

She leaned toward him. "That is not what I'm excited about, Nicolo."

"Tell me then, why are you excited?"

Juliet held back a little. Last time she told Nicolo who the killer was, she got stuck with the killer herself. It was better to play it close to her chest. "It'd be remarkable if she's a Hakim and wasn't part of the wine family, don't you think?"

"Hakim is a rather common name in the Middle East."

She frowned and nodded at the same time. "I did not know that."

"Are you being careful?" He leaned in, just a little.

"Yes, but I don't feel in any danger, just out of place. No one likes me very much."

"You're the boss's daughter. You're snooping around. What did you expect?"

"No one knows I'm snooping around," she told him, adjusting the purse strap on her shoulder. "Well, maybe Beth suspects, and D'Angelo."

He waited.

She stopped talking.

The glass wall between them was back in place. Juliet said, "I guess I'll be off."

Nicolo stepped aside. "Bye."

* * *

Her heart was still bruised from all the butterflies banging around in her chest. She shoved the Fiat into Drive and pulled away from the police station. She'd half expected him to ask her out again. She'd half expected to hear herself say yes this time.

Maybe he won't ask again.

The butterflies came back and bruised Juliet's heart again.

She didn't get the chance to speak to her father when she arrived home. Her mother had guests in the house, and everyone enjoyed wine and double-stuffed *Cornetti con Panna,* which were croissants filled with cream cheese and lemon zest frosting. Paris and Ty were right in the thick of it.

It was the next morning when she cornered her father in the kitchen near the espresso machine. She wore a black and white polka-dotted blouse and pink slacks. It was the best she could find in the casual dress department of her wardrobe.

The warm room smelled slightly sweet with avocado. It was her mother's breakfast, avocado and toast. It sat on the counter in front of Italia.

Tribly was busy rolling out pasta for the lunch meal. She'd already done her hair, and it looked like a black Q-tip on top of her head. Her sweater was neither black nor brown but the mix of some sort of faux animal. Coyote perhaps. Her knee-high socks matched.

Juliet didn't mention the fact. Didn't want Tribly to take off one of those slippers and throw it at her.

Italia, however, was as impeccable as ever in a cream skirt and sweater.

Juliet reached around her father.

Him and his cell phone.

"Still texting Anthony?" Juliet asked, pouring the coffee into her cup.

He glanced at her. Such a handsome man with his gray hair and beard. Tiny lines gathered around his eyes. "It's not so bad with him in jail, eh? I still get my work done."

"I visited him last night, you were texting him then too."

"We are busy people, and I pay him well."

"You should put some of your money into fixing up the West Portland office. The carpet smells like *Bisquick* and bedpan."

Tribly turned around, rolling pin held high. "You've never eaten *Bisquick*. What do you know?"

"I didn't say I ate it, *Nonna*. I said, *smells* like…"

Tribly glared harder, her dark gray eyes penetrating the distance. "You're killing me," she shouted. "I'm on the floor dead over her."

Juliet blinked. "I'm just saying…" She glanced at her father. "The carpet stinks. It's what I *imagine* that *Bisquick* smells like."

Why wasn't anyone curious as to why she knew what a bedpan smelled like?

"Anthony told me that you wined and dined Sebastian D'Angelo before you hired him."

"*Si*," he said, returning to his phone.

"Oh, I was there," Italia put in. "Lovely couple." She took a bite of her toast.

Juliet fit the top on the travel cup and slipped toward the island counter. "Were you? What's his wife's name, do you remember?"

Italia stared off into the distance for a moment. She wore dangling gold earrings and had her straight hair in a bun. "Mrs. D'Angelo?"

Juliet's shoulders slumped forward. "I expect that from

Papà, not you."

"Watch your mouth," her mother said. "I'm not one of your friends."

She grimaced and then gazed at her father again. "Do you remember Sebastian's wife's name?"

He hadn't been listening. "Mrs. D'Angelo," he said with authority.

It is said that a couple eventually meld into one person. Juliet pressed, "What did she look like?"

"How should I know, eh?" her father asked and then blew a kiss at Italia. "I only have eyes for one woman."

Yeesh.

Her mother said, "She was an average looking brunette. It was obviously not her natural color. There were no highlights and her roots were gray, or blonde. She was likely blonde."

"Did she look Middle Eastern?"

Her father shrugged.

So, so like him!

"No," her mother answered. "No, she was an American woman. There was nothing too distinctive about her. She was a little chubby and she didn't speak much. D'Angelo and your father did most of the talking." She pushed her plate away and dabbed her lips with a napkin. "I attempted to engage her in conversation but didn't get much out of her. She seemed, oh, I don't know, possessive of her husband. Protective."

Juliet set the coffee cup on the counter. "*Matri*, have you ever met Beth at the West Portland office?"

Her mother slipped off her chair and took up her plate. She walked around the counter and went to the sink. "I don't believe so. Santos, have I met Beth?"

"Who's Beth?" he asked, dragging his eyes from the phone.

"D'Angelo's secretary... for goodness sake, *Papà*, do you ever notice anything?"

"He doesn't," Italia said, placing the plate in the dishwasher.

Juliet took a paper towel off the rack and wiped her cup, thinking about it all. She said aloud, "I wonder if D'Angelo adopted his son."

Still bent over in front of the dishwasher, Italia said, "I didn't know they had a son."

Her father headed toward the door. "I will be in the office."

"Did you know D'Angelo's son, *Papà*?"

"Anthony doesn't have a son," he said and stepped out the door.

Juliet rolled her eyes at her mother.

"What's this all about?" Italia asked. "Who cares about his son?"

"It's just so strange. Amir must've been adopted, and Gemma came to the party to ask about her son. Maybe she wanted to see him... but why kill her over that?"

"Is this a job assignment?" her mother asked. "It's an extraordinary one. I didn't know our wine business had anything to do with adoptions and murder."

"She thinks she's a detective this one," Tribly said, hanging the pasta to dry on a wooden bar. From another bar, she pulled dried pasta which she'd made last night.

"I thought you were a secretary," Italia said, crossing her arms.

"Never mind," Juliet told them, taking up her lunch sack. "I have to think about this."

* * *

Juliet drove her little red Fiat through the outskirts of West Portland. There wasn't much to the town, even on Main Street. Open fields lined the roads, and then several lovely old homes came into view. There was a small post office and a congregational church on the other side of the street.

Juliet turned her attention to the matter at hand. How was she going to find out whether or not Amir had been adopted, or was the natural son of Sebastian D'Angelo?

Beth would be no help at all, and Juliet didn't think she could ask such a personal question of D'Angelo himself. Well, there was only one thing left to do: break into his house and find the documents she needed to prove it.

Taking her phone from the passenger seat, Juliet pressed speed dial.

An older model Toyota truck on the side of the road caught her attention, and Juliet hung up the phone. She slowed and rolled down her window. "Hi Delia, do you need a lift?"

The young woman stood beside her truck with a cell phone in her hand. She stepped forward in her puffy winter coat and then bent to see inside the Fiat. "I need a mechanic."

"Can't help you there," Juliet told her, moving her purse into the backseat. "Where can I take you?"

"Home, I suppose. I'll call a tow truck from there."

"No Triple-A?"

Delia sat in the passenger seat. The interior was close, and her puffy jacket bumped Juliet's arm. She said, "They dropped me. I've called them too much." Along with the coat, she wore jeans and those cute boots again. She'd tied up her reddish-blonde hair into a bun and left curly strands loose at the sides of her chubby cheeks. She smelled like vanilla and lavender. "Thank you, Juliet. I just tried to call my father, but he didn't pick up."

"We can use my Triple-A."

"No, we'd have to stay by the car, and I need to go to the bathroom. I was beginning to think I was going to go out in an open field somewhere."

Juliet laughed. "Well then, let's get you out of here. Which way am I headed?"

"It's two miles in that direction," she said, motioning with her fingers. "I'll tell you when to turn."

"Shall I speed?"

The girl grinned. "I'll make it."

Juliet shifted gears and hit the gas. "Where have you been so early this morning?"

"I was coming home from a job interview," she said, holding onto the door handle for balance—or for dear life—whichever. "I was there at six o'clock."

"Six? Don't take the job. It's too demanding."

"*If* they offer me the job, you mean." The road curved, and Delia leaned with the movement of the car. She was practically on top of Juliet. She said, "You really don't need to race on my account. I'm not in pain or anything."

Juliet shifted into fourth gear. "Are you out of a job or just changing things up?"

"I was let go from my last job a week ago." She braced her foot on the floorboard. "How are you doing with my dad?"

"Well, he doesn't involve me in anything. He seems

angry with me most times."

"He'll turn around. He's a grumpy guy but loveable underneath. I know you two will get along eventually."

"Does he have a trap door in his office?"

"What?" Her voice had jumped with that last dip in the road.

"Just wondering. I think he's in his office with the door locked. The next minute he's coming in from the hallway."

"Well, he's never mentioned it to me. Turn right up at the next street. Next street… next… THIS ONE!"

Turning the wheel, Juliet punched the accelerator.

"Whoa, whoa… WHOA! It's right here."

She hit the brakes and pulled onto the dirt driveway. Once the dust settled, a monstrous apartment building came into view. It'd probably stood there a hundred years by the look of things. The outside of it was painted clay red with blue railings, and a dilapidated fire escape hung off the building like a broken Tinker Toy piece. Someone had used green paint to trim the windows.

There were two other cars in the parking area. The owner of the paneled '70s van had parked across a line, and took up two spaces. Across from it was a black car with peeling paint.

"Thank you so much," Delia said, her hand still bracing against the glove box.

"Do you want to have lunch sometime?"

She gathered her purse from the floor. It'd started in her lap. "I'd love to, but I don't know what my job situation will be like for long." Sitting this close in the car allowed a good look at the girl's complexion. It was lovely, all pale and pink-cheeked. She didn't need to wear mascara. Her lashes were twice the length of Juliet's.

"How about this weekend? Wait, it can't be this weekend." She waved a hand in a *you don't want to know* manner. "My cousin is having a bridal party meeting. There are twelve of us, and you wouldn't believe how nitpicky Roseline's going to be about everything … and you've got to go to the bathroom." Juliet made a face. "Sorry. Give me your phone number, and we'll figure it out."

After the exchange, Delia hopped from the passenger seat and smoothed one side of her hair that'd come loose during the drive. "Thanks again."

"I hope you do get the job."

"Yeah, me too. Drive safe!"

What a lovely person to care about Juliet's safety. Juliet didn't know why, but she just liked Delia from the start. It had only happened to her one other time in her life, where she'd wanted to make friends with a person at first sight. It was when she'd met Emma.

Juliet had seen her in English class and knew she wanted to be friends with the girl. They'd never spoken, but it was an instant attraction. And now it was the same with Delia. There was so much potential friendship rolled up in those sparkling eyes and chubby cheeks—even though she didn't ride well in the front seat.

* * *

Juliet put her purse on her chair and then turned to peek inside Mr. Leary's office. He was already at his desk. "Delia's car broke down. I gave her a ride home."

And did he appreciate it?

Well, it was hard to tell with that bulldog mug. Today

Leary wore a moth gray sweater vest with a plaid shirt beneath it. "That girl's truck is a piece of crap."

Juliet leaned away. "You should buy her a new one."

He jerked his head back. "I just bought Delia's sister a new car."

"You have three daughters, don't you?"

"Yes, and all of them are a pain in my…" He slammed a drawer. "Shut my door on your way out."

How, how, how did he have such a wonderful daughter? It wasn't natural. Anyone raised by that old man would come out of childhood victimized and with broken crayons.

Juliet sat at her desk, dug the cell phone from her purse, and texted Ty: Will you be home this evening when I get there?

He must've been looking at his phone right then because she received an immediate reply from him. What time do you get home?

Five thirty.

I have an appointment. You can join me.

Juliet cringed. She knew what some of his appointments were like—food eating competitions, sitting around with a puzzle club, or hanging out at the poet's room in Mayville. Where will you be?

Juliet placed her purse in the drawer and set her coffee on the desk. A package had arrived and was on her desk. Maybe it was her new office supplies. Her phone pinged.

Ty wrote back: 1909 Starmeir.

Vague and unhelpful.

* * *

She discovered why he was so vague after she got off

work and drove onto Starmeir. Madame Olei's was in a strip mall that sat on a hill that was off the main highway toward Mayville. It was sandwiched between a tattoo parlor and a nail salon. The sun was about to set, which caused the neon bulbs in Olei's windows to blaze as if it were midnight. The signs were what anyone would expect in a psychic's window: Tarot cards, psychic reads, past, present, and future. Crystal ball.

Juliet was pretty sure the place used to be an H&R Block.

Pushing on the door caused chimes to tinkle over her head. Immediately, Juliet got a *read* herself. The Madame had polished the furniture recently while her codfish dinner fried in a skillet in the room behind the curtain. It didn't take a psychic to smell the fishiness in the place.

Ty sat in the waiting area. The sofa was threadbare at the bottom, and the oval rug beneath it needed a shampoo.

Juliet sat next to him. "When is your appointment?"

"It was ten minutes ago," he said in his usual thick voice. "But some guy jumped the line. Said he had an emergency."

She wrinkled her nose. "Was the guy carrying a Long John Silver's bag?"

Ty never appreciated her jokes. He was slumped on the sofa and stared at the ceramic money cat on a nearby shelf.

"What are you doing here?"

Ty's hair was a thick mat on his head, and it had no sense of direction. His brows were just as black as his hair and just as thick. "I want to talk to Mom."

Her heart gave a little lurch. She reached for Ty's hand and squeezed it. "You think you can talk to her here?"

"She yelled at me last time because I haven't found a job yet."

"You heard Ganozza's voice?"

He waved his free hand toward the black curtain. "She spoke through Madame Olei."

Probably the old fortune cookie took one look at Ty's messy appearance and reasoned he needed to find a job.

No, Juliet wasn't a believer in Madame Olei. She'd run into the woman in different parts of town, and the shyster couldn't even tell where she'd parked her own car.

"Listen, I need you to help me break into someone's house."

"O, look! methinks I see my cousin's ghost."

Chapter 10

"No."

"Well, at least hear me out."

He pulled his hand from hers.

"You've broken into houses before," she reminded him.

His brows formed a V. "For a good reason."

"This is a good reason." She scooted forward on the seat and faced him squarely. "It's about justice."

"Not interested."

She bit the side of her lip, trying to figure out a way to convince him to help her. "It's for Anthony. We need to prove he didn't kill the lady in the cellar."

His shoulders twitched. "I'm sure Anthony has broken into a few houses. Go ask him."

"He's *in* jail. He can't go with me. I need you to cut wires or whatever it is you do to climb through a window."

"You just climb through, Juliet."

She let out a long breath and changed tactics. "Don't you remember how it felt when Detective Le Scalus questioned you about Romeo's death?" She touched his forearm. "You were bothered by that."

"Right. That's why I broke into Montague's house."

"This is the same thing. I'm trying to catch a killer."

His mouth dropped open. "I didn't break in to catch a killer! Why would anyone break into a killer's house?"

She used her last resort. "You owe me."

He blinked hard. "No, I don't."

It had been unspoken between them, her saving his life in a roundabout way. "No one was looking for you, Tybalt Gatti. Nobody but me. I was the one who found you half-buried. *Dying*."

A growl came from his throat. "All right, all right, all right. Whose house am I breaking into?"

She snatched his hand again. "Thank you! It's Sebastian D'Angelo's house."

He shrugged. "Never heard of him. How big is the house?"

"It's probably no bigger than Montague's."

"Will this D'Angelo be home?"

Juliet frowned. "We won't do it if he's home."

"Does he have animals?"

"I—I don't know."

His dark eyes fell on her. "Well, you better do some recon work if you expect me to help you."

"Right. Of course." She gathered her purse. "I will."

The black curtain swished, and there was Madame Olei. She was a tiny woman with red curls held in place with a scarf. Her long skirt was a floral pattern but wasn't long enough to hide those size ten white sneakers. She pointed a finger at Juliet. "You will chase the man you love."

Juliet took a step backward. Of all the things she'd expected a psychic to say, well, that certainly wasn't it. If the shyster had been listening at the curtain, then she might've said something like *you saved your cousin's life*. Or, she could've said something about waiting until the ruling planet is in the first house to commit residential burglary, *blah, blah*...

You will chase the man you love... How did a person respond to such a statement? Juliet smiled and nodded and said, "Thank you."

She drove the rest of the way home in the dark. People already had Christmas lights up on their houses, and it wasn't Thanksgiving yet. Father Jonathon had called such people heretics, which had made Juliet smile at the time. Yet, the colored bulbs and lighted reindeer seemed to brighten her mood at the same time they lit the dead lawns right outside of Mayville.

She cracked the windows and cranked the heat toward her feet. *You will chase the man you love*...

Go on!

She changed gears and changed her thoughts.

Intel, that's what she needed. When does D'Angelo leave the office? Does he go straight home or stop for a drink? Does he sleep at his house every night, or does he stay with Beth?

Oh yes, D'Angelo and Beth were involved with each other. Juliet had connected those dots as soon as her mother described D'Angelo's wife. Beth had followed him from Florida to a tiny town in New York, just to be his secretary. Who does that, but a woman in love?

You will chase the man you love.

"No, I won't, Madame," she said out loud and turned onto Via Cavour.

Back to the main issue. Juliet knew D'Angelo's address. Tomorrow she'd Google it, street map it, and zoom in with a satellite view. A drive-by might be in order, just to check for dogs. Despite Ty's concerns, the break-in should be easy. They weren't going to steal anything, just take a photo of a marriage or birth certificate and get out.

Beth, oh Beth, what can you tell me?

So far, Juliet's attempts to make friends with the woman had been flicked like birdseed out of the cage. That must change. And it would, tomorrow morning.

* * *

The next morning, after setting her purse in the drawer and leaving her espresso on her desk, Juliet went straight to Beth's office with a pastry box in her hand.

It was a no-red-sweater day for Beth. Today she wore a tight leopard skin blouse and black skirt—which was just as tight, and she didn't have the figure to pull it off. She was not catwalk ready.

Beth turned from the filing cabinet. She might've tried to stop her top lip from curling and her face from turning away. She might've, but didn't accomplish it well.

Juliet held out the pastry box. "I've brought a peace offering."

"Why?" She moved to her desk, took a seat, and then pushed a stray hair behind her ear. She was having a good hair day; the golden mass behaved nicely and fell around her full cheeks in waves.

Juliet set the box on the desk. "I wanted to apologize for yesterday, for getting you into trouble with your boss."

Beth still didn't look at Juliet. Instead, she studied the computer screen. "You didn't get me into trouble."

There was a moment of silence.

Juliet pushed the box closer.

Beth glanced at it. "What is it?"

"Homemade Italian cannoli. My grandmother made it. She's one hundred percent Italian."

Beth kept her gaze steady on the box now. "Aren't you one hundred percent Italian?"

"Well, yes, but I don't cook. Never had to because I live with my *Nonna*."

She eyed the box. "I haven't eaten breakfast."

Juliet's mouth twitched upward. "That's perfect. Do you have coffee?"

She nodded to the mug on her desk beside the computer monitor and then gave Juliet a cautious nod. "Thank you."

"Just don't let Patsy see it. She'll take it right out from underneath your nose."

Beth shook her head. "We don't speak to each other."

"Neither do we, but that didn't stop her from grabbing my muffin."

The woman's eyes narrowed. "What?"

"Never mind. Enjoy." She took a step toward the door but then paused. "Is it possible to make an appointment with Seb… Mr. D'Angelo?"

Beth opened the box and stared with soft eyes at the pastry. "He won't be here today. He's in New York City for the weekend."

Suddenly Juliet couldn't stay still. She was ready to hit D'Angelo's house right then. She forced her limbs to keep still and controlled her voice. "Oh?"

"Some trade show."

"Really? I'm surprised my father didn't go."

Beth pushed the box away, the cannoli spell completely broken. "Your father didn't go?" Her voice had turned thin, as though her vocal cords were stretched in a torture device.

Juliet lifted a shoulder. "He was at breakfast this morning."

"Oh, really?" It wasn't an *oh-really-how-exciting* note in her voice, but *oh-really-I'm-going-to-kill-him* tone. She snatched up her cell phone next to the coffee mug and fired off a text.

"I'll be down the hall," Juliet told her, turning. But then she whipped back around. "Does Mr. D'Angelo have a dog?"

Beth shook her head, eyes pinpoints of anger. "What?"

"I'm getting Christmas gifts together and wonder if he has a dog."

"No dog."

But he has you, which is the same thing.

"Cat?"

"What? No!"

"Security cameras?"

Beth's arm dropped onto the desk in a manner that suggested impatience.

"Never mind," Juliet said and stepped out of the office.

Her fingers tingled, just itching to break into D'Angelo's house right that minute. Yet it was daylight. A nosy housewife would see her and call the cops. D'Angelo probably had security cameras, and Juliet wasn't dressed in black at the moment. She'd worn a cute outfit today because she was tired of jeans and tops, and trying to fit in at the office where no one liked her anyway. She'd dressed in a pink sheath dress with a powder blue Chanel jacket, highlighted by a trusty pair of pixel python Louboutins.

Tricia and Patsy were in the coffee machine and refrigerator area.

Juliet almost broke a heel switching routes. She approached Patsy. "I want to know why you think I don't deserve a cupcake."

Patsy's thin brows lifted. She had no more style to her hair than usual, leaving it hanging to her chin and needing a *Ten Voss* treatment.

Tricia's curly hair needed nothing. It bounced on top of the woman's head like a happy cheerleader. "What?" She glanced at Patsy.

Patsy knew what Juliet meant, oh, yes, she did. She shrugged. "I snapped Delia's cupcake out of her hand before she could taste it."

No doubt, Tricia found the idea as infantile as Juliet.

"Haven't you taken enough from her?" Tricia wanted to know, glaring from behind those over-big glasses.

Huh?

The microwave dinged, and Patsy removed the plate. "I made sure she didn't get it. It's okay."

Julie screwed up her features and waved her hands. "Wait a minute, wait a minute, wait ... what do you think I took from Delia?"

Patsy was sprinkling salt on the watery eggs on the plate. "You took her job."

"I took ... what?"

Patsy slammed the microwave door. "Delia was

supposed to get the desk you're sitting in. They eliminated her position in the warehouse, so she was going to assist Leary. She was all set to go until you insisted on having a job. D'Angelo fired her."

Juliet's mouth tasted sour. "I didn't know."

"All because you wanted to work," Tricia said, shoving her lunchbox into the refrigerator, "when you obviously don't need to work. What are those?" She pointed at Juliet's footwear. "Jimmy Choo's? Delia is out of a job, and dead broke."

Juliet's spirits wilted. "And now her truck broke down."

"Well, don't beat yourself up over that part," Patsy said. "She's got another car and it's just as old as that truck."

"But, but, she's so nice to me," Juliet rallied. "Why doesn't she hate me?"

"Delia's not the type of person to hold a grudge," Trisha said. "But here's a thought. Quit and let her get her job back."

Juliet's shoulders stiffened. "Oh, I can't do that. I'm in the middle of… " She gazed at Tricia, at Patsy. "Umm."

Both women waited, leaning in, expecting some explanation.

"I can't quit. I, I just need to stay for a little while longer. But as soon as I leave, Delia can have my job."

"You mean *her* job?" Patsy asked, picking up her plate. "And what are you saying? That you're only here for a couple of weeks, and you've caused our friend all of these problems?"

"No," Juliet said, waving her hand. "No, of course not. I mean, I'll move to another job in the company, and she can have *her* desk back."

"Wow, that's very generous of you." Patsy slapped

Trisha on the arm. "Let's go. You can't reason with someone who has no idea what it's like to have nothing."

Juliet took a step with them. "Maybe I can give her money to tide her over." She was more thinking out loud than to appease them.

Tricia shook her bouncy curls. "Don't do that. Delia will never take money from you. I've tried to help her, but she's an independent woman. Give her back her job if you want to help."

They left her standing in the middle of the hallway and disappeared into their own office.

Juliet slunk toward her own.

She hadn't known what had taken place for her to get a job in the office. But then again, it never crossed Juliet's mind—not once—that to get the job someone else lost the job. The fact sank down around her like a heavy wet blanket of guilt. And, that it was Delia who'd lost the job doubly weighted the blanket down.

And I'm asking her to lunch and worrying about her father's trap door, and she's worried she won't get a job and now her truck is broken down on the side of the road ...

* * *

Anthony's arraignment was held in the Chautauqua County courthouse. The old building reminded Juliet of the Lincoln Memorial and the Capitol Building in Washington, D.C. with its columns and portico, and a domed roof near the back of the property.

Juliet waited in the courtroom as the judge made a decision to set Anthony's bail at seven hundred thousand dollars. Afterward, Anthony came out of the building, searching the small parking lot for Juliet.

She waved to him and then unlocked the car doors and took a seat behind the driver's wheel.

Anthony fell into the passenger's seat and buckled his seatbelt. "Well, have you proved yourself right yet?"

"I'm always right. What are you referring to?"

"You said you'd have proof it was D'Angelo the next time you saw me."

"I thought you'd be in jail a lot longer."

"You have no proof."

"Be patient. I'm working on things."

"That scares me." Anthony tightened the seatbelt and held onto the handle above the door. He closed his eyes. "Okay, I'm ready."

Juliet tossed him a look. "Stop it, I'll drive slowly. And thank you for helping me with everything. I've missed you." And then she hit the gas and roared out of the parking lot.

* * *

Dinner at seven was more formal than usual since Roseline and Dr. Dexter joined the family. Italia had arranged the affair, claiming she wanted to get to know David Dexter a little better since he would soon be her nephew-in-law.

They ate in the dining room, in front of the small fireplace. The candles were lit, and the wine flowed. Dr. Dexter relaxed in his chair with his legs out in front of him—because he was trying too hard.

Juliet had come to the conclusion that Dexter was a nerd. Sure, he looked like the ultra-smooth Nicolas Cage with his chest hairs poking out of that white button-down, but he was a poindexter. Even his name revealed it. Dexter hadn't said so, but there was sure to be a Star Wars collection of something in his nerd cave. He probably had a full-screen television for his World of Warcraft games.

What tipped Juliet off was that Dexter had said something about exploring Hobbit holes in New Zealand on the honeymoon … and if not that, then he wanted to go on an exclusive tour of a Lego factory.

And how was Roseline handling that information? Why, with adoring love and tiny tears in her eyes.

Juliet had so many other things to do than sit there watching them cupcaking and canoodling.

Breaking into D'Angelo's house, for instance, or at least doing some intel work.

Dexter sat on the right side of Juliet. He inclined toward her. "I'm so happy you're going to be in our wedding, Juliet. I know you'll take good care of Roseline and help with the planning and parties."

"It'll be so much fun," Juliet told him. All right, she lied.

Paris sat on the other side of Juliet, and he leaned toward Dr. Dexter. "Where will you live once you're married?"

"Well, I own a house," Dexter said, sitting up straighter in his chair. He still had his hand on the table and he fiddled with the engagement ring on Roseline's finger. He flipped it this way and that. "I'm selling it, though, and Roseline and I will move somewhere new together."

"What a smart idea," Italia put in. "When a woman moves into a man's house, she feels hesitant to make it her own. Best to start out on an even footing."

"I'm looking at houses," Paris said.

Juliet had been in the middle of a bite of *panna cotta*, but it curdled in her mouth.

"Oh," Dexter said, suddenly interested, and swayed their way again. "I'm just outside of Mayville, in the Lagoon Subdivision."

"I looked at a house in that area," Paris said, nodding. He was in a black shirt, which made him even more handsome—or it was the candlelight softening his complexion.

Not that it matters.

Paris put his spoon on the table. "I do like the neighborhood. It reminds me of Venice with the canal running through it, yeah?"

"Yes," Dexter said. "Would you like to see it sometime?"

Juliet set down her spoon, as well. "It's kind of far away, isn't it?"

"Not as far as Martha's Vineyard," Paris told her, eyeing her at close range. The fire in the hearth lit his eyes, making them greener. "You don't want me to continue living here, do you?"

"You may move in anytime you like," Italia inserted.

"A man needs his own space when he's young," Santos put in, nodding to Paris as if to say, *you may not move in anytime you like.*

Paris rubbed a spot on his chin, hiding his smile. He turned to Dexter. "I would like to see it, yes."

Dexter pulled his mouth down in thought. "Are you doing anything after dinner? We can run by, if you like. The cleaning lady was in today, so it should be tidy."

Roseline's laugh sounded like little bells. "You're always very neat, David. I don't know why you need a maid."

"You know how I am, dear. I do like things tidy." He

took Roseline's hand and kissed it.

Wasn't that a bit unsanitary, since he was a self-declared germaphobe?

Paris leaned in. "It's nice that they're in love. One day you will be."

She placed her cloth napkin to her lips, and whispered back, "I'm not going to be so showy about it."

"You will when you fall in love."

"Says the man who loves me but doesn't display any sort of affection at all."

Now what made me say that?

Paris raised one brow. "You want romance, yeah?"

"No, I'm just saying you talk a big show."

"I've been holding back, letting you heal from your past love, but if you're ready now …" He tilted his head and wiggled his brows to finish the sentence.

"Stop it."

Dexter's long face came back into view. "How about it, Nobleman, want to come to see it after dinner?"

"Sure. If Juliet will come along." He tugged her hair as Dexter had done to Roseline.

"Stop it," she repeated.

"O lamentable day!"

Chapter 11

Juliet trailed Roseline's car toward Dexter's neighborhood, which was through Mayville and around the lake, then south. It was an hour away from the Da Vinci Vineyard.

Paris sat in the passenger seat and was in the middle of his passionate debate regarding house hunting. "I'm just saying that I'm not receiving the same level of support as your spy investigation."

"I'm helping you now," she said, ending the argument. She turned the wheel and followed her cousin's powder blue Audi over an arched bridge that led into the subdivision. All the homes were three-story brick with domed windows and flower boxes. The main road curved and dipped, which caused the houses to stand uneven to each other. It was utterly charming.

Paris leaned forward in the seat and gazed at the rooftops. "I was here in the daytime, but I think it's even nicer at night. Look at the streetlamps."

The lights were the filigree type, old-world styling, and each was decorated for Christmas with swags of garland and twinkle lights.

They continued winding around the streets, Pedimonte di Borgoloco, Calle dei Cinque, Paradiso …"

Calle dei Cinque?

Juliet knew that name. Who lived on Calle dei Cinque?

Roseline finally steered into a driveway, and once they were all out of the cars, she took Juliet's arm. "I'm so glad you came with us. It's like a double date."

"It's nothing like a double date. Paris is my friend."

"He's very handsome," she said, eyeing him from a distance.

Juliet's insides squirmed. "Yes, he is, but he's still just a friend."

Dexter led the way and threw open the door to allow Paris to go through first.

Juliet followed, noting the stairway just to the right of the entryway. Crown molding lined the walls and made a chair rail.

Beyond the gleaming kitchen was an enormous living room with a seventy-five-inch screen television mounted on one wall.

The place was clean, sterile like an operating room.

Had Dexter ever been married? There was no feminine touch to the room at all. There was no comfort factor in Dexter's decorating, no pillows, no rugs, and no lamps for softer lighting. Everything was set aright, except for books on the table and two bus tokens on a coffee table.

Paris asked, "I'll have a good look around, yeah, check the plumbing and basics?"

"By all means," Dexter told him, holding out his arms.

Gazing at the air ducts, Paris walked around the room and then stooped in front of the fireplace. He opened and closed the flue, which caused the ashes to flutter. Then he moved back into the kitchen and opened cabinets and looked beneath the sink. Everyone followed him to the front room, where he opened the closet door beneath the stairway.

Juliet glanced inside space too. There was poindexter's bowling bag and shoes.

Paris pushed coats aside and studied the back of the closet. Dexter didn't have much imagination in his clothing choices. Everything in the closet was either black or gray, mostly the same length, except one.

"There's a crack in the flooring," Paris said, backing out of the closet. "Have you had structural damage?"

"No," Dexter said, a note of surprise in his voice.

It astonished Juliet how thorough Paris was in his examination of the house. Did he have construction knowledge? Pipes were pipes to Juliet. Air ducts were air ducts.

They toured the second and third floors next, and Paris was just as complete in his examination.

"So there are six bedrooms in total?" Juliet asked and glanced at Paris. "That's a lot of house for a single guy." Never mind that it was an hour away.

Paris lifted his shoulders. "I'm not always going to be single, yeah? I want a wife and children someday."

Roseline caught Juliet's attention and widened her eyes—as if Paris was proposing right there on the landing.

Julie frowned and shook her head.

The four of them made their way back to the first landing that overlooked the foyer and double door entry. Dexter leaned on the banister. "I've lived here as a single guy for almost twenty-two years, and I've never thought the place was too big." He put his arm around Roseline's waist. "There's plenty of room for guests and family to stay."

Juliet leaned on the railing too and admired the open foyer below. The marble gleamed in the high lighting of the room. The double front door was arched and made of wood and glass and metal. "I'm surprised you want to leave here, Roseline. You could do a lot with this place." And, she meant it. Her cousin had a talent for decorating. She wouldn't need to hire anyone to fix the house up.

"Oh, I know, but ever since the break-in a couple of months ago, I've been a little uneasy in the house by myself."

What's this now?

Dr. Dexter's fingers tightened on Roseline's waist, and he leaned away, eyebrows slanting. "Don't scare away a potential buyer, darling." He said the word darling with just a hint of impatience.

Roseline gasped. "Oh!" She put her fingers on her cheeks, and then she let out a laugh. "I'm so sorry." She eyed Paris. "It's just me. I'm a nervous person." She leaned away from Dexter. "But, you're a big guy, Paris. You won't let a few burglaries in the area bother you, will you?"

There was a strange tension gathering between the engaged couple. Maybe because Juliet knew her cousin so well, she recognized the subtle shift of the girl's attitude. Roseline brought her hands together and crossed them backward, weaving her fingers together. She never liked being corrected.

"Let me tell them about it," Dexter suggested. He led the way down the rest of the staircase, stepping with Paris and pointing toward the door. "I've installed a new security system, top of the line stuff. The police drive by once an evening, and we now have a neighborhood watch in place."

Roseline descended the steps with Juliet, her back straight, but with a dangerous sashay to her torso and arms.

Dexter and Paris reached the foyer first and moved to the center of the room. Dexter said, "I've never had any issues here, it was just one time."

Roseline moved around Juliet and stood apart from Dexter. If her mood were a color, it'd be flaming red.

A wave of pity overtook Juliet, and she sided with the doctor—and for herself as well. "Nice homes are sometimes a target for burglaries. It doesn't matter where you live. You might as well stay here."

Dexter's' face brightened, and he waved his hand toward her. "That's what I told her, Juliet. You've got the right idea."

"Oh, does she?" Roseline asked.

Dexter's eyes landed on his bride-to-be. "Um, yes."

"Juliet is *very* clever," the girl agreed with her voice silky smooth.

Uh oh, here we go.

Roseline tossed a strand of hair behind her shoulder. "How's your little spy business going, cousin?" Her voice clipped with each word she said. "She's gone undercover at her father's wine company, to find a spy. Isn't she marvelous, David? Isn't she the cleverest of us all?"

Dexter seemed to be getting it now. His head slowly pivoted toward his lady love and he leaned just a hair away. "I'm sure she is clever … dear?"

"Oh, she's more than clever." Roseline swept her hand in a graceful arch. "She caught a murderer over the summer. She's a regular Nancy Drew. Remember, I told you."

The doctor's eyebrows came together in the middle of his Nicolas Cage face. "I do remember. Cleverness runs in your family."

Paris seemed to pick up on the tension. He clapped his hands together and rubbed them. "Well, thanks so much for letting me see the house. I am interested in it. When do you think you'll move?"

"January, I think," Dexter said, nodding, glancing at Roseline. "We've set the wedding date for February 14."

"Valentine's Day," Roseline added, stiff through the shoulders.

Paris took Juliet's arm and backed toward the door. "We'll see you soon, I'm sure. We'll discuss the details."

Dexter rushed forward to get the door for them. "That sounds great. Thanks for coming by."

As the door shut, Roseline's voice lifted, "So you think Juliet is so great? Why don't you marry her?"

Paris let out a low whistle and escorted Juliet to the Fiat.

Back in the car, Paris buckled up.

Juliet fell into the driver's seat. "I can answer Abram's question now."

"What question?"

"What does Roseline see in Dexter …" She started the engine. "He's a wealthy doctor, will do whatever she says, and falls apart when she isn't happy."

"You don't know that. He might be in there right now telling her like it is."

Juliet shook her head. "No, he's in there apologizing and groveling. I bet he doesn't have the decency to go down swinging."

"If he's smart, he'll keep an accredited marriage counselor on retainer." Paris had one elbow on the window ledge. "Which brings up the subject of why are you trying to sabotage my house search?"

She pulled away from the curb and did a U-turn. "The least you can do is thank me. I'm trying to stop you from making a bad choice."

Paris patted his pocket. "No, you are in love with me and don't want me to leave. Admit it." He reached into his jacket pocket and then patted the outside of it.

Juliet grimaced. "I'm not in love with you."

"Never mind that now, where is my phone?" He leaned right and felt a back pocket, and then leaned left.

His black hair was very close to Juliet's face and she backed away. "Did you bring it?"

"I took pictures at Dexter's house."

"Oh, you didn't leave it there, did you?" Juliet braked at a stop sign. "I don't want to go back there and witness them making up."

"Don't go any farther. And, let me use your phone." She handed him her cell. "What are you doing?"

He opened the passenger side door and climbed out of the car.

A blast of cold air swirled inside the small interior.

Paris searched the area beneath the passenger seat and then the seat itself. He sat again and turned on her phone.

"I'm using *Find My iPhone*. I don't want to go back to the doctor's house either." He continued tapping the phone screen.

All of a sudden, a beeping sounded, like a microwave going off. It came from beneath the passenger seat.

"There it is," Paris said, stepping out of the car again. "It's …" He pulled at the seatbelt, reached his hand between the seat and the strap, and then pulled out his phone. "Here we are." He handed her back her phone and shut his door.

Juliet made a right-hand turn, watching the street signs for Calle dei Cinque again. She'd remembered who lived there.

"Now, back to our conversation," Paris said. "Your objections about Dexter's house were predictable and trite."

"Uh-huh." She turned right on the next street.

"Why did you turn here?"

Juliet scanned the addresses on the curb. She'd gotten halfway down the street when she saw the numbers 540.

"This one's nice," Paris said, gazing through the windshield and at the house with its glassed-in patio on the easternmost side. There were a few lights on in the windows. "There's no For Sale sign, yeah?"

The street lamps highlighted the manicured lawn and the flowerbed near the front steps.

Juliet pulled into the driveway made of white brick. "We're not here to see the house."

"Oh?"

"I need to know if there's a dog inside and what sort of cameras we're dealing with."

"We?"

She turned to Paris. "This is D'Angelo's house."

"The guy from the Harvest Ball," he said, nodding. He turned his face and watched Juliet in the low lights. "Tell me about *we* again."

She waved her hand. "Me and Ty … and you."

He shook his head. "No."

"Why not?" Juliet faced him. "Don't you want to help catch D'Angelo?" She gazed at the windows of the house again. All the curtains were closed. "How do I figure out if there's a dog inside?"

"You can ask the neighborhood watch when they roll around in their golf cart."

"I watched for them as I pulled onto the street. No one's around."

Paris waved his hand toward the windshield. "We could climb the fence and walk through the yard. Our shoes will find evidence if a dog is living here."

Juliet wrinkled her nose. "I'm wearing Louboutins." She put the car into Reverse, backed a small way, and rolled down the window.

"What are you doing?"

"Listening."

She pressed the horn hard and long.

A dog barked three or four houses away. All was silent in the D'Angelo house.

"No dog," Juliet said, "We haven't broken in yet, so there's no reason for D'Angelo to look at his security cameras."

"Yet. When D'Angelo reports the burglary to the police, they'll look at the footage and see that you pulled in here to case the joint."

"We're not going to give him a reason to check the cameras."

A curtain moved in one of the lower floor windows.

"There may not be a dog, but someone is home."

Juliet shook her head. "D'Angelo is in New York."

"A family member?"

"His son's in Florida and not coming home for Thanksgiving."

"Well, someone's here, yeah?"

Juliet put the Fiat into Reverse and drove around the block. Finding an alley, she slowed the car and rolled past D'Angelo's backyard. She couldn't see anything beyond the fence, but parked right outside the redwood fencing was an older model black Honda with peeling paint.

Paris asked, "Is that D'Angelo's car?"

"No, but I've seen it before somewhere."

"Do you know who it belongs to?"

Juliet bit her lip. "No, but I'll check the West Portland office parking lot on Monday." Pressing the accelerator, she drove out of the alley and back to the highway.

* * *

Saturday evening, Juliet sat on her bedroom balcony, drinking Limoncello to calm her nerves. No, she wasn't tense because she was going to break into D'Angelo's house in another hour. She was edgy because she'd spent too long at the bridal party meeting that morning and afternoon.

Roseline had told the group of women that she was already getting headaches and having tummy issues because of the stress.

Maybe she wasn't marrying the right guy was Juliet's first thought. Then Roseline confessed that she was so nervous because she feared some of the bridesmaids wouldn't be able to fit into the dresses in February. "People gain weight during the holidays," she'd told them. "Please stay away from sweets this Christmas."

Juliet had also discovered that the groomsmen would wear kilts at the ceremony. "Is Dexter Scottish?" she'd asked. Dexter sounded German to her.

"It's an English name," one of the girls had answered.

"So it's not Scottish. What's with the kilts?"

That's when Roseline lost her ish.

Juliet drank the last of the liqueur and gazed at her phone. The battery was fully charged.

Excellent.

She peered at the horizon. Only the sun's halo was left in the sky. The wind off the lake was up and whipping frigid air around the corner of the house.

Standing, she went back into her bedroom. It was time to dress. She'd already laid out her clothes on the bed: black pants, black sweater, black gloves, and shoes. She still needed one thing and went to the dresser to find her black ski cap and face covering. She left the face covering off for the time being and stuffed it hard into her pocket. The thing reminded her too much of her mother's nagging about the upcoming ski trip. Juliet didn't need her mother directing her social life, for heaven's sake. Wasn't breaking and entering a home with her cousin convivial enough?

Juliet stepped out of the room.

Paris stepped out of his room at nearly the same moment. He was dressed in a pale green sweater and jeans. The knit fit over his square shoulders and then hung off his trim body quite nicely, but it wasn't something he should wear while breaking into a house. He asked, "Why are you dressed like a cartoon bandit?"

Juliet's shoulders went limp. "I told you. We're breaking

into D'Angelo's house."

"That's illegal, Juliet."

She threw out her hand. "I'm not happy about it."

"I'm not sure I believe you."

"I don't know when you started to believe such horrible things about me, Paris Nobleman. First, I'm trying to sabotage your house hunt and now I'm a happy burglar skipping off to work."

How she hated a man who laughed uproariously.

She left Paris in the hallway and made for the stairs.

He caught up with her. "And if you get caught?"

"I'm not going to get caught. I'm going about this professionally."

"Yes, yes, Ty is helping you."

They made it to the first landing, and Juliet turned on him. "He's not just a dancer. He's broken into houses."

Paris leaned toward her, practically nose-to-nose. "How many?"

"Er, one."

"That's hardly professional."

She shrugged. "But Ty knows all about cutting wires and smashing glass panes." She leaned away from him. "Will you come with us?"

He stood straighter and shook his head. "Not on your nelly. I can't afford an arrest record right now."

"You've already got an arrest record. I was there."

Ty skipped down the stairs, all knees and elbows. He'd dressed in dark jeans and a black sweater. "Let's get this over with." Ty still hadn't had his hair cut, and it flopped around his ears as he continued his descent.

Paris followed him. "Why are you doing this?"

Juliet trailed after Paris, back straight, listening in.

"She guilted me into it," Ty told him. He was at the bottom of the stairs and turned to face Paris. "How about you?"

"Oh, I'm not going."

Juliet was on the bottom step when the doorbell chimed. Before answering it, she told them, "A little breaking and entering charge would be a first for you," she said, facing Paris. "I expected more. You jumped into the feud over the summer and were so willing to go to jail with me back then. What's happened to you?" Without giving him a chance to answer, she glanced at the front door monitor. "Oh, no." Dragging herself to the front door, she opened it.

Abram Fontana stood in the glow of the porchlight in his tight leather pants, corduroy shirt, and brown jacket. He'd gelled his dark brown hair again, but this time into a peak on the top of his head. The style added an extra two inches to his height. Lifting his chin, he said, "Hey."

Juliet turned on Ty. "Did you ask him to help?"

"What? I don't like him."

Abram bounced from one foot to the other in the cold air. "We're going ice skating. Are you saying that you don't remember?"

Ugh.

She leaned on the door and sucked in a whistling breath. "Sorry, Abram, I can't go. I've got something else lined up."

His mouth dropped. "But you said …" His eyes went from hers to Paris to Ty. "Okay," he said with a nod. "I get it. You've got other friends to hang out with." He turned to leave, to walk back to the enormous black truck in the driveway.

Her conscience stabbed her in the chest. "Oh, just

stop. Stop where you are," Juliet called out. "Are you any good at breaking into houses?"

Abram turned back around, eyes bright. "Are you serious?" He came back to the door. "I'm small and can fit through windows and other narrow places."

She bit her bottom lip for a moment. "Okay, you're hired."

"Juliet," Paris said, stepping around Ty. "The more people you involve, the bigger the chances are of you getting caught."

Abram stuck his head around the doorframe. "I've been arrested. I'm really comfortable with the process."

Juliet pointed her thumb at Abram. "You see there. That's the attitude I'm looking for."

Paris stuck his hands in his pockets.

"Oh, just stay home and out of jail. If that's the way you want to live your life, then live your life that way."

Ty leaned toward him. "Don't let her get to you. She will use every means possible to bend you to her will."

Juliet gasped. "My feelings are hurt. I'm expressing. I'm not bending…"

"Oh, really?" her cousin said, stepping around her and onto the porch. "What was it you said, what is it you said? *You owe me.*"

She shrugged. "Well, you do."

He puffed out his chest. "I know. Let's go."

*"I have no joy of this contract tonight.
It is too rash, too unadvised, too sudden."*

Chapter 12

The threesome paused on the sidewalk—in the twenty-seven degree temperature. Juliet said, "We can't take my car. Someone will recognize it."

Ty nodded, rubbing his hands together. "We can take mine."

"If we take Gatti's car, we'll get caught for sure because it'll stall out in a chase." Abram jerked his chin toward his truck. "We'll take the Freight Train."

"Freight Train?" Ty asked. "What sort of name is that?"

"What? What would you name it, Fred the Ford? Ted

the Truck. You're boring, Gatti."

"Let's just go," Juliet said, leading the way and climbing into the king cab. "Come on, come on. The night's almost over."

Ty climbed into the passenger seat and slammed the door. "It's eight o'clock."

"I don't know when D'Angelo will be back from New York City," she said, fidgeting with the seatbelt.

Abram climbed into the driver's seat and started the engine. "Where to?"

Juliet gave him the address and then sat back in the seat. She still couldn't believe Paris didn't come along. What was going on with him that he cared about an arrest record? Paris was supposed to be her friend, her bestie—her Scooby Doo.

Abram's voice interrupted Juliet's thoughts. He asked Ty, "How's the bakery business?" He'd turned his head toward the passenger seat. Headlights from the other lane hit his face, highlighting the big beak on his face.

"There is no bakery business."

Abram's foot let off the gas. "You're kidding? Your mom's bakery was the best thing in Mayville."

Ty shrugged. "No mom, no bakery."

"Wow, didn't she at least leave you some recipes?"

"I don't know how to bake," Ty admitted. "I dance."

"Dance?" Abram asked with a note of disbelief in his voice. "I'd so open a bakery."

Juliet leaned forward. "You bake?"

"No, but if I had a bakery just sitting there, and had all the recipes in hand, I'd hire someone to bake the *Cassata* cakes. Make a ton of money too. Change out of the dancing dress, Gatti."

Juliet sat up straight. "That's a brilliant idea."

Ty turned and glared at her.

"Not the dress part. The hiring someone part."

Abram nodded. "All my ideas are brilliant."

"Don't ruin it," she said and sat back in the seat again. Juliet knew someone who baked and that someone needed a job.

* * *

They circled D'Angelo's house twice and then parked in the driveway. Abram hit the truck horn.

"I could've told you there was no dog," Juliet said.

"I don't take chances if there's a Rottweiler in the house named Shredder." He shoved the truck into Park, opened his door. "Even Chihuahuas have a mean bite."

"I do believe that part." Ty gazed at Abram. "That you are scared of Chihuahuas." His voice couldn't have been drier.

"I think you need to dial it down a little when you're checking me, Gatti." Abram jumped from the truck. "I'd hate to see you walk home in the cold." His boot heels clunked rapid-fire as he ran on the brick.

"What's he doing?" Juliet asked, grabbing the seat and pulling herself forward.

Abram ran straight for the door and rang the bell. He hopped up and down in the cold air as he waited.

Juliet's stomach tightened. What would she say if D'Angelo saw her in the back of the truck?

She dropped to the floorboard. "What's happening?" she asked Ty.

"He's dancing around, blowing on his hands."

"Did someone answer …?"

The truck swayed.

Abram shut the door, draped his arm over the back of the seat, and told Juliet. "No one's home."

Juliet lifted her head, still kneeling on the floorboard. "Why did you do that? Now the security cameras have seen you."

"If someone asks me, I'll just say I stopped to ask for directions." Twisting back around, he shifted into Reverse. "And you always knock to see if someone is home." He turned around to see her again. "You do care about that, right? This is just a robbery and not an assault?"

Juliet climbed off the floor and back into the seat. "Of course, it's just a robbery. What in the world?"

"Hey, we're just starting our friendship. I don't know what you think is a fun time."

"It's not assaulting people."

He nodded and let off the brake. "See? Another thing we have in common. We'll be best friends before the night is over."

She seriously doubted that. Sitting forward, she said, "Park in the alley, at the end of it, and we'll walk."

The side street was paved and clear of trash bins. Fancy lamps hung off the redwood fences and the lights created a halo glow around each gate.

Out of the truck, the trio moved in stealth mode toward D'Angelo's gate. "I suppose we'll need to climb the fence," Juliet said, gazing at the eight foot structure.

Ty ran his hand over the wood. "It's pressure treated. Smooth. Slippery." He took three steps and tried the gate handle. "Of course, it's locked." He turned on Juliet. "What now?"

"Umm."

"This was your idea," he said, his tone peevish.

Juliet turned to Abram. "Back up the truck and we'll use the bed as a ladder."

Ty shrugged. "That's not bad."

"I'm a thinker," she told him, watching Abram run to the truck.

Thirty seconds later, the truck's engine roared to life. Abram didn't turn on the headlights, but the taillights shone in the dark like red eyes coming straight at Juliet and Ty.

They both crossed the alley and waited for Abram to park close to the fence.

"Someone is going to see us," Ty said, glancing up at the back of the three-story houses.

"No one is going to see us," Abram said, out of the truck and rubbing his hands together.

"Even still," Ty said. "I think I'll stay in the truck."

Juliet gave a start. "What do you mean? You're not coming with us?"

He threw out his arm and pointed at Abram. "He knows what he's doing. Take him. I'll wait in the truck and send a signal if someone comes along."

"Good idea," Abram said. "When we're over the fence, move the truck, so it's not so obvious what we're doing."

Abram handed Ty the keys. "I know you're not used to that much power beneath your butt, so take it easy."

Ty stared at Juliet. "I'm not ready to fall eight feet from a fence. I'm under doctor's care still, you know."

"Your doctor told you not to climb a fence?" Her disappointment came out in her voice. First Paris, and now Ty meant to back out of the plan.

Ty dropped a hand on her shoulder. "I'll come next time. I promise."

She shrugged away from him and climbed into the

truck bed with Abram.

Abram said, "My cellphone is off. Toot the horn if the police arrive and meet us two streets to the north."

Juliet gazed at Abram with a new appreciation. "How many times have you done this?"

"Never mind, Boo-cake. Let's do this."

Boo-cake? Ew.

Ty started the engine.

"Wait a minute," Juliet told him.

Abram stood on the side of the truck and jumped at the fence. He got his belly on the top of it and swung his boot over—then he disappeared.

So, he was a professional fence hopper.

It was a full two seconds before Abram thumped to the ground.

"Wow, that's, that's a drop," Juliet said under her breath.

She climbed onto the side of the truck bed. The slick paint didn't give much traction and her boots slid every second or so. Holding on to the top of the fence, Juliet kicked off. She got her ribcage on the top plank, scrambled her toes against the slick wood …

Ty pulled the truck away fast and drove to the end of the alley.

Absolutely last time I ask him to help me do anything.

Straining and kicking, Juliet finally got her foot onto the top of the wall. She paused a moment. How to get down …

Her hand slipped and she fell into the yard, landing on her back in the grass. "Oww."

"I was going to open the gate for you," Abram said, standing over her and holding out one hand.

She took his hand, and struggled to her feet. Brushing

off her pants, she said. "You might've told me that sooner."

"Keep your voice down," he hissed, and then he took off toward the house.

Juliet adjusted her ski mask and followed him, her heart hammering. She was doing it. She was breaking in to someone's house!

D'Angelo's backyard was large and full of ornamental trees. Paris would love the patio kitchen, fire pit, fireplace, and gazebo.

What am I thinking? I don't want Paris to move.

A fresh wave of disappointment hit her. He should be with her tonight.

Abram held up his arm, like one of those army rangers in the movies. "There are the security cameras," he said, pointing toward the roof overhang.

Juliet crouched down.

He moved forward with caution toward the french doors. "There's no button light. Whoever lives here didn't bother to set them up, or didn't turn them on."

Juliet stood straighter. "Where are all the paranoid people in the world?"

"Pretty expensive equipment to not use it."

"Maybe someone turned them off," Juliet said remembering the flapping curtain in D'Angelo's window the other night. She reached forward and tried the knob on the french doors.

"That's an amateur move."

"I'm wearing gloves," she said, holding up her hand.

"We're not going in through the french doors. There's too much light." He pointed at the alley. "If these people have security inside the house, then you don't want the light coming from behind you. They'll mark you."

"Oh, right. Smart," Juliet told him, and then thought she may well call law enforcement after this, just to let them know that Abram was a person of interest and they might want to follow him around for a couple of weeks.

Abram slunk toward the garage door. He jiggled the door handle. "Do you have a credit card?"

She held out empty hands. "I didn't bring my purse."

"Honestly, woman," he said, digging out his wallet from the pocket of his leather pants. "Why did I bring you along?"

"Because you don't know what you're looking for!"

Abram stuck the card between the door and the frame. He slid it down and then wiggled it back and forth.

I wanted new friends and I got Fast Fingers Fontana.

He turned the doorknob and stepped into the garage. He returned the credit card to his wallet and then turned on the flashlight app on his phone.

The light hit the washer and dryer first. "There'll be a spare key somewhere," he whispered. "Everybody keeps a spare key in a coffee jar."

The double garage was empty of vehicles. Rows of shelving lined the wall nearest Juliet, and she turned her own flashlight app onto the bottles of cleanser and storage boxes. "I don't see a coffee jar."

Abram turned his light toward the door and beamed the flashlight onto the mat. "Here we go." He lifted the rug. "Well, look at that."

Through this door was a large kitchen. The refrigerator gleamed in the alley light coming through the window.

There were lights on the other night.

"He really should leave a radio on or a TV," Abram said. "It's a burglar deterrent."

Juliet couldn't take it anymore. "How many houses have you broken into, Abram?"

"Counting this one?" He spun around to answer. "One."

She leaned away from him. "What's with all the tips?"

"My dad owns an insurance company, remember?"

"Oh yeah," Juliet said, moving faster. "Okay, help me find this guy's marriage certificate."

"That's what we're after?" He sounded let down.

She went around the corner into the front room with her flashlight on. The beam highlighted a television hanging on the wall, then a big couch and chair but no end tables or books.

Turning left, she found a bathroom. It smelled of lemon and lavender. So, maybe it was a maid who'd lifted the curtain the other night. The place was too clean and too fragranced to be the way D'Angelo left it.

She went back into the hallway. Across from the bathroom was a bedroom. The bed was neatly made, with a lamp and side table next to it. Again, no books of any sort. No personal items.

"Either the guy is a minimalist or he's not planning on staying long," Abram said. "Where's all his stuff, the dirty dishes, the clothes on the floor…?"

"We're not at your house." Juliet told him. "This is the way the guy's office looks too. It's so suspicious."

They entered another bedroom. It was utterly empty of furniture, and another bathroom without any scent of lemon.

See, this was precisely the reason Juliet was opposed to Paris finding such a large house. Empty rooms, unused baths. Silly.

Juliet climbed the stairs first and stepped into a bedroom. "Ah, here we go." She went straight to the desk, to a side drawer, and rifled through it, using her phone to see the paperwork.

"Bingo," she said, holding up bank statements. "I mean, sort of bingo. At least this is where he keeps important information."

Abram moved into the room. He turned his flashlight to the top of the desk, the lamp, and a calendar pad. Next, he dug through the wastebasket.

"The certificate is not going to be in the trash," she told him, setting the papers on the desk and holding the flashlight over them.

"Whoa, what do we have here?"

Juliet glanced up from her search. "What?"

Abram laid a single piece of paper on the desk. He'd uncrumpled it enough to read the top part. He read it out loud: *Hey Sebastian, it seems you've found another friend to kiss.*

Juliet turned her own phone's light onto the paper and read over Abram's shoulder. The next line read: *Hear that? It's the sound of your mistake.* The letter had been typewritten with no signature, no address, or a return address.

Juliet took the paper and reread it. "That's creepy." She handed the letter to Abram.

He asked, "What happened to the old way of getting back at your man, taking a bat to his car windows, stealing his credit cards and going shopping…?"

"Never mind. That's not what I'm looking for at the moment." She pulled open another desk drawer.

Suddenly, her phone vibrated. Glancing at the screen, she answered it and whispered, "What's wrong?"

Ty said, "Someone keeps driving by the house."

A small fear jumped into her heart. "What sort of car? A nice one?"

"No, it's a black car. The paint is peeling on the hood of it."

The little fear grew to medium size. "I've seen that car before."

"It's driven by twice," Ty told her. "Slowly."

Juliet nodded as though her cousin could see her reaction. "If that person had legitimate access to the house, they wouldn't circle the place a couple of times."

"You mean like us?"

"Yes."

Abram dropped the creepy letter into the wastebasket and moved toward the window. He must've summed up what was being said from Juliet's side of the conversation. He pulled the curtain back and stared into the street.

Juliet told Ty, "I haven't found what I'm looking for."

"Do it quick is all I'm saying."

She hung up and turned her phone back to the flashlight app.

Abram came back to the desk. "Whoever it is might've seen our flashlights. Maybe it's the scary letter writer?"

That made Juliet's stomach tingle even more. She rifled faster through the paperwork.

Near the back of the cabinet were three folders. Juliet pulled them out of the drawer and turned the light on them. "Here we go, here we go." She set D'Angelo's passport to the side. The next piece looked like a certificate. A pair of doves decorated the top of it, holding a long piece of ribbon in their mouths. The lettering, however, was nothing Juliet could read. Each symbol looked like cursive writing, but all were separated from the other letters. Two names were listed on the page. "Hold your light here," she told Abram.

Abram came back around the desk and pointed the light at the paper. Juliet took the photo and then shoved the certificate—and all of the paperwork—back into the drawer. Turning her phone back around, she dialed Ty's number. "Is the car still circling?"

"I haven't seen it," he answered. "Maybe they've parked. They could be watching from the street."

"The car is not in the alley, though?"

"Not that I can see." There was movement on his end of the line as though he turned around in his seat. "Unless they've parked in the alley directly behind this one."

Juliet worried her bottom lip with her teeth for a moment, and then asked, "Should we leave the house or not?"

"Do you want me to pull to the gate?"

Abram leaned close to Juliet, nearly nose-to-nose. "Move a street over, Gatti, to the north. We'll meet you there."

Juliet backed away from Abram. She shook her head and told Ty, "No, meet…"

He'd already hung up.

"Great, now we have farther to walk. What if someone is waiting for us to leave? They'll see us for sure."

Abram lifted his slender shoulders. "Not if they're waiting out front. They'll never see us leave. Come on, come on. Let's get out of here."

They went down the stairs together.

Juliet eyed the curtains in the living room. They were the thick sort with only a tiny bit of light coming near the curtain rod. She couldn't see the street. What was so wrong with sheers, Sebastian?

It must be Beth out there. No maid came to a job at nine-thirty in the evening.

Did Beth drive a black car with peeling paint? Juliet was sure she'd seen a car similar to it before, at the office, or … somewhere recently.

Had Beth written the stalker letter that was crumpled in the wastebasket? Well, she'd been angry that D'Angelo was out of town, mad that he'd lied about where he was going. And, she'd been angry-typing when Juliet popped into the office.

But, the timing was wrong for that scenario. Beth just found out that D'Angelo lied. If she'd written the letter the other day, then it wouldn't be crumpled in a trashcan tonight. D'Angelo hadn't had time to see it yet.

Maybe she'd been mad-typing for a while now, especially if they'd broken it off and she'd moved all the way to Podunk from warm and beachy Florida.

But wouldn't D'Angelo have fired her for stalking him? He'd fired Delia for lesser reasons.

Out the kitchen door again, Abram slipped the spare key beneath the mat. He followed Juliet to the outside door.

She reached for the knob.

In the glow of her flashlight, Juliet saw the knob turn–on its own.

"God's bread! It makes me mad."

Chapter 13

Jumping backward, she landed on top of an elevator boot.

Abram let out a "Hey!"

The knob clicked back into place. Footsteps pounded and then faded.

Oh no. No, no. Juliet wanted to see who was there; she wanted to see Beth. Turning the knob, she burst outside, jerking her head left and right … there!

A dark figure ran across the yard toward the open gate.

Juliet ran too, straight for the gate and into the alley.

She skidded to a stop, straining to hear something, footsteps, a car door opening and closing.

There was nothing.

Whoever it was must've run to the left. The alley was too long on the other side. The person would still be visible in that direction.

Juliet ran left. In the street, she stopped and listened again.

Oh, there was sound this time: heavy breathing. "What are you doing?" Abram wanted to know.

"I want to see who that was," she told him, flinging her hand toward the next street. "Why did you tell Ty to move the truck to the north? And, which way is north?"

Abram lifted his phone and walked the other direction in the alley. "I'll call him and have him come back."

They were more than halfway down the narrow lane when tires squealed on the next road over.

"Easy, Seabiscuit," Abram said. "I just bought those treads."

Tires hit a curb behind them.

Both of them jerked their heads around.

A black car bounded onto the pavement and barreled forward. Peeling paint covered its hood.

A swell of fear flooded Juliet's chest. "Umm … Run!"

The next cross street was at least thirty yards away. Abram took off, his boots leaving smoke curls behind him.

Juliet ran too, gained on Abram, and then passed him. Her terror was a rocket booster that whooshed her faster.

The Honda's engine revved. The car was closer.

Closer.

"Help me God," Abram screamed. "I'll be in church tomorrow, I swear—ahhhhh."

Juliet got to the end of the alley and with one great leap, jumped into a dirt and rock embankment near the road.

Abram flung himself onto the other side.

The Honda rocketed past them and shot down the next alleyway.

Juliet rolled to her side and watched it go. There was a little light above the New York license, HTF…

Abram jumped to his feet. "I didn't know I needed to do six weeks of combat training before I helped you, Juliet." He'd jumped into a row of evergreen hedge. He brushed twigs from his pants.

"Stop complaining," she said. "The Honda might come back."

But there was Ty, rolling slowly toward them in the truck. He braked and rolled down the window. "Were you two in the bushes?"

Abram grabbed the passenger door handle and yanked it open.

"What happened, what's going on?" her cousin wanted to know.

Juliet climbed in the cab and laid down on the bench. She didn't put on the seatbelt. "I'll tell you when we get home," she said, groaning afterward.

* * *

Safely in her bedroom, Juliet pulled up the photo she'd taken of D'Angelo's marriage certificate. It was a little dark, but it'd suffice, because breaking into a house was on her list of activities to never do again.

Stripping out of her black clothing, she showered and stepped into her star pajamas and her robe. It was too cold to sit on the balcony—and way too cold outside her bedroom door with Paris ready to pop out of his bedroom door, ready to yell at her again for nearly dying.

Those had been his words, not Juliet's. He'd said, "I told you that it was a bad idea, I said to you …"

It hadn't been that bad of an idea, Juliet thought, sitting on the edge of her bed. She'd gotten what she wanted. Now all she needed to do was find out what was written on the marriage certificate. She'd take it to Anthony.

And there was one other thing she needed to do.

* * *

After making sure Abram was in church on Sunday morning, remaining through the service herself, and scheduling confession time with Father Jonathon, Juliet hurried out of the sanctuary.

Her intention was to grab an affogato to go and slip away to show Anthony the certificate photo on her phone. But something–someone–stopped her.

Nicolo's jeep pulled into one of the parking spots near the Cistino del Pane bakery. He wasn't in uniform, but dressed in hunter green cable sweater and black pants.

Look at that, they'd worn matching outfits. Juliet had on her plaid skirt in the same color green, black turtleneck, boots, and tights.

The scruff on Nicolo's face was heavier and more beard-like than his usual look.

Juliet didn't hate it.

He wasn't looking for her, but his eyes flashed toward her and then held.

She raised her hand, but didn't approach. Perhaps he was meeting someone, had a brunch date.

No, Nicolo didn't brunch. If he ate early it was because

he was hungry, and he didn't linguistically blend words. It was either breakfast or lunch, according to his manly manliness.

And, he could date if he wanted to; so could Juliet, if she wanted to date.

She bit her lip extra hard and stepped into the Wake-Up Café.

There was a line.

Someone got in line behind her and Juliet turned.

The green sweater brought out the pale blue of Nicolo's eyes. He nodded. "Detective Da Vinci."

Her heart double flipped. She mimicked his tone. "Detective Montague."

"How's your investigation?"

"Good. Fine. Good." What was wrong with her? She sounded like a repeat rifle.

He tilted his head, not blinking too much. "Is there anything I should know about?"

She shook her head, this time for a long moment. Then she thought of something, "I think D'Angelo was married to Gemma Hakim."

His dark brows went up. "How do you know that?"

"How do I know … do you know it?"

They were a pair of circling fast-draws, waiting to see what the other knew.

"This is the first I've heard it."

"Really?"

"Really."

Juliet waved her hand. "Well, I'm not positive yet. But I will be soon."

"Okay," he said, narrowing his eyes and waiting.

"But, his son, Amir, was born in Iraq, and then the

family moved to the US."

He stared beyond Juliet for a second, at the menu behind the counter, and then brought his attention back to her. "Do you know what this reminds me of?"

"What?"

"When you came and told me about Johnny Doe and his supposed affair."

Juliet straightened her posture. "Can you tell me I'm wrong?"

His brows formed one line. "No, not exactly. But, you're guessing, just like last time."

She leaned toward him. "I wasn't wrong about the information last time, Nicolo. I had the details right."

"Except for who the murderer was."

"Which I remedied by myself," she said with a quick grin and a nod.

Nicolo took a long breath through his nose and then leaned in as she did. "I can tell you that Gemma *wasn't* part of Hakim Wines."

"Oh!"

"Yeah, oh. Does that change your investigation?"

The line moved up and Juliet took a step forward. "Is Hakim a popular name in Iraq?"

His eyes traveled her face. "She may not be from Iraq. I haven't got a birth certificate from the government yet. She could be from one of the remote villages in the Middle East."

Juliet forgot about her hormones for a moment and thought about that. "Maybe she's a relative to the Hakim Wines people?"

Nicolo's frown deepened. "We have no proof of that. And we have no proof that her murder had anything to do with the wine business, remember?"

She shook her head, gazing at cakes and donuts behind the sneeze glass just two steps away. "Everyone at the party had something to do with the wine business."

"No, they didn't. I saw the party guest list, which I was not on, by the way."

Juliet's attention snapped back. "You didn't want to come."

"How do you know?"

She leaned away, frowning. "Because it's not your thing."

"You don't know what my thing is."

"I certainly do. Do you want to come to our Thanksgiving party?"

The shock of the question registered on his handsome face, and he blinked twice. "What will your parents say?"

She lifted a shoulder. "They know all about us or what we used to be."

He shook his head. "I have tickets to the game."

"The party is this weekend, not on Thanksgiving."

He watched the street through the big glass for a moment. "What time?"

"Six o'clock," she told him, holding her breath. "Come, Nicolo."

He tilted his head, and his eyes found hers again. "I need to check my diary."

She teased him, leaning in. "Can't make a commitment, is that it? Are you worried about what your parents will say?"

His mouth tilted upwards at the sides. "Yes, that's it exactly."

"Will you come?"

O' Happy Dagger 175

He wagged his head, as though he couldn't decide. Then, "Sure. Is it fancy? Do I need a tux?"

Her heart jumped into a happy dance. "No. It's dinner, though, so it's a jacket and tie affair."

"I'll see what I've got." He turned and stepped out of the café, moving again toward the Cistino del Pane. And, probably his brunch date.

Her heart raced too fast for Nicolo Montague.

Get hold of yourself. Don't forget what happened last July.

But, there was such a thing as starting over and taking things slowly, right?

* * *

Juliet knew where to find Anthony on Sunday mornings. Since she'd been a child, she'd never been allowed to even speak to him once he had his gear on and left the house.

She knew what she had in her phone warranted the interruption.

Driving toward the lake, she found the marsh road and then turned down a dirt path that led to a small pier on the lake.

Juliet parked and grabbed her phone out of her purse and then closed and locked the car.

It took two minutes to reach the pier because the trail leading to the lake was pitted and only marked by spray paint on this tree or that one. Stumbling along, Juliet thought it might surprise Anthony that she knew where he fished…

"Dammit Juliet," he shouted. He hadn't seen her coming and had nearly come out of those wellies. "How did you find me?" The yellow wellies came up to his mid torso. Colorful straps fit across his chest and shoulders.

Juliet couldn't remember a time when he'd looked so middle class. She held out her cellphone for him to see. "Not important, Angler Man."

He waded forward in the water and glared at her phone. He wore a cap on his head, and there were a dozen fly hooks with little feathers spaced strategically on the top of it.

Beyond him, the sapphire water lay flat on the surface. A foot of fog skimmed the surface farther out. Frogs peeped and grunted in the taller grass to the right of them.

"Why don't you stand on the pier?" Juliet asked.

"Because I don't," he told her.

Testy, ain't he?

"Why are you showing this to me?"

She frowned at him. "It's proof that I'm right. It's D'Angelo's marriage certificate. Can you read Arabic?"

He changed the pole to his other hand. "Yes."

"Okay, well, what's the bride's name there?" Juliet pointed to the phone, at the name at the top.

"I don't know. This isn't Arabic."

She took the phone back and gazed at the certificate photo. "It's not? Well, what is it?"

Anthony shrugged his shoulder. "Could be Kurdish, could be Farsi. The people use the same alphabet, but the letters don't sound the same."

"I've never heard of Farsi."

"There are villages in the mountains, and the villagers speak it, so do the people in Russia and Afghanistan."

"You can't tell if that word is Gemma?" she asked, holding out the phone again.

He glanced at her above his glasses. "You know

nothing about the language, do you? Reading this and knowing Arabic is like you reading French and knowing English. You can see the letters, but you don't know how to pronounce it. The first letter of that particular name sounds like bah. But it could be pronounced jah."

"Jah, as in Gemma?"

"Like I said, I don't know. It could also be pronounced bah."

Juliet stared at the phone screen. "How do I find out what it says?"

"Try Google translate, or put out a request on Reddit. But don't ask for Arabic. Ask for a translator of Persian dialects."

"Oh," she said, tapping the back of the phone to turn it off. "I thought I had something here."

"How did you get that something?"

"The same way you would've if you were trying to get information."

"You tortured someone?"

She flashed him a wide grin. "Things haven't gone so far yet."

"They will if you ever try to find me out here again."

"Right. Gotta go now."

* * *

Back in the Fiat, Juliet drove to West Portland, to a tenant house, off a dirt road. A Toyota truck sat in the grass. Had Delia got it running yet? Had Mr. Leary fixed it for Delia, or was she walking and taking the bus to job interviews.

Juliet parked the Fiat near the truck and then climbed

the rusted fire escape to a single door with peeling paint around the glass.

Someone in one of the apartments played the guitar.

Delia answered on the first knock, her blue eyes wide with surprise. "Juliet?"

"Hi," she said, shifting her weight. "Sorry. I hope it's okay that I stopped by. I should've called I suppose, but I'm excited about something."

"Not a problem. I'm glad you stopped by," she said, stepping back to allow Juliet to enter.

The tiny living room could only handle a loveseat against the one blank wall. Delia had made the most of the space, though, with a white coffee table that looked well made, if not new. She'd draped a chenille throw over the loveseat and tossed pillows of pale blue and white to accent the couch. There was another small chair near the plate glass window that overlooked the back parking lot and open field. In the distance, skyscrapers stood in a misty fog. Delia had draped tiny white lights at the top of the window instead of curtains. She'd hung plants on either side of it.

"Please sit," Delia offered, waving her hand toward the sofa.

Juliet sat on the sofa and placed her purse near her feet on the rug. "What a cute place." The kitchen was on the other side of the room and no bigger than Juliet's bathroom at home. But again, Delia had made the place beautiful. Pots dangled above the stove and floral dishes sat on a shelf above the counter. More plants hung in the kitchen window.

There was a cat too, a fat yellow tabby sitting by the kitchen wall. Its green eyes blinked at Juliet. She assumed the one door led to a bedroom and bath. The place couldn't be more than six hundred feet in total.

Delia took the chair. She looked like she'd been to church since she wore a long flowered skirt and a cute little jacket. She'd piled her hair in an updo and wrapped a colorful headscarf around it to keep it up.

"So," Juliet began. "What are you doing for work these days?"

Delia clasped her hands around one knee and balanced herself on the chair, rocking gently. "Well, I've got an interview at Jack in the Box on Monday, but I've never wanted to work at a fast-food restaurant."

"How about a bakery?" Juliet asked, cutting straight to the point.

Delia released her knee and sat straighter. "What?"

She scooted to the edge of the loveseat, ready to ask but nervous at the same time. "Have you ever heard of Ganozza's Italian Bakery in Mayville?"

"Of course. I used to love that place."

"Ganozza was my aunt."

A wave of sympathy washed over the girl's face. "Yes, I heard. I'm sorry."

"Thank you," she said, a lump forming in her throat. "But, since she passed away, the bakery has been closed. Ganozza had another lady working with her, but Mrs. Castillano is not interested in keeping the bakery going." She took a steady breath, eyeing Delia to judge her reaction. "So, I spoke to my father this morning and asked him if … well, if you could run it." Her voice went up at the end of the sentence, and she winced, waiting for the older girl's reaction.

Delia's mouth dropped open. "Run it?"

"Yes." She held her breath.

Delia's mouth was still open.

"W—what do you think?"

"Oh, Juliet. I don't know…"

"Why not?" she asked, fearing Delia had a good reason that she couldn't do it.

Delia jumped to her feet and paced three steps and paced back two. She stopped and flung out her hands. "Firstly, I have no money to run a business."

"Oh, no. You don't understand," Juliet said, jumping to her feet. "My father agreed to have Renaissance Wines support the operation until it starts making money again."

Finally, Delia closed her mouth and swallowed hard. "Oh, it would be a dream come true, but…"

"No buts, you're a perfect choice."

Delia spun around and grabbed something from the breadbox. "Eat this. What if I can't bake?"

Juliet slumped forward and shook her head. "I know you bake."

"Taste it, make sure."

Juliet pinched off a bit of cupcake and put it in her mouth. Cinnamon crunch melted on her tongue. "Wow." She took a full bite. "It's delicious." Turning toward the kitchen, she put the wrapper in the open trash can. She spun back around, suddenly giddy with plans. "Now, you'd be on your own, and you'll need to find help serving and baking. The place had a big following, so take your time in planning and organizing. All the time you need."

Delia shook her head. "No. Wait. I don't have reliable transportation to get back and forth."

Juliet thought for a moment and stared out the window at the pathetic pickup in the yard. Then she brightened.

"I know! Ganozza had a van. Use the van to get back and forth."

The girl bounded toward her and wrapped her arms around Juliet's neck. "You don't know what this means to me. I can't believe it. You are the best friend anyone could ever have."

Juliet's eyes burned. They were friends, weren't they? Delia was the sort of person she'd had in mind when she thought about making new friends.

Delia finally released her and turned toward the kitchen for a tissue to wipe her eyes.

Juliet told her, "Now listen, it's an Italian bakery. I mean, for now anyway. Later, you may want to change things up."

Delia held out the tissue box.

She pulled one out and dabbed her eyes, too. "My cousin Ty has all of my aunt's recipes. I'm sure he'll give you a hand if you need it. I mean, Ganozza was his mom, and I'm sure he'll love that someone is opening the place up."

* * *

"I can't believe you're letting someone use my mother's recipes, Juliet," Ty told her. They stood in line at the Johnny Rocket's in Mayville.

Juliet pursed her lips and glowered. "I thought you'd be happy."

"Well, I'm not. Why don't you just take a dagger to my heart?"

"Oh, for goodness sake, Drama Boy," waving her hand at him. "I owe Delia a job. I took hers." She brought her purse around in front of her, letting the strap fall off her shoulder. "You'll love her."

Ty shook his head. He really needed a haircut. "I will not love her. Why would I love her? I don't know her."

She leaned away and eyed him. "Well, give her a chance, Ty. You're not opening the bakery. You've done nothing but mope …"

"I've been recovering—emotionally, and physically and psychologically."

The man in front of them glanced over his shoulder, then moved up in line.

Juliet and Ty moved forward too. "Whatever, Tybalt. Maybe this will help you get your life back on track?" She pulled her wallet from the purse. "Do something with yourself."

He swung toward her. "Are you throwing me out?"

"Of course not," she told him, wrinkling her nose. "I'm just saying, get off your skinny butt and away from your cats for awhile. Go help Delia start the bakery." She handed him a piece of paper. "Here's her cell number."

He took the paper and turned sharply toward the counter. "Fine!"

"Fine," she countered with as much vehemence in her voice. "I'm buying."

"Fine!"

"How now, my headstrong, where have you been gadding?"

Chapter 14

Google Translate was unhelpful, mainly because her keypad didn't have letters for Farsi.

So, Juliet took a photo of the first name on the certificate and uploaded it to Reddit. No one had answered the question by the next morning. She checked her phone once more before she got out of her car and hurried toward the office building–all the while keeping her eye out for a Honda with peeling paint.

When she pushed through the office doors, she saw movement down the hall.

It was Patsy's head sticking out from around the corner. "Hey."

Juliet stopped in her tracks. "Hi."

Patsy smiled. Her teeth were straight. White. "Do you want to eat your lunch with Tricia and me tomorrow? I'd ask you today, but I have a thing."

Juliet narrowed her eyes. "Me?"

Her expression didn't change. "Umm, you're the only one in the hallway, aren't you?"

She glanced behind her and then at Patsy. "Sure, let's have lunch tomorrow."

"Good," she said, nodding. Her stringy hair moved back and forth with the action.

"Great." And, when Patsy's head disappeared, she whispered, "Great."

It was only a tiny thrill that hit her bloodstream. Juliet wanted new friends but she wasn't sure about Tricia and Patsy. They were a little spicy, weren't they? Then again, they were fiercely loyal to Delia, and that seemed an essential ingredient for friendship.

Making her way into her office, she placed her purse in a bottom drawer and her coat on the rack, and then just as quickly went back into the hall again and straight toward Beth's office. Had the woman made it in to work yet, or was she delivering more stalker mail to D'Angelo's house?

Juliet waited at the door, pushing it open a crack, and then listened for angry typing.

All was quiet.

She pushed the door wider and tiptoed forward in her black Tieks. Yes, she'd worn a ballet shoe on purpose. After she'd broken into a house over the weekend, Juliet felt liberated by it. Why, she might do anything–unless it was against the law again and she'd be a little slower to try it.

She peeked around the file cabinet.

Beth hadn't arrived. D'Angelo's door was closed and presumably locked.

Juliet's idea was to get to Beth before Beth got to her. The woman's first reaction would tell a lot about what she'd done over the weekend. If she acted her usual awkward self, then Beth wasn't the one who'd tried to mow down Juliet and Abram in the alley. But, if she came across as syrupy and surprised, well, then Juliet knew she had her man. Woman.

Turning, Juliet glanced back into the hallway.

Still no Beth.

Heading back toward her own office, she veered at the last moment toward the front of the building. Was there a black Honda parked out there yet?

I know I saw it — but was it here or somewhere else?

Juliet stood at the glass doors and on tiptoe to check every car … there! Three spaces down from the sidewalk was a compact car. It was black, but it was hard to see if there was peeling paint on the hood. Juliet would need to walk outside to get a closer look at it.

She hadn't brought her jacket with her and turned toward her office again. She'd just pop outside for a moment. Have a little walk around the parking lot.

Delia stood right in front of her.

Juliet jumped back and covered her heart with her hand.

"Sorry," Delia said, trying not to laugh. "Sorry. I didn't mean to scare you. I just dropped by for a quick visit before I head into Mayville." She was dressed in her puffy white coat and maroon corduroys.

"Oh, how nice," Juliet said, massaging her heart muscle.

Delia laughed again. The color on her cheeks was rosy, her blue eyes so bright they twinkled. She reached for Juliet and hugged her. "I can't thank you enough." She stepped away, her cheek color even more pink. "I stayed up late last night working on a business plan and trying to think of who to hire to help me start such an undertaking."

Coming around to the present conversation, Juliet nodded. "Has Ty called you?"

"Yes, he did," she said, in a hesitant tone. "He was a little abrupt."

Juliet squared her shoulders. "I'm going to call him right now."

"No, no, Juliet. Stop." She reached out and took her arm to walk back to the office with her. "I don't want you to yell at him. That will put a bigger wedge between us. I'll charm him, you'll see."

They were in front of Juliet's office door.

Delia didn't go inside with her. "I've got to run and meet him now at the bakery."

Juliet grinned. "Oh, that's exciting. And, I know you'll charm Ty. He's very charmable."

The girl turned away toward the hallway and called over her shoulder. "I'll let you know how it goes."

Juliet turned back into her office, thinking to grab her coat.

Someone sat in the chair beside her desk.

Beth had turned in the chair and draped one arm over the back of it.

Juliet's eyes widened. "Hi, Beth."

No! She got to me first.

"How was your weekend?" Only her eyes moved when Juliet crossed the room and sat behind the desk.

"Great."

Play it cool.

"My cousin is getting married, and I went to her party. There was church on Sunday, you know. Yesterday I helped a family friend." She glanced at her computer screen.

The screen was on.

"That's funny," she said, glancing at Beth. "I didn't turn my computer on this morning."

Fortunately, there was nothing on the screen—unless Beth had looked at the search history.

Beth didn't react. Her features remained smooth, except for that tiny lift at one corner of her mouth. "You must've left it on all weekend."

Juliet nodded, going along with it. "How about you, what did you do over the weekend?"

"I stayed in mostly," Beth said, getting to her feet. She was wearing another pencil skirt, red and black tartan. Very lumberjack-ish. "Well, I just wanted to say hi. I'll be over in the warehouse most of the day since Mr. D'Angelo isn't back from his trip."

As soon as Beth turned on her heel and left the office, Juliet jiggled the mouse and brought up her history screen.

Ugh.

There was all the evidence of checking out Sebastian D'Angelo, the 411.com, the parcel check on his address. The Google map of his house…

Oh yes, and the Facebook check on Amir.

Juliet took a breath and straightened in her chair. So what, right? So she'd done a background check on D'Angelo? What was wrong with that?

Juliet got to her feet too. She grabbed her coat and slipped her arms into it.

She was just buttoning the last button when Mr. Leary came through the door.

He jerked back a little, surprised to see her for some reason.

"Hi, Mr. Leary," Juliet started.

He'd puffed out his blue-shirted chest a little, and gazed about the room awkwardly. "H-hello, Juliet."

She leaned in, waiting for more. He'd never once called her Juliet. When he said nothing, she asked, "How are you?"

"Good," he said, nodding.

"Good." Straightening too, she told him, "I'll be right back. I forgot something in my car."

"Right." Spinning around, he went back into his office.

Juliet stood for a moment, heard his door lock from the inside, and then she moved into the hall. That was odd–it'd been the reaction she'd expected from Beth when she'd tried to surprise her.

Wait.

Juliet stood in the hallway for a long moment. Had it been Leary in D'Angelo's home the other evening? Did he own the Honda that nearly ran her over Saturday night?

She walked to the front of the office and pushed open the front doors. Frigid air lifted her hair off her face and rushed into her nostrils. She was breathing heavily by the time she got halfway down the sidewalk and saw that the black compact car was gone.

* * *

Juliet packed her lunch the next morning because Tricia had told her that they'd eat at their desks instead of going out somewhere. Tucking her lunch box into the refrigerator, she went into her office again, sat in the wobbly chair, and flicked on the computer.

Mr. Leary threw open his door and burst into Juliet's area. He didn't see her at first, was halfway through the little room when he glanced her way, and then jumped back as if he'd seen a gorilla sitting there.

That was certainly a different reaction from yesterday.

He hadn't changed out of his winter jacket, and his cheeks had high spots of color. It was as though he'd just come into the office from outside. "I didn't know you were here."

She narrowed her eyes. "I didn't know you were here either."

"I'm here," he insisted. "Why wouldn't I be here?"

She gazed at the computer screen. "Sometimes I think you have a back door."

His face grew ever redder. "Of course there's no back door. You've been in my office." He bustled out into the hallway, probably in search of coffee. Suddenly, his head popped back around the door. "I want you to make yourself scarce today." He stepped back into the office, sans coffee, and pulled his coat off his beefy shoulders. "You can go to work in the warehouse."

"Doing what?"

"I don't know. You're a Da Vinci and you don't know what to do with wine?" He went back into his office and slammed the door.

She faced her computer again. Oh yes, she'd find something to do after lunch today, like find the back door to his office.

***

"We would've liked you the first day," Patsy confessed, with her mouth half-full of meatloaf sandwich. "If it wasn't for the way Mr. D'Angelo had fired Delia and put you in here instead. You seem like a nice person." They all sat in the finance office, which consisted of two desks facing the door and a long file cabinet in the back of the room.

"Thanks." Juliet had just finished a bite of manicotti. She sat across from Patsy, where the woman had cleared a small portion of the desk for her.

"Besides all of that," Patsy continued, "No one would work for Leary if they had a choice. Except Delia, of course."

Juliet covered the dish with a lid and placed it back into her thermal lunch bag. "She is such a sweet person. She could've been angry at me … is she even mad at Mr. D'Angelo?"

Tricia laughed and then wiped her lips with a napkin. Her desk was much neater than Patsy's, and she'd decorated it with a garland of purple, orange, and red paper leaves. "Delia would never get angry at Mr. D'Angelo. Hurt, maybe."

"Why hurt?" Juliet asked.

Patsy answered, "She's had a crush on him ever since he started working here."

"Isn't he a little old for her?"

Tricia stood, crumpled her sandwich paper, and tossed the ball into the wastebasket. "She's thirty-four. What's D'Angelo, early forties?"

"After high school, nobody cares how old somebody is," Patsy said.

A thought struck Juliet. Was Delia the one who had

come between D'Angelo and Beth? *I see you've got a new friend to kiss...* "Does D'Angelo return the affection?"

"If he did, he wouldn't have fired her."

"I guess not." Juliet got to her feet, ready to put her leftover lunch in the refrigerator. "What about Beth? She's in love with D'Angelo."

Patsy's thin brows came together.

Tricia wore the same expression. She said, "I never got that impression."

She probably hadn't tried to hit these ladies with her Honda.

* * *

Back at her desk, Juliet took her phone from her purse and checked her messages.

Mr. Leary stared at her from his office doorway. "I thought we discussed you working somewhere else this afternoon."

"I'm on my way out." She took her phone with her, and once she was in the hallway, she texted Anthony.

Is there a second door to Mr. Leary's office?

Why?

Is there?

That is top-level information.

Oh please.

Juliet dialed his number. She didn't give him a chance to say hello. "Where is it?"

There was silence for a moment, and then, "There are second doors in all three offices, your father's, D'Angelo's, and Leary's."

"Where do they lead?"

"A passageway."

Juliet paced the hall. "That's where Papà hid from the police last July."

More silence.

"Is there another way out? I mean, is there a fourth door to get out, but not into the offices?"

"Yes."

"Where?"

"The men's restroom."

Juliet frowned at the phone and then stuck it to her ear again. "What if you had a female executive? She wouldn't want to go that route."

"We'll worry about that when a woman becomes an executive."

Before she could fill Anthony's ears with a feminist speech, Sebastian D'Angelo came around the corner, impeccably dressed as ever in a blue suit and tie. His hair, a vision of neatness. He nodded a greeting and then turned into Juliet's office.

"I've got to go," Juliet told Anthony and slipped down the hallway toward D'Angelo's office.

She paused at the double glass doors. What was in the passageway? Why had it been built—just to give executives a clear path to the men's room?

Her father hadn't built the office complex, nor the bottling plant. The address formerly belonged to the Hubba Bubba Soda Company. Juliet had only been a kid when Santos bought the buildings. Still, she remembered the other company because of its connection to bubble gum.

She pushed open the doors and waited a moment, listening for the furious typing of stalker letters.

All was quiet except for the gentle whooshing sound

of heat coming through the vents near the ceiling.

Juliet slid alongside a file cabinet and peeked around the corner.

Beth's seat was empty. A stack of papers sat on the desk in front of the computer. There was the woman's coffee cup.

Slipping forward, she tried her father's office door first. It was locked. Juliet glanced toward D'Angelo's office door and back at the glassed entry. Her belly tingled. She'd been caught in his office last time, and suddenly she couldn't think of a decent lie to tell him if he caught her again.

She slipped forward, tried the door, and then opened it.

Everything was just as she remembered it—except the picture of his son wasn't on the desk any longer. Juliet took in the place. There was the second door right next to the credenza. D'Angelo hadn't tried to hide it with a bookcase or boxes.

Juliet stepped around the desk and toward the door. She turned the knob.

Locked … why? Did D'Angelo think someone might try to enter the room from the passageway? Maybe someone like Mr. Leary? Or Beth?

Unlocking the door, she pulled it open, and then she descended two steps into the darkened room.

It was more extensive than most passageways and sunken down a bit, like a basement area. Juliet had envisioned a narrow space, but it was as wide as her office. Someone had stuck button lights along the ceiling line. Stacks of boxes lined the room. So, it was only a storage area, really, and not a top-level privilege, as Anthony suggested.

There was another door, to the left. Juliet assumed it was to her father's office. She took the two steps up and tried the door. It was locked too.

It was probably twenty steps to the next door. Juliet imagined it was Leary's office door. Or, it was the men's bathroom area. She twisted the knob and started to open it.

Mr. Leary's bulldog voice came loud and clear through the other side of the door. "This is your fault. Put an end to it."

Juliet slowly released the handle.

D'Angelo raised his voice too. "You think that's going to be easy?"

"You did it last time," Leary said. "Do it again."

"I was forced into it."

"Get rid of her or else."

Juliet raised her brows. Or else what? How could Leary threaten D'Angelo?

There was silence for a moment, and then a door opened.

Juliet backed down the two steps, heartbeat irregular. Was D'Angelo on his way back to his office? If so, she wasn't sure how she'd get out of the basement. There was always the men's bathroom, she supposed.

Hurrying back to D'Angelo's door, she took the cement steps.

On the other side of the door, D'Angelo said, "Hold my calls."

Beth must be back in her seat, so there was no picking her father's lock and exiting that route. She stood there a moment, thinking it through.

A door on the other side of the room creaked open.

O' Happy Dagger

Juliet moved fast and crouched next to a stack of three boxes.

Footsteps came closer. They sounded heavy on the cement flooring.

She pressed her back against the wall, held her breath, and waited.

Mr. Leary passed right in front of Juliet, took the two steps to D'Angelo's door, and then pressed his ear against the wood. He faced the other direction.

Move, move, move!

Juliet only had one chance. Once Leary turned around, he'd see her for sure. Half bent over, she slipped toward his door, took the steps, and then moved into the office.

A bookcase blocked the entrance. It'd been moved away from the wall, enough to allow Leary to slip through. Juliet gently closed the door behind her and locked it.

Yes, locked it. That'd give her time to get out of the office.

And wouldn't it give Leary a start when he came back to his door– especially if he was trying to make a fast getaway from D'Angelo.

Skirting the bookcase, Juliet slipped past Leary's desk. Something on the floor caught her eye, and she bent to pick it up.

It was only a piece of paper. Juliet turned it over and read the words. It was her father's fermenting procedure written out, which spoke about some wild yeast her father discovered and used in the winemaking process.

What in the world…?

A sound came from behind the bookcase. The doorknob rattled.

"Jesu Maria, what a deal of brine."

Chapter 15

Juliet set the paper on Leary's desk and opened the door to her own office. She scooted toward the file cabinets and then stopped.

Leary barreled into the office, red-faced as *Yosemite Sam*. "Why are you here?"

He really needed to learn some tolerance and acceptance.

"I forgot my phone," she told him, holding up her cell.

He let out three or four big breaths. "Were you in my office?"

She glanced at the door. "Actually, that's where I thought you were …" She frowned at the door and then at

Leary. "How'd you get out here?"

He didn't answer. Marching toward the door, he tried the knob.

Oops.

"It's unlocked. It's unlocked!"

"I—I don't know. Wasn't Mr. D'Angelo in your office?"

His mouth opened and his face jiggled as though he'd been startled by the question. "How do you know that?"

She pointed toward the hallway. "Because I was still here when Mr. D'Angelo arrived. Maybe he didn't lock the door after he left?"

He narrowed his Yosemite eyes. "I locked the door after he left." Turning, he stomped into his room, leaving the door open behind him.

Juliet leaned around the doorframe–and caught him pushing his bookcase back into place. "How did that get pulled away from the wall?"

Leary jumped. It was a cumbersome movement, and parts of him were still mid-jump when he shouted, "I've told you that you're not allowed in here."

"I'm only making sure you're all right. You seem upset."

Leary eyed the floor and then gazed at the top of his desk. Reaching forward, he picked up the piece of paper on his desk. The one Juliet had found on the floor. "You've been in here. This was on the floor." He shook the paper at her.

Umm.

Juliet asked, "What was it doing on the floor?"

He lumbered toward the door. "You will stay out of my office." And then Leary shut the door in her face.

* * *

Anthony stood in the red section of the cellar beneath the Da Vinci kitchen, pulling out a bottle of wine, examining it, and then pushing it back into place. "Geoff would have a copy of the fermenting process, especially if he'd just been speaking to D'Angelo."

Juliet sat on the third cellar step. "But the paper was on the floor," she explained, knowing that Leary was guilty of something. "Like he'd put it there when D'Angelo came into the office, as though he was hiding it. He knew I'd picked it up off the floor."

Anthony's expression didn't change. Adjusting his glasses, he pulled another bottle from the shelf and examined it.

Juliet leaned forward, elbows on her knees. "And what about the conversation I overheard?"

He returned the wine bottle to the shelf and then turned his dark blue eyes on her. "Juliet, dear gullible girl, they were talking about you."

"Me?" she asked, sitting up straight. "How do you know that?"

"By what you've told me."

She shook her head. "That can't be right."

Anthony pulled a light Pinot Noir off the shelf. "You said Leary wanted you out of the office."

"Insisted on it."

"Tell me what they said again," Anthony said, sticking the wine bottle in an ice bucket.

"Leary said, *This is your fault. Put an end to it.*"

Anthony stood in front of the steps. "Leary thinks it's D'Angelo's fault that you were hired."

"But D'Angelo said, *you think that's going to be easy?*"

Pale light bounced off Anthony's glasses. "I imagine it

would be tough to fire you, Juliet, don't you think?"

"He can't fire me. I'm a Da Vinci. A child of my father, who gave them all jobs, by the way."

Anthony shook his head with a hint of pity in his expression. "He can talk your father into it. And as I recall, Santos isn't crazy about you working there." Anthony pointed the bucket and wine bottle at her. "You told me that. You said Italia needed to talk him into it."

His rebuttal left a bad taste in her mouth, and she pursed her mouth. "I still don't think they were talking about me."

Anthony stepped around her and climbed the stairs.

Juliet pushed off the steps and followed him. "What about the other things they said. Leary said *you did it last time.*"

"He did," Anthony said, continuing to climb. "He fired Leary's daughter last time."

"I know he did. But Leary also said, *Get rid of her or else.* That's very threatening."

Anthony stopped at the top of the stairs. He rested his hand on the doorknob. "Or else he'll quit, and we can't afford to lose Geoffrey Leary."

* * *

If it were true that all Leary wanted was for D'Angelo to fire her, then Juliet planned to figure that out. Fast.

"*Papà*," Juliet asked at breakfast the next morning. "Have you had any reports of how well I'm doing at work?"

He gazed at her over his tiny cup. "No. Why?" He took a sip of the espresso.

"Just curious. I've been filing very quickly and doing a

good job. I thought maybe Mr. D'Angelo mentioned it."

He set his small cup aside. "What's the matter with you? Who cares how good you file? D'Angelo is too interested in how fast we're getting the wine out the door to care about your filing."

"I just wondered," she told him and grabbed the lunch that Tribly had made for her. "Has Mr. Leary said anything?"

Santos placed his hands on his hips. He shrugged before he started with the yelling, "What have you done? Why are you asking these questions? Have you been poking around, sticking your noses into where it doesn't belong?"

"I only have one nose, *Papà*."

"*Basta*!" His brows gathered over his eyes like a threatening thunderstorm. "You have two noses because I say you have two noses, and both of them are into things they shouldn't be in. If I hear complaints that you're snooping around because a woman died, then I will fire you."

Her mouth hung open.

"*Sì*, I will fire you."

Mouth firmly set in a frown, Juliet took her lunch and left the house.

* * *

Setting her purse in a desk drawer, Juliet removed her wool coat and then crossed the room to hang it on the rack near the door. How was she going to figure out if D'Angelo meant to fire her, or if he was going to get rid of someone else … in the *dead* sense?

Juliet took her seat, and after wobbling twice, she

leaned backward. If D'Angelo meant to fire her, then he'd seek her out and ask her to his office so they might discuss her work performance.

Yes, that sounded right. Juliet had never been fired before – because she'd never worked before—but she'd seen movies with the situation acted out. *Leaving Las Vegas* was one example.

How to expedite this situation so she knew whether D'Angelo meant to fire her or kill someone else? Times, they were a wastin', and someone was getting away with murder.

Juliet got out of her chair and walked down the hallway.

Outside the double glass doors, Juliet squared her shoulders for the inevitable confrontation.

I'm a Da Vinci, child of Santos the vintner, nipotino to Tribly by God Da Vinci …

Pushing open the doors, she marched to Beth's desk. "I need to see Sebastian D'Angelo right away."

Beth's golden hair nearly whipped right off her head. "I-I don't think that's possible," she said and pulled out a leather calendar book from her top drawer. "Why do you want to see him?"

"I'm going to ask him to lunch."

Beth got to her feet. She was dressed in a gray knit dress. A wide belt cinched her chubby waist. "You can't do that."

Juliet lengthened her spine. "Sometimes, Beth, I think you forget that my last name is Da Vinci. If I want to ask the man who runs my family's company to lunch, then I will."

The woman took a step back, her mouth ajar. Her eyes had turned to black pools of spite.

Whatever, stalker.

Juliet took two steps to the left and knocked on D'Angelo's door.

D'Angelo nearly pulled the door off the hinges. "Beth, what are…?" His eyes found Juliet's. "Oh, Juliet, hello." He straightened his jacket and buttoned it at the waist.

"I wanted to ask you to lunch."

His straight brows went up, and he flicked a look at Beth. "I - I'm sorry. I have a lunch engagement." His Adam's apple bobbed up and down. "I just got off the phone with Anthony Yeager, and we're meeting at the Landmark Restaurant." He held the door open wider. "But, please come in. We can chat now if you like." He shut the door behind them.

A knot formed in her chest. Maybe Leary did want to fire her …

He waved his hand to a chair and then went to sit behind his desk.

Juliet tucked her dress behind her knees and sat too. "What's happened to your son's photo?"

"I'm sorry?"

She pointed to his desk. "The photo of your son."

The crease between his brows deepened. "Oh, right. I- I took it home." He glanced toward the credenza near the door and then back at his desk.

He doesn't know where it is.

D'Angelo placed his fisted hands on top of his desk. "Is there something on your mind?"

"Well, yes, actually. I spoke to my father this morning, and he's so happy that I love it here. I wondered if you've heard whether or not if I'm doing well and what else I can do to help out here."

"Oh," he said, looking somewhat relieved. "Geoff seems pleased with your work."

"Is he?" Her voice had gone up, almost squeaked. Clearing her throat, Juliet asked, "He said that?"

"No, not in so many words. But I can tell Mr. Leary's pleased. Have you asked him if there is more work for you to do?"

Anthony, you were so wrong!

"Umm, Mr. Leary has been so busy with the new hires. But that's all right. I'll make myself so useful that he'll love me." She forced a smile. "So, you're having lunch with Anthony?"

D'Angelo tilted his head, his eyes studying Juliet's posture for a moment, and then he frowned. "Yes."

She may never get another chance to question D'Angelo, so she continued, "He told me you were in the service together."

He let out a long breath, which made his cheeks balloon out. "Yes. He was much higher ranked than I was."

"Were you in Iraq together? Is that where you met your wife?"

He pressed his mouth together and turned his face a little to the right, as though he was thrown by the question. As if he hadn't expected Juliet to know anything about him. "I did meet her there. Why do you ask?"

"Just curious," she said, shrugging her shoulders. "Anthony mentioned something about it."

"He did?" He put his elbows on the desk and leaned forward. "Anthony never met my wife."

"Oh, I don't know. I thought that's what Anthony said. How did you meet your wife?"

"I was in the army, a ground troop. I went into villages

and secured the area." He nodded as though agreeing with himself. "She was the prettiest girl I'd ever seen."

"What's her name?"

"Jesenia," he said. "Like all the girls there, she had a sad story to tell, and I fell for it. She was so sweet and kind." He stared at a spot behind Juliet's head. "Until she came to the US, and then she realized all the things she'd missed out on. She didn't want to take care of our child. She wanted to live her life. She was so young."

"Did you divorce?"

"We separated, and then she died." He still stared beyond Juliet, as though he remembered something. "I wonder …" He turned those blue eyes on her, his brows pulled together. "I wonder if they got loose from all of that?"

"They?" Juliet asked.

D'Angelo came out of his reverie and gazed at Juliet again. "Will you excuse me, Juliet. I need to … I have some work to do."

"Oh sure," she told him, getting out of the chair. "Thanks for seeing me. Maybe we can have lunch next week before Thanksgiving?"

He stood and then held the door for her. "Thanks for understanding."

Before she got past the glass doors, D'Angelo's voice floated out of his room. "Beth, come in here please."

* * *

In the Da Vinci house, *La Festa del Tacchino,* or Turkey Party never included a dead bird on the table, no. Tribly would stab a fork in her eye before she'd serve green bean casserole. On the table was *Arancini* stuffed with fried green olives, gnocchi with gorgonzola, turkey breast with mushroom, slices of ham, and *Parmigiano* cheese, garlic bread, porcini mushroom risotto, oven-roasted chestnuts, and a *crostata* tart for dessert.

Santos turned up the *classica Italiano musica* from the front room. He turned it up loud, until Italia told him to quiet down, or he would sleep in the spare bedroom.

Italia had set the oak table with china and candles and greenery. The fire was lit in the smaller dining room fireplace, where colored pinecones sparkled pale blue and lime green.

Paris and Ty lined up with Juliet at the door to greet their Turkey Party guests. Juliet wore a fitted beige and cream lace dress with no sleeves. It would only be cold at the door, and she could stand it for the sake of fashion.

Ty leaned around Paris and told Juliet, "She's coming."

"Who?"

"Delia Leary."

Juliet raised her brows at Paris and then said, "I know. I invited her." It was the first she'd actually paid attention to her cousin that evening. And now that she did, she needed to hold back a gasp. "Did you get a haircut?"

He brushed the thick black hair off his broad brow. "What of it?" He'd dressed up too, in a white shirt, dark creased pants, and a striped tie.

Juliet leaned away. "What's going on?"

"He's interested in this Delia woman," Paris said. He'd dressed in a muted plaid suit and blue shirt. Reaching behind Juliet, he pulled her forward again.

The doorbell rang.

Her heart light, Juliet pulled open the door.

Abram allowed his mother to enter the room first, and then he held back. "Why aren't you answering my texts?"

Juliet wrinkled her nose. "I've answered more than half, which is about one hundred of them."

"We went through something together." He'd gelled his hair back. His beak nose came closer to Juliet. "I'm allowed to send you memes."

Right behind Abram, Mr. Leary rode in with a silk top hat.

Delia followed him through the door wearing a long red cape with white fur around the collar.

Ty jumped in front of Juliet. He took Mr. Leary's heavy coat. After he handed off the coat to Juliet, he took Delia's arm and led her to the living room.

"She may want to leave her cape here," Juliet suggested.

"But she looks perfect the way she is." Ty said, gazing at Delia.

Juliet grinned. "May I?" she asked Delia.

The young woman stepped forward and hugged Juliet. She smelled like peppermint and juniper berries. "Thank you for inviting me. I've looked forward to this all week." Stepping away, she removed the cape, revealing a blush-colored dress with long sleeves and white flowers cascading down the sides of it.

Ty walked arm-in-arm with her farther into the living room.

Santos came toward the door and stepped between Juliet and Paris. "Where is Sebastian?"

Juliet handed the coats she'd collected to one of the servers. "I haven't seen him."

"He was supposed to come early." Pulling a cellphone from his pocket, her father turned toward the front living area and pushed numbers on the screen.

Roseline and Dr. Dexter arrived closer to dinnertime.

Roseline already looked like a bride in her white cropped pants and white lace top with a trailing jacket that fell to the back of her knees. She'd pulled her flaming hair into a french braid, wrapping it around the top of her head like a crimson crown.

Dr. Dexter followed her to the dining room, smiling that big smile, that *I'm-marrying-Roseline-Gatti* smile he'd worn since the Harvest Ball.

"Sebastian's not answering," Santos said, coming back into the foyer. "We will eat without him."

D'Angelo wasn't the only one missing.

Where is Nicolo?

Juliet gazed out the door window. No lights came up the driveway.

Her stomach gave a little tug. Nicolo had decided not to come to dinner after all.

At six-forty-five, she stepped into the dining room herself, but first she fired off a text to Nicolo: Where are you?

There were three seats left at the table, but none were near each other. If Nicolo did show, he'd have to sit apart from her.

Paris caught Juliet's eye and lifted his hand. He'd held a chair.

Juliet's stomach tightened. This was going to be awkward. Why hadn't she thought of Paris when she invited Nicolo? Why hadn't she suggested assigned seating? Smiling, she made her way toward Paris.

Mr. Leary sat directly across from Juliet. He leaned toward Ty and then laughed.

Mr. Leary laughs?

What could Ty have possibly said to cause such a reaction? Had he mentioned an earthquake? Given statistical data on how many people died in biological warfare?

"Come, come, let us eat," Santos said, moving toward the head of the table.

Juliet slipped into the seat next to Paris.

He eyed her dress. "You look fetching."

"Thank you," she told him, just as her eye caught Mr. Leary laughing at something else. "What is with him?" Juliet said aloud.

"Who?"

"My boss. He never laughs or smiles. I wonder what's got him in such a good mood."

Paris leaned forward and caught Juliet's eye. "I never seem to hold your attention."

She grinned at him. "You look amazing, too," she told him. "Your wavy hair, your emerald eyes, yeah?"

He set his napkin into his lap. "Get your own pickup lines, lady."

Juliet laughed but watched Leary again.

Something had cheered him up. Maybe it was because Delia had come along with him, and if that were true, then it was rather sweet.

Near the end of the meal three sets of headlights moved up the drive. Juliet wasn't the only one who noticed.

Paris said, "Late dinner guests?"

Juliet was torn. She didn't know whether to be angry at Nicolo or *really* angry at Nicolo.

One of the servants answered the door and then crossed the hallway to the back of the kitchen.

Juliet placed her napkin on the table. She moved into the hallway and stopped in her heels.

Nicolo was there, wearing his policeman's uniform. Two officers stood on either side of him.

Juliet frowned. "Nicolo?"

He nodded. "Juliet, I'm here to see Anthony."

Her stomach felt as though an anchor dropped into the wine in her belly and sank down, down, down. "Oh."

His blue eyes held hers. "I'm sorry I missed dinner," he said in a low voice, without changing his policeman's expression.

It had gone quiet behind her.

Juliet turned to see every eye at the table staring her way.

"Who is it?" her father asked, getting to his feet. When his eyes landed on Nicolo and the other officers, he threw his napkin on the table. "What is this? What is this?"

Anthony came from the back hallway, dressed in a three-piece suit. "You want to speak to me?"

Santos stormed into the foyer. "No, no, no. You've already had him long enough. I spent money to bring him here. You will leave him here."

Nicolo moved aside, and the two officers stepped toward Anthony. One had a set of handcuffs in his hands.

Nicolo said, "Mr. Da Vinci…"

"You better have a good reason to take him away from my home."

Nicolo nodded. His blond hair was in a knot on the back of his head. "You need to know that one of your employees was found dead this morning."

Juliet took a step backward.

Nicolo lowered his voice. "Sebastian D'Angelo was

found murdered. Anthony Yeager was the last person to be seen with him."

"Alack the day, he's gone, he's kill'd, he's dead."

Chapter 16

Juliet said, "Mr. D'Angelo is dead?"

Gasps came from the dining room.

She bit her lip. She had said that a bit loud, but Sebastian D'Angelo was dead! "How did he die?"

Nicolo's eyes landed on her again. "I can't discuss the details."

Her father had his fists on his waist. "Anthony was here with me this week. All week. He hasn't left the house."

He had lunch with D'Angelo.

One of the officers took a coat from the rack near the door and set it on Anthony's shoulders. The other man opened the door and led the way onto the porch.

Nicolo said, "We are taking him to Mayville, and they will transfer him to the Buffalo facility. He won't be allowed visitors until tomorrow sometime." He nodded to Santos and then to Juliet.

Her stomach was a ball of nerves, rolling around and beating the walls of her stomach. Juliet took her seat next to Paris.

Everyone at the dinner table watched Santos return to the room. He said, "Please excuse us, dear friends, but dinner is complete. Thank you for coming."

Chairs scraped on the hardwood floor as the guests got to their feet.

The servants had jackets and coats ready at the door.

Juliet glanced toward Delia. She'd had a crush on Mr. D'Angelo, that's what the girls at work said.

Delia's ruddy features had gone pale. She followed her father toward the foyer.

Mr. Leary didn't seem to notice his daughter's distress. He held out his hand for her to move ahead of him, with a smile fixed firmly on his bulldog mug.

* * *

Despite Nicolo's informing the family that they couldn't see Anthony until the next day in Buffalo, Santos and Italia drove to the Mayville police station with the idea that they'd bring Anthony home.

Paris and Juliet cleared the dishes and helped Tribly put the food away and stack dishes into the dishwasher. Dr. Dexter rinsed the sink and seemed to use excessive caution when handling the silverware. Perhaps he thought germs would jump off the fork tines and slide straight into his bloodstream.

"*Dios Mio*," Tribly shouted, hands raised. "Today is the seventeenth." She'd been present at the dinner table, which didn't often happen when there were more than ten people present. Tonight she wore the necklace. The necklace –the big silver one with the Italian horn dangling from it.

Dr. Dexter leaned away from the old woman. "What does it matter that it's the seventeenth?"

"The number seventeen is bad luck," Juliet told him, taking a dish from his hand and setting it in the dishwasher. She was tense and accidentally clattered the plates together.

"Si, bad luck for our family." She took the green cast iron teapot from the shelf and rapped her knuckles on it three times. "This is good luck," she told the doctor, shaking the teapot at him.

"I'm not Italian," he told her, holding up his hands as if warding off her superstitions—or the teapot.

"You're not Scottish either," Juliet said, remembering the wedding kilt matter.

Dexter frowned. In the kitchen lighting, his hair appeared thinner on top. It wasn't so noticeable in the ambiance of the living area, but near the stove, the lights were brighter, blue-tinged, and more revealing. The bridge of his long nose wrinkled. "What?"

"Never mind," she said, tossing in a soap pellet, and closing the washer's door.

Tribly shuffled toward the side hallway. "I will be in my room," she told them, "ringing the bells."

The doctor glanced at Juliet again.

"Hearing bells at night brings good luck."

He nodded and then leaned against the center island. "I've got a lot to learn about Italians."

"Where is Roseline?" Juliet took a seat on the opposite side of the counter, swinging back and forth in the chair.

"Upstairs changing. Roseline brought another outfit so that we can go to the movies."

Paris sat next to Juliet. "How do you feel?" he asked her.

"I'm shocked," she admitted. "I can't believe D'Angelo is dead." She took a lemon from the basket on the counter and rolled it in her hand. "I didn't know him that well, and only spoke to him a couple of times." She stopped rolling the fruit. "I was so sure he killed Gemma Hakim."

Dexter leaned on the counter, very interested in his unique nerdy way. "You thought he murdered the woman in your basement? I thought you were in the spy business."

"Yes, and no." Juliet put the lemon back into the basket. "I must've been wrong. Unless there are two killers. I'm confused." Getting off the stool, she paced to the end of the counter and then to the other side.

Paris watched her. "Oh, here we go."

Halting, Juliet tilted her head. "Here we go, what?"

He didn't answer and spoke to the doctor instead. "She's thinking it through. She paces when she's gone Sherlock Holmes on us."

Dexter nodded, his eyes brightening. "The game is afoot."

"Settle down, Dr. Watson," Juliet told him and paced again.

"I wonder how he died," Dexter said, leaning his chin into his palm.

"I'd like to know that too," Juliet said, and then stopped again. She was near Paris and grabbed his left bicep. "Wait. Wait, that's it, that's brilliant." She gazed at Dexter. "You're brilliant."

He stood straighter. "I am?"

Juliet tapped Paris' arm. "Sebastian D'Angelo didn't kill the woman in my basement."

"Why not?"

"Because there is obviously a connection between his and Gemma's death. That's why Nicolo rearrested Anthony. If it were two murderers, then the police would've held back and reexamined their case. They would've looked at other people." She patted Paris' arm again because it felt firm and strong. "The police think there is only one murderer." She gazed at Dexter and announced the conclusion, "D'Angelo must have been knifed to death, same as Gemma Hakim."

Dr. Dexter's eyebrows climbed high. He nodded and told Paris, "She's clever."

Juliet retook her stool. "Not that clever. I was wrong about D'Angelo."

"What were your clues?" Dexter wanted to know, leaning in again. "Maybe there are hints within the clues."

"My only clue was a photo of Amir D'Angelo."

"Amir …? I don't understand."

Juliet snatched up another lemon. It was a habit of hers, to scrape the side of the fruit with her fingernail, and then sniff the citrus fragrance. "Gemma Hakim was from Iraq. Amir D'Angelo was born in Iraq." Pulling the lemon from her nose, she said, "At the party, Gemma spoke to D'Angelo about their son. I did a small investigation and learned that D'Angelo was in Iraq during the Iraqi Freedom campaign. For whatever reason, when Gemma confronted D'Angelo at the party, it gave him cause to kill her. Gemma was Amir's mother."

Dexter let out a low whistle. "You got all of that out of a photograph of a boy?" It was hard to know if the doctor was impressed or dumbfoundedly amused.

Heat climbed into Juliet's cheeks. "Yes, but I was wrong."

There was a long bit of silence. Juliet stared at the lemon.

Dexter tapped the counter. "Okay, okay, let's not get defeated. Who else could be the murderer?"

Juliet twisted the seat back and forth, back and forth. "Gemma threw a drink at Geoffrey Leary."

Dexter stood straight again, his brows knotted. "She threw two drinks that night?"

"No, no. Gemma only threw one drink. The one she threw on Roseline was meant for Mr. Leary."

Dexter's dark eyes considered the ceiling as he thought about what she said. "I was standing right there. She threw it at Roseline."

Juliet crumpled a little. "Are you sure?"

"Well, I wasn't expecting it to happen, so I wasn't zeroed in on this Gemma woman, but she said something to Leary and then threw the wine at Roseline."

Paris took the lemon from Juliet's hand and stuck it beneath his own nose. "Why would she throw wine at Roseline?"

"Jealousy? My Roseline is lovely," Dexter suggested.

"Stop being so in love," Juliet told him. "Were you really paying that much attention, or were you thinking about the engagement ring burning a hole in your pocket?"

Color rose on the doctor's cheeks. "I was nervous. I'd told your mother all about my plans, and my idea was to propose near the fireplace … I see what you mean. I guess I wasn't paying that much attention."

Paris turned his attention to Juliet. "So, you think Mr.

Leary killed Gemma because she meant to throw wine on him. That's thin."

"Let me help you understand," she told him, taking back her lemon. "When Anthony and I first considered the situation, he thought—we both thought—Gemma was connected to the Hakim Wine Company that'd tried to take over Renaissance Wine." Juliet got off the stool and stood near Paris. "Remember our conversation in the coffee shop? We thought she'd come to the party to steal secrets from my father." She paced. "I thought Mr. Leary was Gemma's contact at the party. Anthony thinks it was someone else. It was a Tijuana Refund."

Paris narrowed his eyes.

Dexter leaned forward. "Tijuana, what?"

Juliet faced them, hands on her waist. "Anthony thought a company spy took Gemma's money and then killed her so no one could have the information about Renaissance Wine's fermenting processes." She tilted her head in wonder. "The two of you don't know what a Tijuana Refund is?"

They both still had those same confused looks on their faces.

Juliet threw out her hands. "Either that or Beth did it."

Dexter shook his head. "Who's Beth?"

"Beth Holley, stalker, writer of hate mail–she tried to run me over with her car."

Paris' expression cleared, and he nodded his dark head. "Oh, that Beth." Then, "Why would she kill D'Angelo?"

"Because D'Angelo loved someone else."

Dexter still looked confused. "But what's the Hakim connection?"

Juliet sat again. "That's what I've been telling you.

Hakim was D'Angelo's wife. Maybe they'd planned to get back together, and Beth went bunny-boiling crazy and knifed them both."

Dexter slapped his palm on the counter. "That's a much stronger theory."

"That's nightly news," Paris said. "Tell the police about Beth Holley."

* * *

Tell Nicolo about Beth?

He'd want to know when Juliet saw the stalker letters, where she was when Beth tried to run her down with a black Honda.

I'm not lying to him again.

Juliet sat in the front pew of Saint Mary's church for the Sunday morning service. She'd already lit candles for Anthony and for Sebastian D'Angelo. She was now gathering her purse and wool coat to walk into the parking lot.

What if it wasn't Beth in the black Honda?

What if it was Leary?

Out of the service, Juliet crossed the front sidewalks and stepped into the Wake Up Cafe.

Where does Beth live?

Juliet thought she might do a drive-by and find out if Beth even owned a black Honda with paint peeling off the hood. That'd give her proof if she decided to speak to Nicolo about the situation.

While waiting for a Cappuccino Freddo, Juliet typed Beth's name into Google on her cellphone. She read the results while walking back to her car in the church parking lot.

O' Happy Dagger

There were three Beth Holleys in western New York, but only one of them was the same age as Beth, and she lived north of Mayville. The site took Juliet to whitepages.com, and an address popped up. The address wasn't in Mayville but in West Portland.

Does Beth know D'Angelo's dead … if she hadn't killed him, that is? Had Beth been the one to kill Gemma Hakim?

Juliet opened the car door and sat in the driver's seat of the Fiat. How could Beth have killed Gemma? She wasn't at the Harvest Ball.

Starting the car, Juliet drove out of the parking lot and steered eastward toward Plank Road.

Had Beth pulled a Gemma and dressed as a server too? Juliet hadn't known Beth at that time and wouldn't have recognized her.

There would've been more blood.

Maybe Beth lured Gemma into the cellar.

But that didn't account for the blood splatters on the kitchen floor. Someone started a little stabbing business in the kitchen and wound up in the cellar.

Ugh.

A half-hour later, Juliet pulled the car onto Felton Road. It was the same route she took to work every day, the same area she'd found Delia broken down on the side of the road.

Juliet checked the GPS and kept driving toward Propinquity Lane.

Wait …

Juliet took a right—the same turn to the right as when she'd dropped off Delia at her apartment last week.

Beth and Delia live in the same place?

The three-story terracotta building came into view.

Five cars sat in the parking area.

Had there been a black Honda in the parking lot last time she was there?

Juliet didn't remember looking for one. She'd been focused on speaking to Delia and hadn't paid attention to the other tenants in the building.

Well, she was paying attention now. Juliet pressed lightly on the accelerator and rolled forward in the dirt driveway.

There!

Juliet rolled down the windows.

Beth had parked the car backward in the spot. It wasn't really a parking space, but the rear bumper of the Honda was aimed toward the vacant lot next door.

Juliet put the stick into Park and got out of the car. Blame it on the caffeine, but she needed to be a little daring, to figure out if Beth was the one who'd tried to run her down.

"Juliet?"

A jolt of nerves went right through her.

The voice had come from behind Juliet. She spun around.

Delia was moving off the fire escape, dressed in blue jeans and that puffy white jacket Juliet had seen before. Her hair was up in a messy bun, her face was drawn, and her eyes watered. She was either crying or had a cold. "Why are you here?"

Juliet relaxed her shoulders. "I'm actually here to see Beth. I had no idea you two lived in the same apartment building."

Delia wore no makeup. It seemed she'd just gotten out of bed. "We do. I don't see much of her, though. She keeps to herself, comes and goes a lot."

"But she's here now, right?" Juliet pointed to the Honda.

Delia gazed at the car but shook her head. "I don't know."

"She tore out of here early," someone said.

Juliet's eyes found the face of that someone. A man had stuck his head out of a second-story window. Brown hair topped his triangular face and then swept to the side in a long style.

Delia glanced upward too. "Hi, Titus."

"Hey, Deal," he called down. "Beth got herself a big car and squealed out of here this morning."

"That was her?" Delia asked. "I heard the noise."

"Yep," he said, climbing the rest of the way out of the window, his long, long legs leading. He sat on a chair on the fire escape. "She looked up at me before she got in the car. It was Beth."

"And she hasn't come back?"

"Not that I saw, and I've been here all morning. I just went inside for a second to get my sandwich." He held it up.

Delia turned back around. "Is there something else wrong, Juliet?"

"No, no," she said. "I just didn't know if anyone told her about Sebastian's death."

Titus got out of the chair and leaned on the fire-escape railing. "I told you she looked up at me. Her makeup was all smeared and her hair…" He circled over his head with his free hand, "it looked like a rat's nest."

Delia shook her head. "Titus!"

He shrugged. "It was."

Delia gazed at Juliet and gave a rueful shake of her

head. "I'm going back upstairs. Do you want to come up?"

She could tell her friend didn't need company at the moment. Delia had dark circles beneath her eyes. Her natural pink complexion was pale. She hugged the jacket to herself as though she were still cold despite the down coat.

Juliet moved toward her car. "No, I'll see you later this week." She glanced up at the fireplace. "Bye, Titus."

He held up his sandwich in return. "Bye, Jewels."

Juliet reversed out of the driveway and drove to the end of Propinquity Lane.

Beth seemed more and more guilty in Juliet's mind. Titus had said Beth looked hysterical when she left the apartment, and who wouldn't be hysterical after a murdering spree? Beth had rented a car and driven off, likely to hide from the police. Where would she go? D'Angelo's?

Juliet turned left onto the main drive and pulled out of the neighborhood. She picked up speed on Felton.

But, Leary…

He was guilty of something. He'd argued with D'Angelo, threatened him with an or else. And what was with the smiling when he'd learned D'Angelo was dead?

Juliet wouldn't smile at such news, ever. She'd never liked Mariotto Romeo, but she hadn't smiled. She'd been sick and sad.

Who killed Gemma Hakim and Sebastian D'Angelo— Beth, or Leary? Both Leary and Beth?

She put on her blinker and took the exit toward Mayville. There was nothing but trees behind the guardrails. The cold air swept purple and red leaves across the road. Maybe because it was Sunday, there were no other drivers on the road.

Juliet glanced in the rearview mirror.

There was one vehicle behind her. It was a black car, one of those hefty luxury cars with a big grill on the front. It was maybe fifty feet behind the Fiat.

Juliet relaxed into the seat. Someone else was on the road. With the low gray clouds and the lonesome two-lane stretching out in front of her, she'd been put in the mind of the horror flick, *The Hills Have Eyes*.

I've developed post-cinematic paranoia.

She glanced in the rearview again.

The black car was ten feet away.

Juliet sat up straighter and glanced at the speedometer. Had she been musing so intently that she'd slowed too much?

I'm going sixty-eight ...

Slowing the Fiat, Juliet pulled over to the shoulder of the road to let the car pass.

The black car braked hard—and then pulled right behind the Fiat.

There is a taste to fear. It was like holding a Duracell battery in your mouth. Juliet had tasted the same battery last summer. She twisted in her seat to see out the back window.

She couldn't make out the driver. It was as if the seat and head all came together in a shadow.

Juliet's index finger found the lock button and pressed it.

The locks clicked.

They were already locked, but she pressed the button again to feel more secure.

But, Juliet didn't feel secure at all. The nerves on her forearms danced all the way up to her shoulders. She picked up her phone on the seat and tapped the screen.

Suddenly, there was a crunching sound, and Juliet's seatbelt locked her against the seat as the Fiat jumped forward.

Juliet pressed the brake harder and stared wide-eyed into the rear view.

The black car's engine revved twice.

"Oh no, huh-uh," Juliet said and punched the accelerator. She was born for this. She'd practiced tearing out from zero-to-ninety every day since she was sixteen years old.

The Fiat's tires squealed. The back of the car fishtailed.

The black car's tires squealed too.

Juliet watched the rearview.

The black car was gaining.

"I see thou know'st me not."

Chapter 17

Juliet took the curves fast, gripping the steering wheel tight.

The other car's bumper hit the Fiat again. The steering wheel jumped.

Fear tasted like a battery, but it was also the color blue. It tinted everything in Juliet's line of sight. She heard her own breath ripping out of her throat, and smelled her own tires on the cement.

Where was she, exactly? She'd lost her place on the road between towns. Was she near Mayville?

She blew into the next curve. Her left side pressed against the driver's door as she kept the wheel jammed to the right. Tapping the brakes, Juliet held the wheel to the right on the next curve, bending into it, and then stomped on the brakes.

The Fiat screeched to a stop on the shoulder of the road again.

Juliet held her breath and prayed the black car would fly past her.

The driver of the other car braked too and stopped even with the Fiat.

Lightning fast, Juliet shoved the stick into Reverse, held the wheel to the left, and made the quickest U-turn she'd ever dared to take. She kicked the accelerator to the floor and the Fiat tore down the road. She watched the rearview mirror and the road ahead, back and forth.

The black car didn't bother with a U-turn and sped down the hill after her.

"You're crazy," Juliet yelled at the driver.

Whoever it was, was pretty good at driving in reverse—but was falling behind.

Juliet grabbed her phone off the passenger side seat and panic-dialed nine-one-one.

"Nine-one-one, what's your emer—"

"SQUIRREL! GET OUT OF THE WAY SQUIRREL!" Juliet was at the S-curves and dropped the phone on the floor. "Crap, crap, crap."

The black car hit the Fiat again.

Juliet's seatbelt locked her down.

"Good car, good car," she told it.

At some point, the black car had turned around.

Juliet screamed toward the phone on the floor, "If anyone is there, I'm on Felton Road, heading … I don't know, north, I think. Someone is trying to kill me." She took the next curve at ninety miles per hour. Where was a damn onion field when she needed one?

The black car hit her bumper again, harder.

The steering wheel leapt out of Juliet's hand.

She grabbed it—but she'd taken her foot off the accelerator.

The Fiat slowed, careened ... hit the guardrail.

There was nothing for it. Juliet knew she was going over.

She hit the gas.

The Fiat roared down a rocky bank and into a boulder field.

She drove for her life, steering around a large tree trunk and into a small clearing. She stomped the brakes the rest of the way down the hill.

The car slid to a stop about a foot in front of a pine tree.

Spinning around in her seat, Juliet stared out the back window. Her seatbelt nearly cut off her circulation at her throat. She clicked it off and jack-knifed in the seat.

Did the person intend to follow her down the bank?

Juliet couldn't see anything but brush and dead grass. She clicked the door locks again, double-checking once more. Breathing hard, she pulled the keys out of the ignition and fingered the pepper spray—which wouldn't do her much good against a gun.

No. The killer was dagger-happy. They would come after her with a knife.

Her breath was loud in the quiet car.

"Hello? Hello?"

Juliet reached to the floorboard for her phone. "Hello! Someone rammed my car. I'm in a ravine off of ... I don't know. I don't know where I am. I was heading south, and I'm on the west side of the street in a ravine."

The dispatcher's voice remained calm. "We're triangulating your call. We'll find you. Is the other car gone?"

"I don't know if the other car's gone or not. I can't see beyond all the trees."

"Stay in the car. Stay on the line. Did you see the driver?"

"No," she said in a loud voice. She couldn't stop yelling for some reason. "It's cloudy, and the road was tree-lined."

"What color is the other car?"

"Black, newer, luxury model. Large grill on the front," she told the woman, keeping her eyes on the windows all around her. "Should have some damage to the front bumper."

"Remain in the car. Stay on the line."

"I'm not going anywhere."

* * *

It was the longest twenty minutes of Juliet's life.

She heard a helicopter first–and then three police officers trudged down the slope toward her car. One of them tapped the trunk before approaching the driver's window.

Juliet opened the door and stood on shaky legs. "Is the other car gone?"

"Long gone. The helicopter's circling," one of the officers told her. They were all young looking. All wore guns in unclipped holsters. "Let's get you up the hill."

Two hours later, she was still in the Mayville police

department, giving a statement to Detective Marshall.

Marshall was a barrel-chested man with a bald head and a thick neck. He told her, "A tow truck just pulled your car out of the ravine. It's at Joe's Towing Service whenever you're ready to haul it to a garage."

Juliet nodded. The desk sergeant had brought her tea. It was cold in the cup on the desk in front of her. "When can I go home?"

"As soon as your ride gets here."

* * *

Paris held the passenger side door for her, and Juliet slipped inside the Jaguar. He hadn't said anything, but she knew she was about to get an earful. Yes, the usual happy Paris had a grim look on his face as he slammed the door shut.

The shouting commenced as soon as he shut his own door. "What is *wrong* with you?"

"I didn't …"

He twisted in his seat, green eyes blazing. "You had to go to West Portland to see that Beth woman who you think is a *murderer*?"

All of her muscles tensed. "I only went to see…"

"I don't care, Juliet. I don't care what was in your mind. I *swear* you are crazy. Why do I care about you if you don't care about yourself?"

She opened her mouth. Nothing came out the first time. Then, "I… I do care about…"

"Why didn't you ask someone to go with you?"

"Because…"

"Because you don't trust anyone, that's right. You don't

trust me. Just say it."

She shook her head, blinking two, three times. "I trust…"

"Stop talking. You are not going to say anything that I think is okay. Nothing. Stay quiet over there." He twisted back around and started the car.

The engine click, click, clicked because he held the ignition down too long.

Paris hit the steering wheel. "You pig car!"

Her throat had a lump in it the size of her own fist. "It's a very nice car."

He held up one finger. "Stop talking. I used to believe you were one of the smartest people I knew. Now I need to rethink everything. You're not up to the job, Juliet. I cannot have a woman who is so dangerous to her own self…" His words trailed off—or were cut off by the car's screeching tires.

When they arrived home, he got out of the car before she did and stormed into the house.

WHAT in the world?

Inside, Juliet grabbed two bottles of Limoncello and went to sit on her balcony.

Once there, she cried. A lot.

* * *

The next morning Juliet avoided everyone in the house. She was out of the kitchen before Tribly packed her a lunch. Because she was running early, she had the time to stop at the Wake Up Cafe for coffee. She took a different route to work, the Lake highway. She drove her father's car, the Lancia. This was the car Juliet should've driven yesterday—when the crazy person chased her off the road. The Lancia was a smooth, fast ride.

Juliet didn't drive fast though. Not because she was scared, there was no tingling or nerves running through her body. No, it was just that she was having a hard time feeling anything other than the heavy weight in her chest that Paris had put there.

Of the friends Juliet had lost and of the people she desired as friends, Paris was the keeper.

Yes, he'd put the heaviness in her heart because he was being so, so concerned and cautious and unsupportive.

I'm not a danger to myself.

He'd not let her explain that she hadn't gone after Beth and that she'd only driven out that way to look at the Honda's license plate. Was it her fault that someone drove her off the road? Was that a reason to stop being her friend?

Maybe it wasn't even Gemma's and D'Angelo's killer— had he thought of that? Road rage could've been the reason the black car slammed into the Fiat.

As soon as she thought that last bit, Juliet knew. That was no road rage incident. She'd been stalked and targeted.

She tightened her grip on the Lancia's steering wheel and glanced in the rearview mirror. Who'd been in the black car? Why would they try to drive her off the road?

To scare me, to make me stop nosing around.

Right. So that meant she was close to figuring things out. It meant someone she knew didn't want her snooping around any longer. Juliet was on the right track.

Beth.

Okay, possibly Mr. Leary.

Either way, she needed to figure it out before whomever

it was tried to kill her again. She needed to solve this before Paris completely cut her out of his life.

The heavy feeling lifted a bit and in its place came a subtle nagging fear. The killer would probably try again to stop her snooping around.

She pulled into the parking lot of Renaissance Wines and waited in the car, watching the plant and office workers arrive.

No black luxury car pulled in. Neither did a Honda with chipped paint on the hood.

She watched the gate through her rearview mirror. No other cars pulled into the parking lot, so Juliet got out of the Lancia and hurried toward the office.

Juliet bypassed Tricia and Patsy and slipped into her office. Mr. Leary's door was closed. She leaned toward it. There was no shuffling of papers, no clearing throat, no murmuring.

She put her purse away and took off her coat, and then slipped out the door again.

"There you are."

Juliet jumped and spun around.

"Sorry, did I scare you?" Tricia asked. She stood at the door of her office with her curls wild on her head.

Juliet stood straighter. "No, not at all."

"Come down and see us. We want to know what's happened. We heard Mr. D'Angelo died."

Juliet didn't know what to do with her hands, so she stuck them awkwardly behind her back. She never stood with her hands clasped behind her back!

Tricia's brows gathered. "Everything okay?"
"Everything's great. I just need to go down the hall for a minute."

"Okay. Come see us soon." She disappeared into her office.

Juliet knew she needed to avoid gossiping with Patsy and Tricia. If someone was after her, then they might think she was sharing information with the ladies and try to take them out too.

Turning, she went straight to Beth's office.

The woman wasn't there. The desk was clean. All paperwork was off the top of it, and her coffee cup was gone too.

Beth had taken off. She'd rented her big car and raced back to Florida.

Possibly.

Juliet walked around the desk and pulled open drawers. There were the usual objects: pens, pencils, extra tape, and staple refill boxes. In the bottom drawer, there was the framed photo of D'Angelo and his son.

What was it doing in Beth's desk? Had she stolen it from D'Angelo's office to obsess over it?

He'd been surprised the photo was missing.

Yes, he had ... did he suspect Beth took the picture? Had he finally figured out that the best secretary he'd ever had was obsessing over him and fired her for her stalker ways?

The glass doors opened at the other end of the office.

Juliet's heart jumped into her throat. Had Beth come to work after all?

Geoffrey Leary stood there, his wonky brows up near his hairline. "What's going on?"

His presence did nothing to calm her nerves. Was it Leary, standing there in his wooly coat, the one who'd tried to run her off the road?

He leaned in. "I asked what's going on Miss Da Vinci."

"It looks as though Beth cleared out," she told him. "Did Sebastian fire her last week?"

"Why don't you ask your father?" He plodded forward and twisted the handle on D'Angelo's former office door." He jiggled the knob even though it was obviously locked.

For the first time, Juliet figured out who Leary looked like … what was the actor's name? He was an older man, too, possibly dead already. Walter something or other. "Why are you trying to get into Mr. D'Angelo's office?"

He turned back around, with his eyes narrowed. "The same thing I imagine you're doing going through Beth's drawers. Things need to go forward, don't they? I need to figure out what D'Angelo was doing so that I can keep the office going."

"Oh."

Juliet didn't believe him. His job had nothing to do with Mr. D'Angelo, they didn't cross paths at all. There was no reason for him to figure out what the director had been doing. Leary couldn't keep the office going, even if that was what was really on his mind. That was her father's job.

He asked, "Isn't that what you're doing?"

She straightened her posture and lied, "That's exactly what I was doing."

Matthau. Walter Matthau, that's who he looks like!

"But there's nothing to see," she told him. She went around the other side of the desk and then out the double glass doors.

Mr. Leary followed her.

Once they were back in the office, Leary unlocked his door, went inside, and slammed it shut.

He was going to go in the back way, wasn't he? He was

going to find something to break a lock and then open D'Angelo's second door.

What was he after?

Juliet sat at her desk again, in her wobbly chair, and finished her coffee. Why would Mr. Leary kill Gemma Hakim?

Well, there was the spy business and the refund something or other.

But, why would he kill D'Angelo?

Throwing her cup in the trash, Juliet stood, meaning to follow Leary and there was only one way to do it.

Go through the men's bathroom to the passageway.

But first, she needed to get past Patsy and Tricia.

Once she got near their door, she took off running. It was a touch dramatic, but since she had no other ideas of how to avoid them, it didn't seem so extreme.

"Hey," someone called to her. It wasn't Tricia or Patsy. It'd been a man's voice, and slightly familiar.

She turned around.

Nicolo stood ten feet away. He must've come into the office and stopped in the ladies' office first. He walked right toward her, very purposely, dressed in his uniform and bomber jacket. "I want to speak to you." His eyes were half-closed and his jawline firmly set.

Juliet's heart just couldn't get a break. It was pounding away again.

She waited for him by the water fountain, right outside the men's bathroom.

Nicolo kept the same stride, took Juliet's arm, and dragged her toward a private corner at the end of the hallway. Swinging around to face her, he said, "You need to tell me what you know about Anthony Yeager and

Sebastian D'Angelo." He held up his hand, to finish with, "I don't care how you know it, which laws you broke…"

Juliet blinked at him. "Really?"

"Why?" he asked, his eyes narrowing. "What did you do?"

She gasped—more on the inside than audibly. Had that been a trick question? "Nothing," she squeaked. "Nothing."

"I don't believe you." He pulled a notepad from his jacket pocket. Unsnapping the pencil, he waited.

Pulling her shoulders square, she told him. "I know Anthony is innocent."

He sagged a little and lifted his eyes to the ceiling.

She went on. "I know Beth Holley had some sort of relationship with D'Angelo. She came from Florida and pretended to be his wife."

"Not a crime."

"No, but it's wacky."

"You mean like pretending interest in your dad's business just to catch a killer, that kind of wacky?"

Juliet pressed her lips together and took a breath. "No, not like that. Something split Beth and D'Angelo up. Maybe he figured out Beth is living *la vida loca*, or he started seeing someone else. She stalked him and wrote creepy letters to him."

Nicolo shook his head. "Which one is Beth?" His blue eyes gazed down the hallway as if maybe the woman was nearby.

"D'Angelo's secretary."

"Full figure, high-pitched laugh?" He wrote the name Beth on his paper.

"Yes!" she said, finger pointing upward. "D'Angelo lied to her about where he was last weekend and she broke into his house a couple of times. She might be there right now because she rented a car and left her apartment with her makeup all smeared … I'm pretty sure she tried to run me off the road."

Nicolo shook his head. "She's not there. We've been in his house all weekend."

Juliet nodded with enthusiasm. "Then, you saw the crumpled stalker letters in his wastebasket?"

Nicolo turned his head a little and brought his brows together. "When were you there?"

"Oh," she said, dampening the wick of zeal. "Right, well, I was there … the other night. What was it, Friday or Saturday?"

His expression didn't change. "When he was out of town?"

She opened her mouth twice, nodded. "No."

"You're nodding your head. That means yes."

"I swear I didn't take anything."

"These griefs, these woes, these sorrows make me old."

Chapter 18

"You broke into his house." It wasn't a question. "If you didn't take anything, then why did you go?"

"To find a marriage certificate or a birth certificate. I was convinced D'Angelo was married to Gemma Hakim." She shifted her weight under his intense stare. "He may have been. I don't read Farsi."

"He wasn't married to Gemma Hakim. He was married to Jesenia Wasim. We saw the marriage certificate too and didn't need to break into his house to find it."

He'd definitely put emphasis on the words *break into*.

"You said you didn't care what laws I broke."

He raised one brow. "I do care, but I'm going to forget

about it this time."

"Oh." She stuck her hands on her waist. "I still think Beth is someone to look at."

"What else you got?"

"Geoffrey Leary," she said in a softer tone, glancing over her shoulder at the men's bathroom.

His blue eyes flickered in that direction and then back at Juliet. "Why?"

"Two arguments." She held up two fingers. "One with Gemma Hakim at the Harvest Ball, and one with D'Angelo in his office where he told D'Angelo to get rid of someone, or else."

Nicolo gave a small shake of his head and shrugged. "That's it?"

Juliet gaped at him. "Or else, as in *or else I'll kill you*."

One side of his mouth lifted, and he gazed off for a moment. "Or else is suggestive of an alternative. He could've meant, or else I'll throw you a party."

She screwed up her face. "Oh, come on."

"You think Leary killed him?"

"I don't know, but Leary is so sketchy. He sneaks around using a back door, has information in his office that he shouldn't, top-secret information…"

"Top secret? This is a wine company."

She ignored that and thought it through for a moment, letting her eyes drift toward the ceiling. "If it weren't for the fact that Mr. Leary stopped a company spy this year from damaging Renaissance Wines, then I'd think he was guilty of corporate espionage."

"We are way off topic," Nicolo said.

Juliet came out of her reverie and blinked. "He could've killed D'Angelo because D'Angelo caught him doing something illegal. He could've killed Hakim in a Tijuana Refund situ…"

"What do you know about a Tijuana Refund?"

She twisted, uncomfortable. "I know what it is."

"It usually refers to prostitution," he said, all judgmentally.

"Watch your language, Nicolo."

He took a steadying breath. "When was the last time you saw Sebastian D'Angelo?"

"I was in his office."

"Did he know you were?"

She nodded. "Funny."

"Did he say anything about his plans that day?"

Juliet wasn't going to reiterate D'Angelo's plans to eat lunch with Anthony. She said, "No, but he ended the conversation abruptly. He'd remembered something."

"Like what?" He held his pencil at the ready.

"He said, *I wonder if they ever got untangled*–and something about a divorce."

"Who was he talking about?"

"I don't know. But as I left, D'Angelo called Beth into the office."

"Because she was his secretary."

"Maybe," Juliet admitted. "How did Mr. D'Angelo die?"

Nicolo shook his head. "I can't share that with you."

"Just nod if he died the same way Gemma died."

Nicolo nodded.

Juliet's heart rate picked up. "Did you find another knife?"

"No," he said and then closed the notebook and stuck it back in his pocket. "Where is Geoff Leary?"

"That's a good question."

He turned his face to the side, waiting.

"We can try his office."

"Lead the way."

Patsy and Tricia were at the door of their office watching her and Nicolo with their brows raised. How much of the conversation had they heard? Neither of them smiled when she passed by. Actually, their expressions reminded her of the first day she'd met them at the coffee pot. They looked at her suspiciously, and with a touch more anger to their eyes and brows.

Once inside the office, she tapped on Mr. Leary's closed door, knowing he wouldn't answer. He was in the passageway.

Should I tell Nicolo about it?

Leary's door flew open. "What is it?"

"Oh!" Juliet said, taking a step backward into Nicolo. She frowned at him. "Sorry." To Leary, she said, "He's here to see you."

She got out of the way fast and went back to her desk. It was as though she was in a tornado. Her head was spinning.

I don't know anything, do I?

Did she?

I know enough that someone tried to kill me.

She grabbed her purse and pulled out her wallet. Extracting a credit card, she went back to Beth's office and straight to her father's door. Juliet had no idea what Abram had done to open the garage door at D'Angelo's house, but she meant to mimic it. She stuck the card into the space between the frame and the handle and wiggled it back and forth … back and forth, while twisting the knob at the same time.

The door opened!

"No way," she whispered, checking the glass doors behind her. Patsy and Tricia were likely following her around at this stage of the investigation. They'd looked so wary of her in the hallway.

Juliet stepped into her father's office and shut the door. She'd been in the room before, and it looked the same. A big mahogany desk was in the center of the room with plush chairs in front of it for visitors. One wall was covered with a bookshelf that held more of his miniature car models and books and wine glasses and bottles. It smelled like him, citrusy and earthy.

If she'd seen the second door in his office in the past, Juliet hadn't paid attention to it. Yet, there it was against the opposite wall from the bookcase.

Juliet locked the office door and then went through the second door into the same small basement area she'd scooted through the other day. Wow, that seemed a lifetime ago. In reality, it had only been a week. She left the door unlocked and tucked the credit card into the pocket of her wool slacks.

She stepped up to what she now knew as Mr. Leary's second door.

"I know D'Angelo went to see Mr. Yeager on his lunch break. That's what he told me anyway." It was Leary's voice coming through the door.

Nicolo said something, but it wasn't as audible.

Juliet caught the word, *Hakim*.

Was he asking him about Gemma then? Was Nicolo suspicious of Leary too? Was he questioning putting Anthony in jail?

Leary said, "I don't know anything about her other than she threw wine at people. I wasn't really paying that much attention to her."

A chair moved backward with a scraping sound. Nicolo said something.

"Anytime officer. I wish I could help more. I rather liked Sebastian D'Angelo."

Juliet scrunched her face. Leary didn't like D'Angelo, he didn't like anybody.

Off the step, she headed back to her father's office, slipped inside, and then held the door half-closed. Leary would come out of his office soon and try to get into D'Angelo's.

Does he know the credit card trick?

But Leary didn't come out of his office.

Should she go back, listen at his door?

The glass doors in the front office whooshed opened and closed.

Tiptoeing forward, Juliet reached her father's other door and listened.

A doorknob rattled. Was Leary trying to get into D'Angelo's office again?

Other noises came through the door: drawers opening and shutting. He was at Beth's desk, searching for something…

"Ahh," Leary said. He sounded satisfied with whatever he'd found.

A door opened and then shut. He'd gone into D'Angelo's room!

Juliet skipped out of her father's back door fast and went around to D'Angelo's door.

Again, the sound of drawers opening and closing sounded. Papers rustled.

She leaned closer.

A familiar rattling sound, as though he'd picked up the phone receiver. Whoever he called took thirty seconds to answer.

While he waited, Leary made soft grunting noises and grumbling sounds, as though speaking to himself. He shuffled papers. Then, "I've got it." There was a pause. "No, don't come here. The police have been here today, asking about D'Angelo." Another pause. "I didn't say anything. I'm not going to tell anyone. This is your little venture. You decide what to do. Yes, yes, all right. I'll meet you at four ... where? The old library, why?" After another moment, he said, "Fine. Let's meet in the romance novel area." Leary laughed as though he'd made a hilarious joke and hung up the phone.

Juliet practically ran back to her father's door and shut it behind her. She twisted the lock. Leary was a spy! He'd found something, and he was turning it over to the spy.

Wasn't he?

She sat in her father's chair behind the desk and waited.

Should I tell Nicolo?

The idea made her insides squirm.

She'd have to catch Mr. Leary in the act. Juliet nodded to herself. She'd sneak into the library and take photos of Leary handing over the formula and receiving money.

Was that how corporate espionage worked? Hand over the formula and receive a suitcase of money?

Her phone buzzed. Pulling it out of her pocket, she checked the display.

Paris' number and face were on the screen.

Her heart gave a little jolt, but she pushed the button. Keeping her voice down, she said, "Hey."

"You left early this morning."

Juliet played with the knob on the top desk drawer. "I didn't think anybody would notice."

"I did. Where are you?"

She gazed at the bookshelf and the miniature cars. "In my father's office."

"Have lunch with me. I'll come there."

"Bring something with you. I forgot my lunch."

"Can't we go out?"

"There's not much around …"

"I'll bring something. I'll be there early."

"Paris."

"What?"

"Stop being angry with me. Please."

"I already have," he told her and hung up the phone.

* * *

At eleven-thirty, Juliet waited for Paris by the doors at the front of the building.

The blue Jaguar made its way through the gates. Paris stepped out of the car with two boxes of food in his hand and walked toward the door.

Behind Juliet, Patsy said, "Do you only know good looking men?"

Juliet turned and smiled at her. "That's just Paris."

She nodded, then frowned at Juliet and moved away.

* * *

They sat at her desk and ate the Tortellini Alfredo Tribly had sent along. She'd packed forks and knives, and bread and butter.

Paris ate quietly. It'd never been awkward with him, and Juliet hesitated to bring up yesterday's argument. She was just happy he was there, sitting with her.

Patsy was right. Paris did look handsome in his gray sweater and jeans. He'd combed his wavy hair away from his face and kept his eyes on his food. He asked, "Did Detective Montague visit you today?"

"How do you know about that?" Juliet asked, wiping her mouth with the cloth napkin Tribly had sent along.

"He stopped by the house first."

She nodded. "Nicolo wanted me to tell him everything."

His green eyes found hers. "Did you?"

Nodding, she said, "I did. I even told him that I broke into D'Angelo's house."

For the first time since he walked through the door, Paris grinned. His eyes brightened. "What'd he say?"

Juliet moved her wobbly chair back and forth, grinning too. "That he'd forget about it this time."

Paris raised his brows. "Wow, you really do have it in with the cops." He took another bite of his food and then asked, "Did you tell him your theory on Beth and Mr. Leary?" He turned around toward Leary's door and shot a glance that way. "Is Leary here?"

"Somewhere. I heard Mr. Leary tell someone that he *found it*, and he's meeting them at four o'clock to hand it over."

Paris sat up straighter. "What did he find?"

She shook her head. "I don't know. But I'm going to follow him and take photos..." Juliet sat straighter. "Will you come with me?" she asked, remembering what he'd said yesterday about not going it alone and not caring about her own safety.

He sat straighter too. "Where?"

"The library, for some reason."

"Do you know who he's meeting?"

She shook her head. "No clue."

Paris reached into his pocket and pulled out his phone. He tapped the screen and then put it to his ear.

"Who are you…?"

Paris held his index finger to his mouth. Then, "May I speak to Detective Montague?"

Juliet pushed to her feet. "What are you doing?"

"Detective, this is Paris Nobleman. Juliet and I'd like to meet with you right away regarding Geoffrey Leary's upcoming meeting."

Juliet sat down hard–immediately sorry because her chair nearly dumped her onto the floor. She breathed hard through her nose. Paris Nobleman was a turncoat.

He hung up and gathered the utensils and boxes. "Let's go. He's meeting us at the H&R Block parking lot."

"He's not going to believe me. I don't have proof yet."

Paris pulled her lunch box away from her and then leaned in very close.

Juliet sat back in the seat.

"If you don't care about your safety, then it's up to the rest of us to protect you. Now come on." Placing the rest of the boxes in a bag, he headed out the door.

* * *

The H&R Block was Madame Olei's spot now. The old charlatan stared at the cruiser before she went into her shop–as if she knew something of what they were talking about.

Nicolo didn't pay attention to the old woman and stared at Juliet.

She sat in the passenger seat of the police cruiser.

Paris stood beside Juliet's door with his arm on the window ledge.

Nicolo asked, "What did you hear exactly?"

She glanced at Paris and then at Nicolo. "He said, *'I've got it'*."

"What?"

She raised her shoulders. She sat with her back against the seat to see both men. "I don't know, I couldn't see him. He was in D'Angelo's office on the phone."

"Then how do you know…? Never mind. What else did he say?"

"Umm," Juliet started, trying to remember. The way that Nicolo–and Paris–stared at her messed with her speech mechanism. "He said, *No, don't come here. The police have been here…*" She shook her head, staring at the dashboard instead of Nicolo. "He said *I didn't tell them anything…*" She glanced up. "And then he said he'd meet the person at the old library."

Nicolo placed his forearm on the steering wheel and thought about what she said for a few moments.

Which gave Juliet time to glare at Paris.

"No, no," Paris said. "You don't get to be mad at me. No. You don't do this on your own ever again."

Nicolo shot Paris a look and then offered his fist for a fist bump across Juliet's lap.

Paris' fist hit Nicolo's.

Nicolo said, "That sounds like a plot from a bad movie."

"It's still true," Juliet told him. "And you know what, I'm going to go to the library."

"No, you're not. If you set one foot out of this car, I'll leave you here. You can stay at the tattoo parlor while I figure out what's going on."

Juliet sat straighter. "You believe me?"

"I believe you. Of course, I believe you," Nicolo told her, shaking his head.

"You didn't believe me this afternoon."

"Because you were lying. You said you didn't know anything, and you had a bunch of information you'd kept from me."

"Because you're so bad-tempered."

"Basta!" Paris practically shouted.

He'd shouted it wrong.

Nicolo and Juliet both frowned at him.

"Your accent could use some work," Juliet told him. "You are angry. The word *Basta* is an adjective."

Paris kept his mouth straight during her speech. Then, "All I'm saying is, will you two stop fighting about it and make a decision about what's next?"

Nicolo seemed to appreciate the logic. He nodded. "I'm going to the old library at four o'clock."

Juliet leaned forward. "Me too."

He shook his head again. "I can identify Leary without you."

"But, you can't identify the paperwork he's going to sell."

"I don't need to identify anything. As soon as money passes hands, I'm on it."

"I'm still coming."

Nicolo checked his radio display, which read three o'clock. "You'll stay completely out of the way." He glanced at Paris. "Keep her out of the way."

*\ *\ *

Nicolo and Paris decided to change cars, knowing a police car would throw Mr. Leary off and ruin the deal. They all piled into the Jaguar and drove past the Army-Navy store on the outskirts of town.

Nicolo said, "Pull over here. I need to change my shirt."

"Stay in the car," Paris told Juliet. "I'm going with him."

Bromances.

Her nerves had switched into high gear. What if there was no deal in the making? What if Leary was entirely on the up and up, and there was no spying going on? Nicolo would never trust her again, that's what would happen.

Nicolo came back to the car, wearing a camouflage jacket. He'd pulled his blond hair back into a small knot at the back of his head.

Paris had pulled on a green jacket too and held a hunting hat in his hand. He tossed it to Juliet and then fell into the driver's seat.

She held the hat in her hand and frowned at it. "Someone is going to think we're terrorists. They're going to call Homeland Security."

"We don't look like terrorists," Nicolo told her, pulling on his seatbelt.

"Who picked this out?" she wanted to know, holding it up.

"Not your color?" Paris asked, watching her from the rearview. "Stuff that mass of hair under there."

They'd come so far since he'd said she had enough ringlets for five princesses. She shook her head and stuffed her hair under the hat.

*\ *\ *

Paris pulled the Jaguar into the library's parking lot and parked in the farthest spot away from the door. Not that it helped much. The library was a dinky building.

"Okay, this isn't going to be too easy to stay out of sight," Nicolo said. "You two stay in the car."

Juliet's grimaced. "I don't want…"

"Stay in the car," he barked.

"Go to the romance section," she called after him and then asked Paris, "Do you think he heard me?"

Paris raised a shoulder and stared out the windshield.

Juliet got out of the car.

Paris opened his door. "What are you doing?"

"Moving to the front seat."

He sat again and shut the door.

She climbed into the front. "I want to go inside."

"Why?"

"Because Nicolo doesn't know what to listen for. What if the money is transferred to Leary electronically? Maybe he's just handing over a piece of paper."

"How will you know anything?"

"Because I know what's been said up until now."

He shook his head, "Juliet. You're reckless. And you don't trust anyone."

"I have good reasons."

"No you don't."

She glanced at him. He'd meant himself, and she knew it. But she didn't want to have that conversation right then; she wanted to watch for Leary.

And there he was, getting out of a silver-blue car. A big one.

"Be patient, for the world is broad and wide."

Chapter 19

"I guess Leary's not the one who tried to run me off the road," Juliet said. "Unless he has another car."

"What?"

"The car that tried to run me off the road on Sunday was a big black car."

"So, Leary's not the killer."

"Unless…"

"Right. He could have a second car."

Juliet slunk down in the seat. Even with the hat on, she feared Leary would see her.

Paris kept his eyes steady on Leary until he was in the building. "Okay, he's in."

Juliet straightened and pulled on the door handle. "Come with me. I'll follow you in and hide behind your bulk."

He frowned at her. "My bulk?"

"Your bigness. It's a compliment."

He gazed out the windshield and shook his head. "Being around you does nothing for my ego."

Out of the car, Juliet followed Paris up the five steps to the double doors.

"Where to?" Paris whispered over his shoulders.

"Romance section."

Paris' shoulders caved. "Well, where is that?"

"Let's ask," she said and stayed behind his big beige coat.

The room smelled like old carpet and Pumpkin Air Wick. Paris approached the half-circle desk that gleamed in the recessed lighting above it. The woman behind the counter was dressed similarly to Juliet in a black turtleneck and skirt. She was a bottle blonde, however, and somewhere in her fifties.

"That's so funny that you ask. You must be the third or fourth man to ask for the romance section."

"There's a contest coming up," Paris lied. "Men only."

"Oh," she said, bobbing her head. "That makes sense." She pointed ahead of her and said, "Up the stairs. On your right."

Juliet poked her head around Paris' shoulder. "Is there a back stairway?"

The woman jumped back, startled at the sight of Juliet.

Paris pushed Juliet's head back again. "Sorry. Thank you."

Juliet straightened the hat. "You messed up my hair."

"The poor dear about had a heart attack." Paris stopped

at the bottom of the steps. "I'll go first, check it out, and call you upstairs."

Juliet bit her bottom lip and waited. Paris was right, of course, but Juliet felt exposed. What if someone came in that she knew?

Probably not in West Portland.

"Psst."

Juliet glanced at Paris with her foot on the first step.

Paris waved her forward.

She joined him and then stood behind him again. "Do you see Nicolo?"

"Yes." He nodded to the right.

Paris led the way and then slipped down one of the aisles. The knitting books aisle. He leaned in and then nodded to the opposite side.

Juliet peeked out.

There was Mr. Leary, hands in his black pants and wearing a white button-down and a beige sweater.

Juliet pivoted to stand behind Paris.

Suddenly, a knitting book moved on the shelf in front of her.

Staring out from the other side of the bookshelf was Nicolo. His blue eyes were bluer because of the purple book covers next to his face. He whispered, "I told you to stay in the car. Don't blow this, Juliet."

"How am I going to blow it?"

"By saying anything at all. You're Leary's secretary. He knows your voice."

Paris said out of the corner of his mouth, "He's staring over here now, if anyone's interested."

Juliet clamped her mouth shut.

Nicolo replaced the book.

And then he came around the end of the aisle and stood on the other side of Juliet.

It was so lovely the way Paris blocked them, him and his big green coat. He turned a page on a knitting book he admired. He said, "Someone just passed the aisle and went to stand on the other side of Leary."

Nicolo slipped back into the next aisle.

Heart beating out of her chest, Juliet peeked around Paris' jacket again. She'd been right. It was happening!

She couldn't see who was on the other side of Leary. It was a woman, though, dressed in puffy white jacket...

Juliet's heart stopped beating altogether.

Mr. Leary held out an envelope and handed it to Delia.

And then Nicolo slipped up behind them. "What's going on here?"

Delia backed away. "What do you mean?"

Leary said, "What are you doing here, Detective?"

Juliet's entire body shook. Leary was meeting Delia at the library? Why? And what was in the envelope?

"May I see that?" Nicolo asked, holding out his hand.

Delia's face paled. "I can explain." Her eyes glistened.

Juliet stepped around Paris and into the aisle. Delia saw her. "Juliet?"

Nicolo held up the piece of paper. It was a typewritten note, it looked as though it'd been crumpled at one time, but straightened out and folded.

Geoff Leary's face went purple. "What is going on here?"

Nicolo brought his brows together. "That's what I'd like to know. Maybe we should head down to the station, and you can explain this."

Leary's eye fell on Juliet. "This is your fault, isn't it?

You've been snooping around behind my back. I knew it."

"Let's go," Nicolo said, glancing at Juliet too. "You too."

* * *

Nicolo drove Mr. Leary's car to the Chautauqua County Sheriff's Office back in Mayville. The building took up half a block on Chautauqua Street.

Paris and Juliet followed in the Jaguar, and once they were all inside the old building, Nicolo pointed toward a room with a table and four chairs.

Paris waited in the large reception area with four or five other people who seemed to be waiting to speak to the desk sergeant.

Nicolo sat beside Juliet, facing the Learys. He pulled the paper from the envelope again and asked, "Where did this come from?"

Mr. Leary took a big breath and said, "D'Angelo's office. I'd been looking in his office, trying to find something, anything on his receptionist, Beth Holley. The woman has been threatening my daughter."

Juliet fell back in her chair. "What?"

Leary's jiggly face turned toward her. "That's right. Ms. Holley is a sick woman. When Delia and D'Angelo started seeing each other, then Beth stalked Delia."

"She stalked you?" Juliet asked. "Delia, I had no idea."

"Why should you?" she asked, with a half-laugh. "Beth is so odd. And Dad, Mr. D'Angelo and I weren't dating." She set her eyes on Nicolo. "Detective, Sebastian and I had lunch together one time. Beth was watching me and hanging out near my apartment." She shrugged. "We live in the same building, but suddenly she was there when I opened my door in the morning. She watched me from my fire escape."

Leary leaned in. "Delia thinks she's a detective herself. As soon as D'Angelo died, Delia thought Beth killed him and asked me to find something in the office to prove Beth was up to something." He pointed to the paper. "Well, I found this in Beth's drawer. Beth was stalking D'Angelo, too."

Juliet tapped the letter. "This is the same as the letter in D'Angelo's house."

Nicolo sat, picked up the paper. "Okay, okay. Has anyone seen Beth recently?" He gazed at Delia. "Has she been back to the apartment house since D'Angelo's death?"

Delia shook her head. "I haven't seen her. My neighbors and I are all pretty close. We're friends. Everyone's been watching for her."

Juliet asked, "Does she own the black Honda with the peeling paint?"

"Yes, that's her car. She's left it in the parking lot at the apartment." She asked Nicolo, "Would you like to see her car? I can lead you to the apartment building."

Nicolo stood.

Everyone else got to their feet too.

"Okay," he agreed. "Let's run past the wine offices for my cruiser. Then we'll head to your house."

He turned to Juliet. "Go home." Not waiting for an answer, he stepped into the reception area.

Juliet faced Delia. "I'm sorry."

"You're sorry?" Mr. Leary asked. "You've spied on me, got it all wrong, and you're *sorry*? What were you going to do, have me arrested?"

"No," she said, shaking her head. "I didn't know exactly what was going on."

He drew himself up with a satisfied look on his face. "You're fired, Miss Da Vinci."

Juliet gasped. "You can't fire me."

"Yes I can. And I'll make sure your father knows why." He stormed from the office to join Nicolo in the reception area.

Yep, I'm fired.

She smiled at Delia. It wasn't a genuine smile, more of a smile-grimace thing with a lot of guilt stuffed into it. "I'm sorry, Delia."

Delia nodded. "It's okay, Juliet. I understand."

"Will you please still work for us at the bakery?"

Delia blinked a couple of times. Red splotches highlighted her cheeks. "Oh, um, I don't know Juliet. Let me think all of this through okay?"

* * *

Paris drove Juliet back to the office parking lot to collect her car. She drove home slowly, not relishing the idea of facing her father.

She didn't make it into the house. Her father was in the garage when she pulled into the spot.

Juliet shut off the engine and got out of the car. "*Papà?*"

He was dressed in an old shirt and jeans. It seemed he'd been polishing the side of the Alfa Romeo he'd been restoring for the past nine months. His hair was messier than usual. Messier because he'd grown it out longer for the winter. He held up the cloth. "You're fired."

"I know." She shut the car door and leaned against it.

"What'd you mean you know?" he asked, waving his hand. "I just fired you. I'm lucky Geoff didn't leave the company. He threated to quit; did you know that?"

"No," she said, putting her purse on the counter. "He doesn't have to quit. I'm out. I'm not going back."

"Because I fired you, *capiche*? Here's what you're going to do, you're going to stay home forever."

"Okay."

"Okay? Okay? You will because I said so."

* * *

Compared to the usual Da Vinci gathering, Thanksgiving day was a smaller and more casual affair eaten at the kitchen island and dinette table. Tribly served pumpkin soup, spinach and prosciutto stuffed turkey breast, fennel in bechamel sauce, and chocolate chestnut cake. The older Da Vincis sat at the small table, which left Juliet to dine with Paris and Ty.

Pressing her feet against the stool's foot bar, she arched across the counter for a plate of cake.

Ty smacked her hand. "No cake for you." He'd sulked all day.

Juliet thought those were his actual first words to her that day. She might've been okay with it if he hadn't smacked her hand. With her fork raised in protest, she asked, "Why not?"

Ty leaned toward her smelling of no-shower-since-Tuesday. He glanced at the dinette area, and then hissed, "Because you are a sucky, suck-suck cousin."

She didn't react, didn't give him the satisfaction. "Three sucks?"

He lifted his heavy eyebrows. "You suck to the third degree."

"I know, but why do you think so?"

"Because you've ruined my chances with the only girl I will ever love."

"Try not to die, Dramatron. And, you don't know Delia well enough for that sort of devotion. *Dios Mio*, she's at least ten years older than you. Get your life together."

"Me? My life together?" He stabbed the turkey on his plate. The tines of his fork hit the plate, causing them to scrape like fingernails on a chalkboard. Ty didn't lose a beat. "You who go around destroying other people's lives because you're poking your nose where it doesn't belong, that sort of getting my life together?" His voice had gone up on the last words.

Everyone at the dinette table stopped, their forks mid-air, and stared across the kitchen.

Juliet smiled at her father.

He lowered his gray brows and narrowed his eyes.

It was a tough crowd tonight. Even Paris hadn't sat next to Juliet. He was on the other side of Ty, chewing his food like he needed to kill it first.

Someone knocked on the back door.

Everyone turned around, but no one got up.

It didn't matter because Roseline pushed open the door and presented herself, arms wide, as though she meant to twirl. She wore a red sweater dress and red boots with fur.

Dr. Dexter followed her in. "Happy Thanksgiving," he said. "Oh, we've come at dinner time. Sorry. We were on our way to dinner ourselves."

"There's plenty here," Italia said, coming off her chair. "Come and sit. We'll bring in another chair."

"Oh no," Roseline said. "We didn't stop by to beg food."

"*Basta*," Tribly said. "You don't think my food is good enough for you? Sit, sit." She got up, too, and pulled plates from the cabinet. "I said, sit. My food will come to you and you will enjoy it. You want turkey? You want the fennel?"

Dexter smacked Paris on the arm. "Been relegated to the children's table, have you?"

Paris turned his eyes toward Ty and Juliet. "It certainly feels that way. Say, I was just about to text you. I'm putting in an offer on your house on Monday."

Juliet's heart nearly stopped.

Dexter threw out his arms. "That's fantastic news." He still wore his overcoat. A polka dot tie showed itself.

Italia was back in the kitchen and dragging a dining room chair behind her. She stared at Santos. "Your highness, will you get another chair for the doctor?"

Juliet's father threw his napkin on his plate and stood.

Dexter waved his hand. "No need, no need, I will pull one in."

"Take off your coat, Doctor," Italia instructed. "My husband is getting the chair." She stared at Santos. "Because I'm his wife and said so."

Her father rolled his eyes and marched out of the room.

"Isn't this fantastic, darling?" Dexter said and then glanced around the room. "Hello, Juliet."

She nodded and smiled.

"Everything all right?" he asked.

"Stop teasing her," Roseline said, pulling his arm to her. She stopped next to Juliet. "We've heard all about what happened on Tuesday."

Juliet winced. How could Roseline possibly know what happened between Leary and her father and Delia and …? She turned in her seat.

Tybalt!

He pursed his lips and turned up his nose.

"It's all right, Juliet," Roseline said. "I'm glad you got fired. Now you can concentrate on our big day. It's wedding dress shopping time."

Could her life get worse?

"Oh no," Italia said. "This weekend is Juliet's ski trip."

It just got worse!

"I never said I was going, *Matri*."

"I'm your *Matri,* and I said so. I've sent the flight itinerary to your email. You leave tomorrow morning at eleven thirty-eight."

"*Matri*, I don't want to go."

Her mother stood beside her chair. "Juliet," she said softly. "You are going. You need a break from all of this. Go skiing."

Juliet opened her mouth, but nothing came out.

Roseline said, "No, no, no. I have an appointment at Kleinfeld's."

Italia spun on her. "What day?" She'd used her curt voice.

Juliet sat up straighter. She hadn't heard her mother use that tone since Juliet was about sixteen years old.

Roseline's face turned red. "On- on Sunday." She pointed at Juliet. "She promised to go with me. She's my maid of honor."

"She'll be done with her ski trip on Sunday. She'll meet you at Kleinfeld's."

And no one dared to say anything more about it.

Ty left the counter and went to sit with the rest of the family at the small table.

Juliet scooted over one chair and gazed at Paris. "Yay, bridal dress shopping."

He shrugged without looking at her.

"You're buying Dexter's house?"

He gave her his full attention. Twisting in his seat, he placed his elbow on the counter. "I am."

"The house is too big, Paris."

"I've seen fifteen other houses, and all of them are the same size. I want a big house."

She leaned away from him. "Fifteen?"

"And you've seen three of them."

She felt the reprimand all the way to her toes. "But Dexter's is farthest out."

"What does that matter?"

She didn't have an answer, other than it was too far away. This was what she knew would happen. Paris would move away, just like he did before. He swore he loved her, but he didn't. Heart in her throat, she answered his question. She let out a long breath. "It doesn't."

He leaned in. Paris smelled like a citrus tree with flowers of vanilla. "That's all you have to say to me?" His eyes were green fire.

What did it matter? He was like everyone else. "That's all I have to say." She got off the stool and left the room.

* * *

In the end, Juliet decided to go to New York. There wasn't one person at home who was happy with her.

Matri wasn't mad but she was, in a way, worse than the

others. Italia was concerned about Juliet, as though she was mentally disturbed or something.

Staring out the window of the plane, Juliet watched the landscape change from brown and orange and red to white along with the mountain ranges.

I don't have to ski. I can hole up in the lodge and stay under the covers all weekend.

She'd tell Olive and Emma she was sick.

I am sick.

She hadn't helped Anthony, she didn't figure out who killed Gemma or Mr. D'Angelo either. Nicolo thought she was an idiot. Delia thought the same. Leary... *Ugh*, smarmy Leary. But Leary hadn't been in the wrong, had he? Juliet just didn't like him, and now that was out in the open.

Papà fired me!

And Paris...

His disappointment and anger bothered Juliet the most. The only friend she had in the world disregarded her advice, thought poorly of her, and was rethinking his friendship with her.

I'll be self-dating from now on. Table for one, drinks for five, please.

* * *

Once off the plane and through the gate at Lake Placid Airport, Juliet found Olive and Emma in the luncheonette. They rented a car and arrived at the Vienna Resort a half-hour later.

It was exclusive, and the luxury accommodation was a private chalet four minutes away from the ski lift.

A fire was already lit in the hearth by the time the

porter dragged their luggage inside.

Juliet picked an upstairs bedroom with three sets of french doors that overlooked a magical forest of pine and snowdrifts. The sauna was housed on her patio, along with a covered bar and seating area.

She wandered back into the living room area and fell into a soft couch and stared at the fire.

Olive was already sitting in the big chair. Her auburn hair was cut knife sharp at her cheekbones. She was already in ski gear, puffy blue pants, and an unzipped jacket. She wore sneakers, though, and a ribbed tank top beneath the jacket.

"I don't want to ski," Juliet confessed. "I'd much rather stay in this weekend."

"Your mother said you'd say that."

Juliet wrinkled her nose. "Oh, did she?"

"Yes. But we're dragging you out, Juliet. You're not allowed to stay in. I promised Italia."

Emma handed Juliet a glass of wine and sat beside her. "What's going on with you, Juliet?"

"Oh, nothing," she lied, but then everything tumbled out of her. "I'm just completely screwed up. I've lost all of my friends. Nicolo's angry, Paris is angry, my father…" She shook her head. "Abram Fontana won't text me. Patsy and Tricia … I got the wrong guy in a murder investigation."

Olive held up her hand. "Whoa. Abram Fontana?"

"I actually kind of like the guy," Juliet confessed.

"I don't want you to be sorry," Emma said, leaning forward. "Last time, when your father was arrested, you turned away from us." There was a sad note to her voice, as though she'd really been hurt for some reason.

Juliet wrinkled her nose. "No, everyone turned on me."

"No. Your shallow friends did," Olive said, standing up. "We were in the Caribbean if you'll recall. We weren't home for the events. But when we came back and reached out to you, you'd cut everybody out."

Wait, what?

"You lumped us all into one category and avoided all of us," Emma told her. She'd dyed her hair pink since Juliet last saw her. It was in a spikier cut too.

Olive said. "And you never told us about your crush on Nicolo Montague. That makes me angry with you to tell you the truth."

Juliet blinked at the girl. "But, he was my family's sworn enemy."

Emma said, "We never cared about that, Juliet. We love *you*. Your family is nice and all, but we wouldn't have taken their sides in the matter. If you loved Montague, we would've helped you elope."

She sat up a little straighter. "Oh."

"Oh?" Olive sounded much angrier. "You've pushed us away, and all you can say is, *oh*?"

"Umm."

Emma took her hand. "I am so sorry I wasn't with you over the summer to face everything that you faced. But I'm here now, and I'd like you to tell me what is happening."

A lump formed in Juliet's throat, blocking her airway. She tried for a big gulp of breath but squeaked instead.

Emma narrowed her eyes. "Come on, out with it."

And so she told them everything, beginning at the Harvest Ball all the way to traveling to upstate New York to be with them.

"So, you did it again?" Emma asked.

Juliet winced. "Did what?"

"You're such a jerk," Olive said, taking a poker from the tools beside the fireplace. She poked a log with gusto. "And you are a lousy friend. There are so many people around you willing to help you and you shun us all. You do what you want, put yourself in danger, and almost get yourself killed." She put the poker away and faced Juliet. "Do you know what it would do to us, to your friends Paris and Nicolo, if you died? What if this killer got to you and knifed you too? How do you think your mom and dad and Tribly would get through that?"

Juliet was dumbstruck. She stared open-mouthed at Olive.

The girl pointed at her, "You're a bad friend."

"Me?"

Emma touched her hand. "Do you think you've been a good friend?"

They were right, weren't they, and Juliet felt it all the way to her bones. She was, she was the jerk. She'd been the one sneaking around, leaving people out of her life, not forgiving people …

Her throat hurt so badly that she couldn't swallow.

You've got to be a friend to make a friend.

"What do I do?"

Emma glared at her, hands on her hips. "First, you can say you're sorry."

"I am sorry," she said in a small voice–because she felt the weight of the guilt pressing on her shoulders and pushing her into the couch. Her eyes burned. "Please forgive me."

Emma reached her first and wrapped her arms tightly around Juliet's neck. "It's okay. We're back together now and better than ever."

Juliet hugged her back, hard. As soon as Emma released her, Juliet got off the couch and reached for Olive. "I'm sorry."

Olive grabbed her even harder than Emma.

* * *

After dinner at the lodge, Juliet sat in her room and watched the snowfall outside the tall windows. She'd brought along thicker pajamas, the striped ones with a matching robe. Taking her phone from the bedside table, Juliet phoned Paris. She'd neglected him and expected his support when she hadn't involved him in her troubles–even though he'd asked her to—been angry with him because he didn't break into a house with her.

He picked up on the first ring.

Because he's my very best friend!

All he got out was "Juliet?"

"Paris, I'm so sorry for the way I've acted. I've been a terrible friend to you. I should've never asked you to break into D'Angelo's house with me or gotten mad at you for calling the police. I should've involved you more in what I was doing."

"Whoa, whoa, whoa," he said. "What's going on? Are you okay?"

"No, I'm horrible. Wretched. Say you forgive me."

"Juliet, I've never been that mad at you. Well, a little."

"Yes you were, you yelled at me."

He started to say something.

She cut him off. "And, you should have. I deserved it. I deserved more. Yell at me now."

"No."

"You're my best friend."

He made a choking sound and then said in a pleasant voice, "Oh. Yay."

"Mega best friend," she told him, grinning to herself.

"Even better, yeah?"

"I'll help you move. I'll carry the couch."

Off the phone with Paris, she scrolled through her contacts and found Abram's number and sent him a *Shen Yun* meme, knowing that would get him texting again.

* * *

The next morning, Juliet went skiing with Emma and Olive. The sun was high and the temperature had reached the thirties. All the new-fallen snow hung onto the branches and glistened like diamonds.

She'd already taken the same downhill course once that morning, but she wasn't familiar enough with the trail to know that the marker had been moved. Juliet only knew that suddenly there were more trees than she remembered, and the trail itself had disappeared.

She skidded to a stop and glanced around in the dead, dead sound of nothing.

"Come, gentle night; come, loving, black-browed night."

Chapter 20

She glanced up the hill again. She'd come quite a way down. Obviously, she'd made a wrong turn.

Turning, she gazed ahead. There was nothing but more trees and snow.

Juliet didn't want to ski forward. Something inside told her not to go ahead.

Instead, she side-marched up the slope as quickly as she was able, digging in her ski poles and dragging herself upward.

At the top of the hill, Juliet glanced downward again.

Something moved.

She stared harder.

Nothing was there.

She waited.

There! Someone in a white snowsuit moved among the trees.

***

She made it back to the lodge and waited inside for Emma and Olive. She sat staring out the windows, watching every person who came down the hill in a white snowsuit.

Sure, the person in the trees could've been anyone. They'd skied off in a different direction and hadn't followed her up the hill to pull a knife on her.

Juliet rubbed her cheeks with both hands. No one at the lodge knew who she was, not enough to trick her into coming down a wrong hill.

No one knows me here…

Juliet gazed around the room, at the guests buying food at the restaurant and purchasing ski passes.

The police hadn't caught Beth, as far as Juliet knew anyway. Had the woman stalked her to the lodge?

Or, had someone tortured her mother and father and found out where she was…

Get a grip!

Regardless of whether she got a grip or not, Juliet dialed her mother's number.

"Juliet?" Italia asked, answering on the third ring.

"*Matri,*" she said, relief flooding her body. "Everything fine there?"

"Of course. How's the ski trip?"

"Good. I'm – I'm happy I came. I have a funny question. Did you tell anyone I came here?"

"No," her mother answered, sounding distracted. "But

your friend stopped by, Geoff Leary's daughter."

Juliet smiled. "Really, Delia came by? What did she say?"

"Nothing much. The girl was surprised you'd gone skiing for some reason. Ty came downstairs and they went off somewhere together."

"Okay, thanks. And thanks for sending me on this trip. You're right. I need to be a friend to have friends."

"Oh? Who said that?"

"You said it!"

"Because I'm the clever one in the family."

* * *

It was nine o'clock in the evening and Juliet was in the great room, in front of the fire, texting Paris.

Emma and Olive were in the big kitchen, making pizza.

Paris texted back: Who moved the course marker?

I don't know for sure that someone did. I'm just telling you it happened because I want you to be involved in my life Mega Best Friend.

She'd grinned when she sent it, knowing he'd enjoy the drama of it.

Her phone rang. Juliet hit the green button. "Hello, Mega Bestie."

"What do you mean, someone moved the marker?"

She sat straighter. "I don't know that someone did, Paris. I got back up the hill before I saw someone."

"What?"

"Calm down, Scooby. I'm fine. I shouldn't have told you." She swirled the wine in her glass. "Wait. I'm glad I told you, but you've got to start taking blood pressure pills."

"Who was down the slope?" he asked, his voice sharp.

She shrugged as though he could see her. "It could've been anybody, Paris. There are trails all over the place."

"All right, all right," he said. "But if something else like that happens …"

"Like what, I take the wrong trail again?"

"Don't do that anymore. When are you coming back?"

"Tomorrow evening sometime. I've got to go dress shopping with Roseline."

* * *

It was after two in the morning, and Emma and Olive had piled onto Juliet's bed and caught up on each other's news.

They fell asleep there, after three o'clock.

A scream woke Juliet. It sounded as if someone had electrocuted a coyote.

Juliet was out of the bed in a heartbeat.

But, nothing was wrong. The light was on.

Emma slapped her sister's arm. "Why did you scream?"

Olive's voice trembled. "There was someone at the window. I swear there was."

Juliet glanced at the window and french doors. They were on the second floor. If there'd been someone out there, they'd been on the balcony.

This is not good.

Emma lay back on the bed again. She was in silky white trousers and a cami. "You dreamed about it. You ate too many slices of pizza."

"No, I was awake. I just went to the bathroom and laid down again."

Juliet slid along the wall until she stood next to the

window. Carefully, she reached out and touched the lock above the window. "It's secure." She pulled the drapes closed and then ran back to the bed. "You did lock the front door, didn't you?"

"Umm," the girl said, her pink spike looking redder in the low lights of the room. "I don't remember."

"Okay," Juliet said, getting out of bed again.

Neither of the other girls moved.

"I'm not going by myself, ladies," she told them, her nerves in a mild panic.

Forming a line, they held onto each other and navigated the stairs. There was a glow coming from the fireplace. The log hadn't burnt out yet.

"There's the door," Emma whispered as if the other two didn't recognize it.

Olive made a *tsk* noise. "Good one."

"If you're so brave, then you go first," Emma told her.

"Juliet is our leader. She always has been. Go on, Juliet. Go check the door."

She made a face. "Oh, yes. I'll run right over and do *that*."

"Come on, let's keep moving," Emma told her. "I need to go to the bathroom too."

Juliet led the procession down the steps, her toes feeling for each level, thinking she might fall if the human train behind her skipped the track and lost their minds. She strained her eyes to see the door.

The top lock had been turned and set.

She relaxed, ready to turn around again.

Something hit the door hard, hard enough to make the door vibrate.

Juliet jumped.

Emma hit her from behind.

Juliet slid the last three carpeted steps to the floor.

Olive screamed, "Someone's out there. I told you, someone's out there."

"Call the police," Emma said. "Where's the phone? Where's the phone?"

Juliet dashed back to the bedroom.

Olive and Emma ran behind her.

Then they all hurried back downstairs together. Olive went to the kitchen and grabbed several knives. "Here, take these." She held them out like playing cards.

"I don't want a knife!" Emma told her, holding up her palms.

Juliet held her finger to her ear, waiting for the police dispatch to answer.

Instead of the knife, Emma snatched the iron poker from the toolset at the fireplace. She held it on her shoulder like a baseball bat. "Somebody open the door. Open it! I'm ready to engage."

"Everyone stay calm," Juliet screamed. "If anyone is going to freak out, it'll be me." Then, "Hello 9-1-1?" she asked in her calmest voice.

* * *

Three police cars arrived within minutes. Lights flashed through the trees, through the windows, everywhere.

Juliet and her friends stayed in the house until the officers came back to the front door.

"Come in," Emma said, stepping out of the way, holding the door.

A cold whoosh of air blew through the foyer and all

around the front room. The dying log got a fresh wind and actually lit again.

The first officer, a woman, said, "Someone was out here. But whoever it was is gone now. We checked the entire area."

Juliet stepped forward. "Did you see footprints?"

"Yes," one of the other officers said. He was as big as a football player.

Juliet considered asking him to stay for their entire vacation.

He said, "They were snowshoe prints, so it was hard to tell much about them."

The female officer, Brandt, her name badge read, nodded. "The shoes sank down in the snow pretty far, so the person was heavy.

"Weight challenged?" Olive asked. "We got someone weight challenged outside?"

"Um," Brandt started. "A man or a heavy woman, perhaps."

Olive nodded. "Okay, they were on the balcony upstairs. I screamed, and they ran. Maybe you can see prints up there?"

"We checked," the football player told her. "They were scuffs only."

The police officer nodded. "What would you ladies like to do? We can give you a lift back to the lodge."

Juliet shrugged, glancing at her friends. "Maybe we should go?"

"No," Olive said. She asked Officer Brandt. "The person's gone now, right?"

"Yes, and we'll do a drive-by if you like."

Juliet was torn. She wanted to go home, but she didn't want to leave Olive and Emma here by themselves. Perhaps they needed to hear about the car chase again. "You need to know…"

"We'll leave early tomorrow. We won't stay another night," Olive told her. "It's already four-thirty. If we sleep for a couple of hours, we can ski once more and then go."

* * *

Juliet didn't sleep. She kept her eyes on the french doors while Emma and Olive slept. Every noise caused her to sit up and study the stairway and wait for another sound.

And she texted Paris.

I'm coming to you, he texted in return.

We're leaving early. The sun will be up soon. I'll stay in the lodge, and then I'll meet Roseline at Kleinfeld's.

It took a few moments for him to text back. I booked a flight. I'll meet you at the lodge. The plane gets in at ten after ten at Lake Placid.

Paris!

Going to take a shower and get out of the house. Stay close to your phone.

* * *

They were out of the chalet and in the lodge by seven o'clock.

After breakfast, Olive and Emma decided to take a couple more runs on the slopes since Juliet wanted to wait for Paris to arrive.

Juliet remained in the dining hall in her sherbet-colored ski suit. She crossed her legs and stared out at the snow. The window created a mirror, and Juliet could see behind her as well as out to the mountains. She really wasn't looking behind her at first. No, she was looking at the slope nearest her, trying to see Olive's metallic ski jacket. It should be visible from a mile away. It shined like the sun.

Then her eyes shifted toward the mirror image in the glass.

Beth?

Juliet jerked around hard.

A woman with golden hair moved toward the exit of the lodge and then stepped outside.

Juliet got to her feet and rushed across the room.

"How will you pay for your breakfast Miss Da Vinci?" the maître d' asked. "On my tab," she said, still rushing.

"You've closed out your account," he reminded her. He was the same height as Juliet, but round as a butterball.

Juliet snapped her purse open and handed him a credit card. "Hurry, please."

She waited by the windows, trying to see where Beth disappeared to–if it was Beth. Juliet had only seen the woman's reflection in the window.

There, in the yellow jacket!

The woman turned and looked at the lodge, maybe to see if someone followed her.

Juliet stood on tiptoes. She still wasn't sure if it was Beth. The woman was too far away. Then she stepped inside the Cigar Shop.

Moving toward the edge of the dining room, Juliet decided to come back later for her card.

But the maître d' was there, holding her up again, and wanting her to sign a receipt.

Finally, Juliet raced onto the sidewalk outside the lodge.

There were cars in the valet parking line, two young men unloading suitcases, and a bellman pointing and issuing orders.

Juliet stepped into the Cigar Shop and glanced around the small store. The woman who looked like Beth was not in the shop.

Juliet walked around the building and then stepped onto the boardwalk sidewalk, where a line of shops lured winter visitors with specialty foods and clothing. Cobblestone walkways led to a wine market.

She entered one store and then another.

When she came out onto the sidewalk again, she gazed at the fountain where several people stood speaking to each other.

All at once, the hair on Juliet's neck rose up. She could feel it, someone watching her.

Her eyes scanned the parking lot and the shops again.

No sign of Beth. No one seemed to watch her.

Back in the lodge, Juliet went into the common area where a fireplace the size of a house blazed with a bonfire. She sat by the front doors and surveyed the cars, and people coming in and out of the lodge.

A black sedan pulled up next in line in the valet line. The only reason Juliet noticed it at all was the front bumper was dented in several places.

Swallowing hard, Juliet got to her feet.

Two valets stepped forward to open the driver and passenger doors.

A redhead popped out of the passenger side first.

Juliet stopped breathing. She couldn't blink.

The other valet stepped out of the way for David Dexter to get out of the car.

"And smilest upon the stroke that murders me."

Chapter 21

Dexter was dressed in a black suit. He buttoned the jacket as he walked around the front of the car to meet Roseline on the other side of the vehicle. He held her arm, and they stepped toward the shops together.

Juliet stepped outside again. Her breathing was so fast that she couldn't catch it. She wanted to see the fender of the car. Was it …?

She was so nervous she almost fell. A fire went through her ankle, and she leaned against one of the rock pillars that held up the covered valet drop off.

One of the young men plopped into the driver's seat

and pulled the sedan forward.

Juliet waited, leaning forward.

The car came closer.

There were three dent marks on the front bumper …

Then Juliet saw it. Red paint marred the very edge of the right side of the chrome.

Her stomach twisted, and she breathed hard again. Reaching for her phone, Juliet pushed the icon next to Paris' name. While his line rang, she crossed the cobblestones toward the shops along the boardwalk.

Snow sat on top of the short bushes outside each shop. Twinkle lights danced atop the snow.

Paris' phone went to voice mail. Was he still on the plane?

Walking on her boot tiptoes to see inside the shop windows, Juliet left a message, "Paris, it's me. I'm following Dr. Dexter and Roseline into the shops. They arrived here for some reason. I was supposed to meet Roseline for a dress appointment at four, but they're here … Paris, it was Dexter's car that pushed me off the road last Sunday."

The message limit beeped in her ear, and Juliet ended the call. Stuffing the phone into her jacket, she hurried to the next shop.

There!

Dexter's long-faced profile leaned toward Roseline's upturned face. He smiled and said something to her.

Juliet slipped inside the gift store. Twinkle lights draped across the cash register and the display window. She pretended to look at designer purses and then moved around a display toward the sweatshirt wall.

Roseline turned toward her.

Juliet ducked behind a spinning shirt rack and then

crept around the other side of it.

Roseline said. "Every time I call her, it just goes to voice mail."

Who was she talking about? Juliet?

Dexter said, "Well, she is on vacation, dear. She's probably skiing."

"I don't think I should've picked her as my maid of honor. She's never available. When we were kids, she begged to be a part of my wedding."

Juliet made a face–she couldn't help herself. Roseline made stuff up all the time.

"Well, we're here now, and we can all drive together to Kleinfeld's."

"You can't see me in my wedding dress, David."

"I don't want to see you *in* your wedding dress," he told her in a sultry tone.

Gross.

"How will we know where to find her if she won't answer her phone?"

They stopped talking for a moment.

Juliet scooted forward and took a peek around the display.

There was Roseline, her long red hair falling over her left shoulder as she held her cellphone to her right ear.

Juliet's phone rang in her ski jacket.

She fell back into the display. *Shut up, shut up, shut up…*

"That's funny that a phone would start ringing in here," Roseline said. "Maybe she's here."

Juliet stopped breathing and remained still beneath the hanging shirts.

Her phone went silent.

"See, right to voicemail," Roseline said. "I am going to

O' Happy Dagger

pick another maid of honor. Juliet will be lucky to be in the wedding party at all."

It was silent again.

Juliet breathed again, in gasps. She covered her mouth with both hands and held completely still. She was hyperventilating.

She uncovered her mouth and slipped forward.

They were gone.

She got to her knees and then stood. Still stooping though, she peeked over the shirt rack.

Roseline was outside.

Dexter had just stepped outside–and turned around.

His eyes locked onto Juliet's.

Juliet fell to her knees and crawled away from the shirt rack as fast as she could. To her right was a pair of swinging doors and she charged through them like a slow cat on cobblestones.

Once inside the backroom of the shop, she got to her feet and ran. She hit the backdoor safety bar, spun around with the force of it, and fell on her butt into the alley.

There were more shops out this way with awnings and twinkle lights. A ski clothing shop was opposite her, and then a ski rental shop.

Her phone rang again.

Juliet got to her feet and pulled the phone out of her jacket, intending to turn off the ringer.

Paris' face appeared on the screen.

She hit the button and yelled, "I'M OUTSIDE! I'M RUNNING IN AN ALLEY. I DON'T KNOW EXACTLY WHERE I AM. PARIS! IT'S DEXTER. HE SAW ME."

Then she dropped her phone.

"Oh crap, I'm sorry, Paris." She found her phone and pushed it to her ear again. "Are you there?"

He wasn't. The phone screen had gone blank.

She pressed the on button.

Nothing.

Stupid cobblestones!

Juliet stuffed the phone back into her pocket, missed, tried again. Her hands shook like leaves in a blizzard.

Think! Juliet, come on.

She ran forward, went into the ski rental shop. She waited at the desk while the clerk waited on a couple in front of her. She watched the gift shop's back door. Would Dexter follow her?

Why would he run her off the road? Had he killed Gemma Hakim, Sebastian D'Angelo…? Why? He doesn't even know them, right?

"Can I help you?" the clerk asked. His name badge read Chris. He was only a few inches taller than Juliet. The hair on the sides of his head was blond and military short.

"How do I get back to the ski lodge from here?"

"Follow the road around the backside and then take the alley…"

"Thank you," she told him and rushed out of the shop.

Juliet had to get back to Olive and Emma. Dexter knew them now, didn't he? He'd seen them through the window last night. Dexter had been on their deck…

What if he grabbed them to get to her?

She ran faster, took the back street, and then cut up the alley, which brought her right back to the valet drop off. She glanced left, toward the shops, for Dexter and Roseline.

Strangers walked on the cobblestones.

O' Happy Dagger

Juliet went slowly through the doors of the lodge. Was Dexter already inside, waiting for her, ready to pop out at any second?

She went quickly to the hearth and sat on the stone seating. It was the best spot to see everything in the open room. The dining room was to her right, the reception desk to her left.

Juliet watched the window and the glass door area.

A tall figure came out of the alley and into the valet drop off area.

Dexter!

His eyes were on Juliet as he walked toward the doors. He didn't blink, kept his jaw in a hard line, his mouth downturned.

* * *

She should've screamed, caught people's attention …

Well, that was an excellent thought now that she was running across a vacant game room with a pool table and hot tub in it.

There was a door at the end of the room, one of those flimsy types with louvered fronts. She opened it.

It was a closet.

She glanced behind her. Had Dexter seen which way she ran? She'd turned a few corners.

A noise sounded on the other side of the room.

Juliet stepped into the small room and shut the door and locked it.

The small closet was walk-in size with shelves on either side of Juliet's head. Behind her were a janitor's bucket and mop – no other door.

She held her breath and listened.

Her body shook violently. She didn't know how long she could stay on her feet.

Something beeped.

She twirled slowly. What was beeping? There were no red lights, no electronics that she could see …

A fist slammed through the louvered door.

Juliet screamed and jumped backward, knocking the bucket and mop over.

A hand reached toward the knob and twisted it.

The door opened.

Dexter's big mouth turned upward. "Hi." He glanced to his left and right and then took a full step into the closet. He blocked the only exit.

Her heart nearly exploded. Juliet braced her forearms on the shelves just to stay on her feet. If he thought she was going down without a fight, he was crazy. She'd make it look like a fox and a wolf fighting in a mailbox.

His eyelids dropped halfway over his eyes. "You think you know something?"

"What are you talking about?" She moved her hand to the shelf, too, toward the bleach bottle.

"Sure you do, Juliet." He put his hand on the shelf next to hers, pinning her in place.

The beeping sound came again.

Juliet was hardly aware of it this time. Her breath came fast. She needed to stall for time. Someone would come into the recreation room, wouldn't they? A janitor would come for his mop.

If she screamed for help, Dexter would probably kill her quicker.

She said, "I'm confused. Do you know Beth?"

He lifted his face toward the ceiling and let out a laugh. "Oh, that's right. Your little investigation. You need to tie up loose ends, is that it?" He lowered his face again and stopped laughing. "Okay, I'll play. I don't know Beth."

"Remember, I told you about her. She worked for D'Angelo. She was in love with him."

"Psycho Beth, yes, I remember her now."

"Did you kill D'Angelo together?"

God, her chest hurt from the labor of breathing so hard.

He looked at Juliet sideways. "Hey, I don't know Beth *that* well to murder people with her."

She straightened a little, kept her hand steady on the shelf. "Why did you kill D'Angelo?"

"Because he asked too many questions."

"He asked you about Gemma Hakim?"

Dexter let out a noise, like a harrumph. "He thought I'd married her, as he'd married that stupid girl he got pregnant. Sebastian thought I'd asked Roseline to marry me when I was still married to Gemma." He straightened his features and lowered his face toward Juliet's. "You need to know Juliet; I would've never asked your cousin to marry me if I was married to Gemma."

As though that mattered. As if Dexter was such an upstanding guy.

"D'Angelo knew you?"

His eyes flicked over Juliet's body. "Yes, sure. We were all there together. D'Angelo, Anthony Yeager …" Dexter shook his head and smiled again. "Between you and me, I can't stand Yeager. He thinks he is so clever, doesn't he? Mr. Intel. Though I am grateful that he introduced me to Roseline." He leaned closer to Juliet.

She leaned away.

"They're going to electrocute him, you know?"

She narrowed her eyes. "You set Anthony up? You framed him?"

He stood a little straighter. "No, not really, but I'm not sorry he's getting charged with the murders. And with you out of the way, there's no one to tell anybody differently." He stuck his hand into his suit pocket and pulled something out.

Juliet stiffened. Was it a knife?

No, it was blue … blue surgical gloves.

Stall … stall … please, God, send someone to help me.

"How did you know Gemma?"

"I met her the same way D'Angelo met his wife. They knew each other, Jesenia and Gemma. Gemma had a baby." He dropped his hand from the shelf and shook the glove out. He fit it onto his hand.

"She had your baby?"

He frowned and shook his head. "Never determined. The kid died. She came here to the states about a month ago, wanted me to know about her son, wanted another kid like him." He let out a breath of a laugh. "As if we'd produce the same kid again or something. She was crazy." Dexter eyed Juliet while shaking out the last glove. "You can't replace a kid, Juliet."

The endless beeping, what was it?

She asked, "Did the two of you try to…?"

"Sure, we tried, but Gemma kept wanting, again and again, wouldn't leave me alone. I'd met Roseline and Gemma wouldn't leave me alone."

"Gemma lived with you."

He shrugged. "I let her stay."

O' Happy Dagger

It came to Juliet clearly. *Nonna* would be proud. "You don't have a maid. Those were Gemma's bus tokens on your table. That was her jacket hanging in your closet."

He raised his thin brows. "Wow, I'm impressed, Juliet. Very good. You don't miss much, do you?" He nodded, his eyes back on hers. "I threw her out, and she started stalking me. She followed me to the party, threw wine on Roseline." He shook his head again. "Can't have that. Not my precious Roseline. So, I found her in the wine cellar and got rid of her forever. And now it's your turn, Juliet."

"Someone will catch you," she told him, leaving Paris' name out of it.

"Your police boyfriend? The cop doesn't believe anything you say anymore." He blinked. "Wait, do you mean Paris? You think Paris will come after me?" With both hands flexing, he changed his expression again. He became very still. "Always carry gloves, Juliet. The world is a germy place."

Dexter reached into his pocket again.

The hilt of a knife appeared.

Juliet grabbed the bottle of bleach and swung with all her might.

The bottle was full and hit Dexter on the side of the head.

He fell sideways, striking his head on a shelf. Dexter fell to his knees.

Juliet jumped past him and flew out the door.

Dexter's hand gripped her sore ankle.

She fell, but she kicked, kicked and screamed as loud as her voice would go. Spinning onto her belly, she kicked Dexter in the face and on the nose.

His hand lessened its grip on her ankle.

Juliet pulled away, got to her knees, and scrambled toward the other side of the room.

Shoes, she saw shoes coming at her. "There!" someone yelled over Juliet's head. "There! Him, that's him!"

Juliet scrambled forward. Someone had her by the arms and lifted her.

Paris!

"You're here," she blubbered. "You're here. I knew you would find me." Her eyes were so wet, she could barely see him. "I knew you'd find me."

He pulled her close and held her, stepping away from the men wrestling Dexter on the floor.

More people piled into the room.

Juliet pulled away to watch the scene.

The police were among the crowd, guns out, and billy clubs.

One man looked like the maître d' who'd taken Juliet's credit card. Had he brought it back to her? No, he held a bottle of liquor over his head, ready to slug Dexter if he moved the wrong way.

Dexter fought them, even face down on the floor. He kicked. He punched.

"He's got a knife," Juliet warned.

The maître d' stomped hard on Dexter's hand.

Dexter screamed in outrage.

The police officers were on him then, jerking his arms behind his back, putting the handcuffs on his wrists.

Juliet watched, wide-eyed and hanging on to Paris at the same time.

The football player police officer hauled Dexter to his feet and shoved him forward.

Officer Brandt stepped in front of Juliet. "We'll need you to come to the station."

"I'll bring her," Paris said, nodding to the woman.

"Fine. But come now."

"Right," he said, pulling Juliet after him, but then he stopped. "Take the phone out of your pocket, Juliet."

She shook her head. "What?"

"Your phone," he said, reaching for her jacket. "It's still beeping."

She grabbed her pocket too. "My phone?"

He nodded, wide-eyed himself. "I used Find My iPhone to get to you, yeah?"

She gasped. "That was the beeping noise."

"Right."

She started to cry for real then.

Paris pulled her to him again. Raising his free arm, he called to the officer, "We'll be there soon."

Ten minutes later, Juliet was still sobbing, but Paris forced her to walk with him. "Come on, we need to go."

"All right. Paris. All right. You're my best friend. I love you."

He grimaced. "Yeah, I love you too. Please don't say those two things in the same sentence again. Juliet, you have to move your feet."

They made it to the front of the lodge.

"Juliet!" a female voice called out.

She glanced toward the reception desk of the lodge.

Emma and Olive stood near with the rest of the crowd of onlookers. Emma broke loose and started to move toward Juliet.

A blur of red flew in front of Emma, blocking the girl's path. It was Roseline..

Roseline. Dios mio, Roseline. She'll be devastated.

"You!" she screamed at Juliet. "What have you done?"

"Roseline …"

"They're taking Dexter to jail!" She pointed one blood-red nail toward the doors.

Whirling blue and white lights flashed through the windows.

"I can't marry him when he's in jail."

Juliet stood taller and let go of Paris' arm. "Roseline, he tried to kill me. He pulled a knife …"

"Well, what did you do to deserve it?" Her eyes were nearly the color of her fingernails, and just as shiny from tears. "You always have some sort of smart comment to make." Her top lip curled over the top of her teeth. She pointed at Juliet. "You don't like his house. You don't like him. You're just jealous of everything we have together."

Juliet took a step backward. "He tried to run me off the road with his car a week ago, so, no, I don't like him."

"He never did such a thing!"

Juliet pointed now, toward the windows. "Did you see his car? Did you ask him why his car bumper is damaged?

Roseline let her head fall back. "Ugh," she yelled toward the ceiling. "He hit a deer last weekend. Of course he told me about it. But you think this is all about you, don't you? Not happy to be the bridesmaid again, right?"

"I think it's about two people dying. What is wrong with you?"

"What is wrong with me is that you've ruined everything. I hate you."

"Roseline," Juliet started again. "He's a murderer."

"I don't care. We were going to be married, and you ruined everything. I hate you. I HATE YOU!"

The football police officer took Roseline's arm and pulled her toward the doors.

"I HATE YOU, JULIET!"

O' Happy Dagger

* * *

It was after Christmas when Ganozza's Bakery reopened with Delia running it. She'd changed the look of the customer seating area to heavy white tables and pink striped upholstered chairs. She ordered white wood shelving, too, to display packaged items. But the best was behind the sneeze guards … Ganozza's baked goods, all the old recipes, cookies, cannolis, *Torta Della Nonna*. It was all there.

And, as Juliet predicted, the place was packed with customers. Everyone in the family was there, working behind the counter. Delia was in the back, baking. Ty ran food to the customers and went back and forth between the kitchen and the shelves. Juliet handed out baked goods and Paris ran the register. Santos and Italia greeted the customers with free coffee. Even *Nonna* was there, supervising the ovens.

Abram stood with Juliet behind the counter. He wore a pink apron like the rest of them. "Well, I've met my goal. I've made new friends."

"Yes, and I've met my goals too. I've made new friends and kept my old ones."

"What sort of goal is that?"

She shrugged.

He lifted his chin in an upward nod. "How's your crazy cousin?"

"Seeing a counselor."

"And how's your boyfriend?"

She shook her head. "Nicolo is not my boyfriend."

"I wasn't talking about Montague. I was talking about

the cashier."

Juliet glanced around Abram to spy Paris handing change to a customer.

Paris caught her staring and winked.

What's next for Juliet?
Find out in *Thus With A Kiss,*
Book 3 in this delightful series!

Everyone is convinced Paris Nobleman is on the verge of proposing marriage to Juliet Da Vinci. However, Juliet is not sure how she'll respond if he does. The big question recedes to the back of her mind when two murders take place and witnesses put Paris at the scenes of both crimes.

Forget working with the police. Paris goes on the lam and Juliet follows right behind him with questions of her own. Such as, who's the girl Paris has kept secret for the past nine months?

Cue the hotel staff impersonations and the scary cooks at the Jinlin Dine-in because Juliet decides to figure things out on her own. Maybe, while she's at it, she'll discover if Paris is just a good friend or something more.

Thank you for taking the time to read *O' Happy Dagger*. I hope you enjoyed reading it as much as I loved writing it. Please consider telling your friends or posting a short review online. Word of mouth is an author's best friend and is much appreciated.

Thank you!

C.J. Love

Visit CJ Love's website at

https://lovecj316.wixsite.com/cjlove

And her blog at https://thatacus.wordpress.com/

Sign up for her free mystery newsletter and receive advance information about new books, along with a chance at prizes, discounts and other mystery news!

Contact by email: thiajwhitten@yahoo.com
Follow CJ Love on Twitter, Pinterest, Instagram and Facebook

Printed in Great Britain
by Amazon